THE PROMISED LAND

THE PROMISED LAND

A WESTERN DOUBLE

UZZIAH MOUNTAIN MAN
BOOK SEVEN

J.J. BONHAM

The Promised Land: A Western Double
Paperback Edition

Wolfpack Publishing
1707 E. Diana Street
Tampa, FL 33610

www.wolfpackpublishing.com

Paperback ISBN 979-8-89567-357-7
Ebook ISBN 979-8-89567-804-6

THE PROMISED LAND

THE PROMISED LAND

1

That winter, which had started out so mild as to almost be unbelievable, changed strides once Uzziah had gotten home. Immanuel had not planned well, let it be said that his health did not prepare him for the amount of work that was required for planning well.

Uzziah was sitting in his cabin, and the potbellied stove was doing its job, and the fireplace was also going well. Uzziah's blood had grown thinner, and his ability to bear the low climes of the Rockies had been compromised. He was looking at the dummy that Immanuel had made and placed in his rocker when there came a knock at his cabin door.

"Enter!" Uzziah yelled. It irritated him that Immanuel was knocking now before he entered Uzziah's cabin.

"Hey," Immanuel said as he came in and closed the door behind him. He looked at the fireplace and the potbellied stove and frowned.

"I know, I know, I gotta stop burning the proverbial

candle at both ends," Uzziah apologized. Immanuel had gotten onto him about using too much wood.

"It's okay," Immanuel said, grabbing the coffee pot on top of the stove and pouring himself a cup of coffee. He blew across it and then took a sip. "Yer coffee's better than mine," he said as a compliment.

"Why do you bother?"

"Whatya mean?"

"To make coffee. Yer always over chere drinkin' mine, and I seen ya pour yers out 'cause it's lousy."

"Maybe I gets up afor ya, maybe I want a cup afore ya get up," Immanuel said.

"We're both wasteful in our own ways," Uzziah concluded.

"Yeah, but yer wasteful can get us frozen, while mine just runs us outta coffee," Immanuel said, smiling as he sat at the table with Uzziah.

"How long ya been at that weight?" Uzziah asked Immanuel.

"Why? What weight? Whatcha talkin' 'bout?"

"Yer arms resemble chicken wings," Uzziah said.

"When did ya see my bare arms?"

"When ya took a bath the other day, and I walked in on ya."

"Start knocking," Immanuel grumbled.

"No, I won't, we didn't come up chere to practice good manners with each other, we came up chere to..."

Immanuel looked at Uzziah, who had stopped mid-sentence and was staring into the fireplace. Immanuel joined him in his staring as they both sipped coffee and watched the dancing flames.

"I been chere longer than ya, and I still ain't got chere," Immanuel admitted, knowing that coming back to the physical mountains was not the same as coming back to the fact of being there, really there.

Uzziah looked at the older man, who really did look older now, especially since he'd dropped a hundred pounds, and he wondered if coming back had been a good idea, after all.

"I been wonderin' the same," Immanuel said.

"How ya know what I'm wonderin'?"

"Just do."

Uzziah stared back into the fire and started to speak, but the only thing that happened was his mouth opened, then closed again.

"I can't believe I'm saying this, but I miss New Orleans."

Uzziah looked up at his partner and smiled. "Is it the whores or the booze?"

"Not fair."

"Maybe not, maybe so."

"Well, yer missin' got more roots than mine, I'll admit that, but neither of us will survive up chere, ifn we get lost in the past, ya know?" Immanuel said as he got up and walked toward the door.

"Where ya goin'?"

"To feed the hosses."

"Dun fed 'em."

"Oh."

"Well, maybe I'll chop wood," Immanuel said.

"Don't, it makes me tired watchin' ya."

"Then, don't watch," Immanuel said as he grabbed at the latch.

"Stay, ya need to eat, and I need to cook."

Uzziah got busy cooking, cutting the thick slices of bacon, grating the potatoes he found at the Vrain, and making another pot of coffee. He looked over at Immanuel, who had taken up reading one of the newspapers he brought from Jeff City. He smiled to himself, thinking of Porter, who now looked more like Immanuel than Immanuel did. The weight he sluffed off had been a wasting of his largeness as well as a wasting of who the man ultimately was. Uzziah felt it was his duty to put some weight back on his partner's bones, which were prominent enough to remind him of the bones that underly all our bodies, but which we'd rather not see on a daily basis.

"What ya starin' at?" Immanuel asked, Uzziah hadn't even noticed that he'd looked up from the newspaper.

"You."

"Why?"

"Sorry, just thinkin' things," Uzziah tried to explain without explaining.

"Says here, ya was a hero of Jefferson City. From what's written chere ya coulda had yer way with a lot of things there," Immanuel said, and then he read. "*Uzziah O'Bannon, the big Mick, that came to our fair city from Nauvoo, may indeed be a Latter-Day Saint, but his deportment in Jefferson City had convinced this editor that he came in a hero and only proved it later.* Damn, young son, who the hell did these people think ya were?"

"Nobody but me, nobody but me," Uzziah said, throwing the grated potatoes into the hot bacon grease in the large skillet. He had had some of these potatoes in Jefferson City, and they had been called hash browns.

"It's 'bout being bulletproof, ain't it?" Immanuel said.

"I told ya, after what happened, yer not allowed to ask about that anymore. We had the discussion and our friend died," Uzziah said, throwing some cut-up onions and jalapeños in with the potatoes.

They ate the fabulous breakfast, and Immanuel did, indeed, like the hash browns, though he complained about the peppers, said it gave him such bad heartburn that it reminded him of his angina pectoris. Uzziah made a mental note not to use as many next time.

They made it through the winter, but not without the help of Max and Frederick. They hated to ask, but they were going to have to tear down part of the new barn to have wood to burn. They had already scavenged all the wood from the other blown-up cabins, which Immanuel hated to do. In point of fact, there were only two cabins now, and the evidence of the other ones were literally gone up in smoke.

Immanuel tried to organize a reading of Shakespeare's A Midsummer Night's Dream with Max and Frederick, but both were such poor readers that by the time they finished their speeches, both Immanuel and Uzziah felt like they were back in grade school. Immanuel thought for a second that he would teach these two *backard* men the art of reading, but dismissed it after the first attempt. He realized he'd have had a lot more fun shooting both of them than trying to teach them to read.

But they were grateful, and when the spring finally

announced itself, and Immanuel had gained back about half the weight he lost, when he'd been sick with the heart stuff, the boys decided that they would go down Vrain Trading Post and see what was shaking. Who knew, maybe Jean Baptiste would sponsor another horse race.

Uzziah had sent a message by way of tumbler a few days into spring, it would be much warmer at the settlement, and when the tumbler returned, it seemed everybody was ready for something besides sitting around their fires and dreaming of doing something else.

At Vrain Trading Post, they picked up some supplies they needed, and saw that Jean Baptiste was sponsoring another race, and he was going to use some meadows near the settlement as a place to race.

They left for the settlement, happy they'd been right about a Trading-Post-sponsored race. The winner would get $100, and who couldn't use a $100?

"Ya know why we're adoin' this, right?" Immanuel whispered as they rode down in the mud toward the trading post. Max and Frederick were riding up ahead, and this particular topic of conversation wasn't meant for their ears.

"Yeah, I know," Uzziah whispered back.

"No, ya don't."

"I do," Uzziah said and patted Shadow's neck.

"So, ya do, okay. Wanna make a little side wager just between the two of us?"

"I do not," Uzziah said out loud, wanting this particular conversation to come to an end. He did not like the idea of two friends racing their excellent horses against each other. It was a recipe for the end of that friendship, at least that's what Uzziah believed.

Immanuel looked at Max, who had turned in his saddle. "What ya two girls arguin' 'bout now?" Max asked.

Both Uzziah and Immanuel pretended that it was only a fart they heard and nothing more.

They camped the one night and figured they'd get in late the next night at the settlement. Uzziah cooked because both of the boys felt obligated to Frederick and Max for saving their bacon that winter, and neither of them like the idea of an obligation any more than they liked the idea of a boil on their arses.

Immanuel had downed a good-looking buck, and the venison steaks that Uzziah fixed, along with the other fixings, made Uzziah think of how he'd cooked when Hannah needed a break when she was pregnant. The meal of steak, field greens literally picked that afternoon from around the campsite, bacon, and beans was good, and of course, there were always Uzziah's Dutch oven johnnycakes, which were appreciated, but not as much as his biscuits.

As they sat around and ate in front of the fire, Immanuel spoke up.

"These boys wanted yer biscuits."

"Nah, no, no," Frederick started in, "we're happy with the johnnies."

"Liar," Immanuel said to Frederick's face.

"Well, that ain't nice," Frederick said, which proved he was lying.

"I seen the look on yer faces when the top was taken

off the Dutch, and ya can't tell me that weren't disappointment," Immanuel said.

"Well, hell, U's biscuits are legendary," Max said.

"Ya don't even know what that means," Immanuel teased him.

"It means they be talked about, don't that mean that?" he asked, looking at his partner, Frederick.

"Yep, that what it mean."

"Both of ya may have rescued our arses this winter, but the association has been good fer yer vocabulary, don't ya think?" Immanuel asked.

"We ain't even got one of those 'round chere, Immanuel, besides, yer remedies are better than most store ones," Max said, looking right at both Uzziah and Immanuel.

"Yer thinkin' of apothecary, not vocabulary," Immanuel said, eating and looking down into his plate. He wondered sometimes how men like Frederick, who admittedly was smarter than Max, since obviously only Max had gone over a waterfall with a whore in the back of a schooner, how men like that managed to survive regardless of their ignorance. Robert Spells could read and had hisself a good set of words to speak from, but when push came to shove and the ice was forming on his mustache, he didn't know shite from Shinola!

"Is that what I'm thinkin' of?"

"I'm sure of it," Uzziah said, not wanting to embarrass the men who had been generous with their wood and grass hay.

"Yeah, me, too," Max said, and he helped himself to seconds on the johnnie cakes.

The ride into the settlement the next day was wet and cold. It started to rain just as they broke camp, and the thunder and lightning, which no horse really likes, kept the time they made down to a minimum. It looked like they were going to arrive really, really late that night, or, maybe if they camped again, early on the morning of the third day.

They decided, with the rain, and some of it coming down as snow and sleet, that camping that night would be as miserable as riding the rest of the way in, so they rode.

Uzziah took a look at his chronometer when the settlement was in view, and it recorded the time as three in the morning. Horrible time to wake anybody, but people with kids, inexcusable. They pounded on the fortified stockade gate anyway, until Willet ran out with a poncho over his dead, and swearing like a sailor. They rode in, and he quickly closed the gate and put the log lock back down.

Evidently, things had really changed in the settlement, since they were shown to a third cabin which had recently, as in the last two years, been built and was unoccupied at the time. It had a fireplace that had been stoked, and the fire whooshed back up, once logs were added. Willet said little, grunted something, and left.

There were bunks in the third cabin like a bunkhouse, and they were certainly more comfortable than lying in the wet. All four mountain men were asleep before the fire died down.

2

Children love to torture adults in the morning because adults who order them around deserve it.

Evidently, Willet had left the latchstring out, and all the kids at the settlement, and there looked to be at least ten of them, were running around the bunkhouse and making noises vaguely resembling attacking Injuns.

This noise brought pistols and rifles up, till it was realized the source of the attacking noises. Uzziah and Immanuel got jumped on, and Uzziah thought he recognized Cubby, Oscar's kid, and he was tall and weighed a lot. He had jumped on his grandpa's bed, and Immanuel had had the wind knocked out of him, and was trying to catch his breath, which the cruel children thought was very entertaining as they laughed and pointed at the wheezing old man.

Uzziah could see that some of the Injuns were half black, and some of them were just Crows. He reckoned correctly that this idea of horse racing had gotten as far as the Crow villages, and Beckwourth had shown up with his four wives, and some of the other Crows had joined him. He wondered why Standing Bear hadn't put them in the third cabin, this bunkhouse, but when he chased the screaming—with delight—children from the bunkhouse, he saw that there were more than a few teepees pitched in the back part of the settlement around the pond, and woodsmoke was traveling through their smoke holes nicely since it looked like they had been allowed to sleep in longer than anyone. He imagined correctly also that it was Standing Bear who had sent the children in to awaken the guests.

He looked back in on the bunkhouse and all those in there, the three other mountain men, had rolled over after Uzziah had chased the kids from the cabin, and the snoring had started back up again.

Uzziah put his boots on, pulled up his suspenders, and with the top of his long johns as his shirt, he made his way to the big cabin.

When he opened the door, which was always opened to anyone who was in the stockade, Cubby, Will, and Charlie came running over, and all of them exclaiming, "Uncle Uzziah!"

They surrounded him, and he hugged all three. Will was nearly twelve years old, and Charlie wasn't far behind, with Cubby being about the age of Will when Uzziah first met Oscar, when he'd saved the two mountain men's lives.

"These kids are growing like weeds," he commented to Standing Bear in Crow. He figured she was still committed to that way of life, since she was still dressed as a Crow woman would dress.

"They are worse than weeds, they are briars, Uncle

Uzziah," she said back to him in Crow. His Crow was a bit rusty, but he could make most of it out just fine.

He noticed at the big table sat Jean Baptiste, the owner of Vrain Trading Post. He was naturally surprised to see him and wondered if he and Standing Bear had gotten together over the winter. Immanuel sure wouldn't like that!

"Baptiste! Whatcah doin' chere?" Uzziah asked good-naturedly and came over, and the two men shook forearms, the Injun way.

"I'm offering a $100 reward to the winner of today's race, and ifn an Injun wins and don't want the money, they can take it out in honest trade," Jean Baptiste said, and Uzziah looked at Standing Bear, and she shook her head *no*. How was it that women always knew what you were thinking?

"Say, since we missed ya when we were at the post, got something ya might wanna see out in the barn," Uzziah said to Jean Baptiste.

They walked out to the barn, and Uzziah had the Girandoni air rifle wrapped up in some oiled cloth. He took it out and showed it to the Frenchman.

"Merde! What in the name of Caesar's ghost is it, a club?"

"Nah, it's an air rifle and it shoots with no smoke and hardly any sound."

"Ah, the Germans call it the Windbuchse!" Jean Baptiste said, then added, "Is this a gift?"

Uzziah just looked at him.

"Okay, okay, can't blame a guy fer tryin', can ya?"

"No, I can't. Ya think ya can ya sell it fer me?"

"Maybe, I've heard of them fer years, but this is the first time I see it, the caliber?"

"Forty-five, and there's a mold in the bag fer making more of yer own bullets."

"Okay," Jean Baptiste said, and he put the rifle in the extra scabbard of the saddle he rode.

They walked back into the big cabin, and Uzziah saw all the hungry faces.

He looked around the kitchen and made the Indian sign for cooking. Standing Bear clapped her hands, and the children squealed with delight.

"Is that why ya sent them in there to wake me?" Uzziah asked.

Standing Bear blushed, and Uzziah realized how much his cooking was appreciated in the settlement. No sooner had Standing Bear blushed than Leah and Willet came in with a little girl, dressed as a Crow baby. She looked to be around three years old.

"Hello, uncle," the little girl said in Crow.

He looked between Willet and Leah, "She's crazy about Injuns," Leah said in English, "and we figured what harm could it do?"

"Let me guess, you guys are hungry?" Uzziah asked them in Crow.

Willet expressed himself in Crow. "Yes, and when a great warrior cooks for you, you'd better sit down and prepare yourself."

Uzziah, who had never really cared that much for Willet, saw a different part of the man who had come to be with his younger brother, only to lose him at the buffalo run. Uzziah grabbed Willet and gave him a nuggy on the top of his head. Willet tried to get away, but Uzziah had his head in a headlock.

"Your brother would be so proud of you," Uzziah said to him in English.

Leah gathered over by Uzziah and looked up to him. "I'm gonna learn how to do these johnnycakes," she said.

"What ifn I'm cookin' biscuits?" he asked her in English.

"Then," she retorted in English, "I shall learn both!"

He was up to his elbows in flour and had potatoes cooking on the griddle and the eggs ready to scramble when the rest of the crew wandered in. He had been told by Standing Bear that the Crows would cook in their own homes. He would only be responsible for the six or so who lived permanently at the settlement and their new guests. Uzziah did a quick count and came up with fourteen, if Beckwourth had brought all four wives. When he walked in, there were five Crow women with him, and Uzziah guessed correctly that he had married again. *Hey*, he thought, *it wasn't just the Mormons who liked more than one wife*!

Then the men were shooed outside to wash their grubby hands, who wants dirty hands all over the biscuits and johnnycakes going around the table?

Max started to grab at the johnnycakes, and Immanuel swatted his hand with the back of his Bowie knife.

"Damn, old man, that hurt!" Max complained.

Immanuel just pointed to his partner Uzziah, who had already bowed his head.

As all at the table bowed their heads, and the steam was coming off all the fabulous food that Uzziah had fixed, in his heart of hearts, he sincerely wished that he had Hannah and his son, George, with him so they could meet his incredible extended family. People don't really know each other till they know their families.

"Heavenly Father, we gather here today to celebrate Your creation, and the wonderful foods which You supplied us on this earth. Make us ready to meet our deaths as they are right here with us, and deliver us from shying away from their presence. Give us the grace to race the horses we have gathered like the good sporting men and women that we are. Forgive us for falling short in the things that we misunderstand and do backward. May this day be filled with the love that we all have for everyone that we call friend. In my Brother, Your son's, name we pray, Amen!"

When he looked up, Beckwourth was staring at him, and he nodded, thanking Uzziah for giving the life and energy gathered the proper blessing. The food was going around and was diminishing with each hand that touched it. When all were served, the talking dropped off as it always did when good friends and family sat down to take on their chuck.

As the seconds were being appreciated, Beckwourth spoke up, "Immanuel, what disease has attacked you of recent?"

"It's called angina pectoris, sir," Immanuel said, not wanting to discuss it.

"I have heard of it, nothing to be shamed by. When strong men partake of the life which God has offered them, they often go too far sometimes. I wish ya a quick recovery."

"He's on the mend," Uzziah said. "He just needs to put back the weight."

"He looks fine in his leaner state," Beckwourth said and said something to his Crow wives, and everyone at the table laughed.

"I miss most of it, it's been a while fer me," Immanuel whispered to Standing Bear.

"He asked his wives if you were not a man that they would share their buffalo robes with?" Standing Bear said, and Immanuel blushed.

No more was said about Immanuel's state of health, and he was glad for that, but when the dishes were being cleared and cleaned, Standing Bear grabbed Immanuel's hand and pulled him to herself on the other side of the big room.

"You have no reason to be ashamed of sickness," she said to him in English.

"The heart attack, as some call it, made me as weak as a kitten when it happened, and if an enemy had been near, I would have perished," he told her.

"But Uzziah told me, even though he had left you on the paddle wheeler, there was a French doctor there," Standing Bear said.

"Damn! Ya can't tell that man nothin' less he's spoutin' it off to everyone," Immanuel said, glaring at Uzziah, who was cleaning up what he had cooked.

Standing Bear hit Immanuel on the arm, and he looked at her. "That man loves everything about you. You are not just his brother, but his older brother, who has taught him everything he knows, and he will always look up to you."

"Ya think?"

"Thinking has nothing to do with it. If you were dying and he could give his life to save you, he would be the dead one," Standing Bear said.

"Maybe. What's Jean Baptiste doin' chere, ya take up with him?" he asked her in English with just a twinge of jealousy in it.

"How is the white snake?" she whispered to him in Crow.

He looked at her as if he had misunderstood. They had quite a relationship when Immanuel had returned from the buffalo run, but that was when he was in his prime, and although she had grown older, there was nothing about her that suggested that her powers of heat had not diminished any.

"Well, that is an unexpected, but not unwelcome question," he said more to clarify than anything else.

She reached down and affectionately squeezed his Johnson, and the shock that it sent through his body almost made him weak-kneed.

"Standing Bear," he said softly to her as he gazed into her eyes.

"You will meet me by the pond tonight, please?" she said and walked away.

What the hell! Immanuel thought. He wasn't sure he was up to the shenanigans that she could get up to.

"All right," Jean Baptiste said, "it's time to see all the ponies that will race!"

The settlement had built a nice big corral, and all the *ponies*, as Jean Baptiste put it, who were going to race were invited into that corral. The Crow brought their literal ponies first, and Uzziah and Immanuel were both sure that there were some racing ponies among them, but then Beckwourth brought his baled-face paint from the barn. It was enormous, almost as big as Stygian the Great. His eyes were blue, his haunches and buttocks were high, and his thighs were thick, but not enough to slow him down. The advantage he would gain would be tremendous when that horse started pushing his back feet along the ground as he lengthened his stride.

Of course, many had seen Shadow, not only in person but also in action. He was without a doubt a very fast horse, but no one had seen him in the long distance, and the race which Jean Baptiste purposed wasn't just a jaunt around the settlement. There were many whistles and whoops and hollers with Shadow's appearance, but all his thunder was stolen when Immanuel led Stygian out of the barn. Even the horses already in the corral sort of moved away from Stygian, as if they feared the huge horse, but Shadow moved over, and the two horses reared up on their back legs and pawed at the empty air together.

Hopes of winning were being greatly diminished among the Crow, and their frowns and conversing with one another showed it.

Ululations came from the women, who had come out to see what men thought was only their purview. The horses, all of them, reacted to the sound of the tongues, and they raced around the corral snorting and biting at each other's arses. The men and braves had to get out of the way of the almost stampeding horses.

"This is gonna be one hell of a race," Immanuel said to Uzziah as they took refuge on the porch that surrounded the big cabin.

"What are we racin' fer? I know these Crows are cash poor," Immanuel said.

"We race to win the $100 prize," Jean Baptiste said.

Both Uzziah and Immanuel looked at each other, and both wondered why Jean Baptiste wasn't racing.

"Ain't ya gonna race?" Immanuel asked the Frenchman.

"No, no, I will be here with the women and children when ya return," he said in his thick Frenchie accent.

Immanuel couldn't help but wonder what that meant about being with the women, but he let it drop. They weren't going to be gone all day!

3

The time of the race had arrived. Jean Baptiste had picked out the route the racers would take a few days before. Uzziah figured he must have been out for a ride and seen Chimney Rock sticking out, then rode out to it. He told everyone that all they had to do was ride to the meadow, and they would see Chimney Rock, and then ride to the top, turn around, and come back to the compound of the settlement.

"How will we know that the man who wins had been to the top?" Immanuel asked, and everyone chimed in with grunts and uh-huhs.

"I left something up there, and if ya don't return with some of it, then we'll all know ya cheated," Jean Baptiste said, smiling.

"What d'ya expect he left up there?" Uzziah asked Immanuel.

"It sure weren't his pride now, were it?"

"How long a ride ya suspect it is?" Willet asked.

"It's probably five miles, so however long it takes yer horse to cover that ground," Beckwourth said.

"And a lot of it will be straight up and straight down," Immanuel said. "Sorry I got involved with chere race, Jean Baptiste's gonna get some horses hurt, ifn he ain't careful."

The men, Braves and White men alike, plus Beckwourth, had all eaten a good breakfast, and the horses seemed ready. Everybody was mounted up and Standing Bear was holding onto the log lock waiting to open it. She looked at Immanuel and smiled. Uzziah noticed that and turned to his partner.

"What's 'at all 'bout?" Uzziah asked.

"What's what all 'bout?" Immanuel asked, hoping Uzziah hadn't seen him and Standing Bear smiling back and forth at each other.

"Ya done got in her bed agin, didn't ya?" Uzziah whispered.

Technically, they had been out by the pond in the cool night breeze, so no, he hadn't gotten her in bed again.

As Immanuel turned to Uzziah to tell him just that, Standing Bear took the log lock down, and the gates were pushed open.

Neither Uzziah nor Immanuel thought it was important to be out of the stockade gate first, after all, they had the fastest horses without a doubt. Really, the only way they could lose was if their horses got hurt, and they weren't about to let that happen in the rush to exit the settlement.

There were yips, hollers, and a couple yee-haws as the majority of riders squeezed through the stockade gate, one Brave was scraped off his pony, and his leg was bleeding when Uzziah and Immanuel dog-trotted their blacks past him.

"That looks like it hurts," Immanuel said, and they both took off down the narrow trail after the others.

The evening before, miles away in the shadow of Chimney Rock, as the sunset was splashing its colors all over the small river, a group of Blackfeet buffalo hunters had rested well and now they were breaking up their camp and about to go out again in search of the elusive beasts. The leader of the hunting party, who had been at the buffalo run that Beckwourth and both the mountain men had played a part in, looked up at the top of Chimney Rock and spoke to a warrior friend of his. This particular Brave took off up the trail that led to the top of the chimney.

"Where's he going?" another Brave asked in Blackfoot.

"If those who have enhanced our lives are around, surely on such a clear day, he will see where they are grazing," the leader said, and everyone relaxed.

The group of hunters had ridden hard and far from their village, which was in the Montana territory, and they were glad to sit for a while, smoke a pipe. There was a stream nearby, and before long, nearly all of them were down there fishing. And, as fate would have it, the fish were biting.

The lone Brave who rode to the top stopped several

times to rest his pony. They had ridden hard the days before, and his pony was a bit older than some of the others. He loved this pony that he called Lightning Strike because the day it was born, when he was dragging it from its mother and the colt had not yet stood, a storm had rolled in fast, and a nearby tree had been struck by lightning.

He had hoped that the horse would be fast—a sure sign had been given him. He was when he was younger, but now, the years had taken steps away from the pony as it did all living creatures. The horse seemed to have gathered his strength again, and they continued up the steep path to the top of Chimney Rock. When they got there, he felt as tired as his pony, not really, but it had been a chore to stay on the horse's back all the way up.

There was a flat spot at the top, and he released his pony to feed on what little grasses there were up there, but instead the pony scurried over to a pile of fresh hay. How strange. Who could have done this? Unless the Sun, which had given them all the means to live, had done such a thing, but then again, maybe Napi, the old trickster of Blackfoot legend, was playing one of his tricks.

He covered his eyes with the shadow of his hand and looked down to where he could see. He had very good eyesight, and it was probably the reason that the hunting party leader had sent him up there. He could see they were fishing, and he hoped they were catching some because the buffalo search had been most disappointing. Which reminded him, his fellow braves were east and south of his position on the rock, and he rotated toward the north, still no buffalo, but they had come that way, then to the northwest, nothing, then directly west, and he noticed there was dust rising from the prairie. Perhaps these were the buffalo they so eagerly hunted?

He squinted to help his vision, and when the wind had blown the dust from the trail, there they were! Not buffalo, but at least twenty or so riders, and they were in the traditional dress of the Crow nation, and behind them, White men were hot on their heels. These White men, these mountain men, must be fierce warriors if their small number were chasing so many Crow.

He jumped on Lightning Strike and was veering down the steep slope that led to the bottom. He could have screamed or shot an arrow in warning, but the others would not have known the danger that was coming their way.

He made it before the wave of Crow braves saw him. He shouted to those fishing and the leader of the hunting trip, and everyone thought, because of his excited behavior, that he had spotted buffalo.

When everything was hurriedly explained, the hunt leader got everyone to take their horses into the trees on the other side of the river, then the Blackfoot braves hid along the worn-out banks of the river. They would see who was coming, then deal with it on their own terms.

The first large group of riders were Crow, a dreaded enemy of the Blackfoot, then shortly afterward, not firing their weapons at them, but certainly armed to the teeth, came the mountain men, four of them. One of them was a man who was very dark, and some of those with the Blackfeet recognized the black man as one who had come to the buffalo run years before.

As the mountain men spurred and encouraged their

horses up the slope, the Blackfeet mounted up and rode after them. They would catch the mountain men as they attacked the Crow, and be at their backs, destroying them.

As they neared the top of Chimney Rock, the Blackfeet saw the Crow riding with gusto toward the White men, and the White men seemingly letting them slip on by. It was very strange. Okay, so the Blackfeet would kill the Crow warriors, then take on the White men.

But as the Crow came thundering toward them, they did not raise up weapons, but only held sheaves of hay in one of their hands. *This is not a good sign*, the leader thought. It was obvious that the Crow had a strong medicine in the wheat which had made them invisible to the White man, and perhaps even, invincible to all who attacked them.

The Blackfoot leader rode his horse off the side of Chimney Rock and began the precipitous ride back down the tall mountain, but this time, with no road and straight down. Sometimes the best way to deal with strong medicine was to avoid it! The other Blackfeet followed, and there were yips and hollers as Blackfoot riders lost their seats on their ponies and ponies tumbled after their hapless riders.

The Crow saw what had happened, and they mistakenly thought that these Blackfeet had entered the horse race late and were going for the finish line without the requisite hay to prove they had topped Chimney Rock. In order to impede their progress and not let them get ahead, the Crows went over the side of the mountain and ran their ponies headlong toward their enemies.

From the bottom of the mountain, it looked very much like two separate groups of Injuns had lost their good sense and were basically throwing caution, all caution, to the wind to see who could, with breakneck speed, make it to the bottom of Chimney Rock in one piece. Not many did, riders were rolled over by tumbling ponies, riders ran into other riders, and in the process, almost all the Crow had to use both hands on their war bridles, and there was a lot of hay flying down the mountain along with tumbling Injuns and shrieking horses.

When Immanuel and Uzziah had grabbed their hay and turned around and were coming back down Chimney Rock, they saw what was happening along the nearly cliff-like side of the rock. The Crow had abandoned the road for a straight line to the bottom. They looked at each other quizzically. What could have made their friends, the Crow, take such chances? The hay which the mountain men had retrieved was in their saddlebags as they hotfooted it down the trail toward the bottom.

Some of the Crow had made it safely down the side of Chimney Rock, and so had some of the Blackfeet. At the bottom, there were trembling horses and shaken-up Injuns, but amazingly, none of the horses or Injuns were seriously injured. Riders were chasing after doubt-ing, already tumbled ponies, as both Blackfoot and Crow were mounting up on whatever horse came their way. The result being, as the Crow had made their way back toward the settlement, the Blackfeet were in pursuit and trying to shoot them off their ponies.

When Uzziah and Immanuel heard the gunshots, the first thing that came into their heads was the fact that someone wanted that $100 a lot more than someone else. Some were willing, and it seemed able, to shoot their competition from their ponies with no qualms whatsoever. Which reinforced the notionality of all Injuns!

At the bottom of Chimney Rock, Immanuel pulled his spyglass from his saddlebag and glassed those riding away.

"There's Blackfeet shootin' at unarmed Crows," he said as he turned Stygian loose and laid down on some flat rocks, followed by Uzziah.

They knew the difference between the two tribes, hadn't they done battle with the Blackfeet right after the buffalo run a few years before? Well, almost!

Both Hawkens went off simultaneously, and up ahead of them, a great deal ahead of them, two Blackfeet tumbled off their horses.

So, thought the leader of the buffalo hunt, *the mountain men did have a prowess beyond the normal range*. He yelled something in Blackfoot to the others, and they all peeled off and took to the surrounding foothills to get out of range of the long rifles.

"What the hell's goin' on!?!" Beckwourth shouted at Uzziah and Immanuel.

After having reloaded, they mounted back up.

"To be perfectly clear, we have no idea," Uzziah said.

"What he said," Immanuel said as the two of them spurred their black mounts toward the settlement.

Willet still hadn't made it down Chimney Rock, and he wasn't sure if Immanuel and Uzziah were killing off their competition or what. He made a mental note to tell Jean Baptiste of the fouls in the race.

Back in the settlement, Jean Baptiste was the least surprised when Immanuel and Uzziah didn't come in neck and neck. After shooting the Blackfeet and wondering what in heaven's name that could have been all about, they let both Beckwourth and Willet pass them as they loped in easily to the settlement.

Immanuel had taken the scalps off the two dead Blackfeet and presented them to the Crow, who whooped and hollered and told him they would celebrate that night.

Uzziah was worried that the Blackfeet would retaliate, but Immanuel just sluffed it off.

Besides, one of the Crow had won the prize and decided he would take it out in trade before he went back to the village north of them.

They broke down their teepees the next morning, and like all good Crow, the place looked no worse for wear once they were gone.

Uzziah stayed in the smaller bunkhouse cabin, but cooked meals for everyone. He liked cooking, and it gave him a sense of service that he got in no other manner.

That night after the Crow left, he was preparing dinner, and his mind was a thousand miles away. He wondered if the Mormons were getting persecuted further by the Gentiles who lived around them. He worried about Hannah and George's grave, and wondered if the Gentiles would go so far as to violate the sanctity of hallowed ground. He wished he had thought and simply brought their bodies with him when he left Nauvoo, but he didn't know how that could be done. And, who knew, maybe it couldn't. Regardless, Hannah and George were in Nauvoo, and he supposed that they would rise from their graves and join Jesus in the air at the second coming. He didn't like to think about things like that when he was cooking, but he supposed it was all right as long as those he was cooking for didn't know.

There were many compliments on the venison steaks and the golden spuds he'd grilled, along with the greens which the children had gathered. His johnny-cakes were always a treat, and since Leah had joined him in their making, they also made big, flaky biscuits.

That night, when most of the children were in bed except for the older ones, and the women were cleaning up the kitchen, Immanuel, Uzziah, Willet, and Beckwourth were on the porch smoking.

There was a clamor at the stockade gate and someone shouted out in Crow, "Something here," or something like that.

When they all went, armed again to the teeth, to the gate, and Willet pushed up the lock log, the warrior who had won the race held out an envelope.

Immanuel reached for it, and the warrior said in Crow, "No, for Wolverine!"

Immanuel knew Uzziah's nickname among the Crow, but he wasn't sure Uzziah knew it.

"It's fer ya," Immanuel said.

Uzziah took the letter and the rider rode off, and they put the lock log back in place.

"How'd ya know it was fer me, he said it was fer Wolverine?" Uzziah asked.

"That be yer sobriquet among the Crow," Immanuel announced.

"Since when?"

"Not sure," Immanuel said.

"I heard him called that way afore we met," Beckwourth casually mentioned.

"What kinda nickname is that?" Uzziah asked, having put the letter in his vest pocket.

"A damned good one," Beckwourth said. "Ya ever try to kill one of them sonsabitches?"

"But wolverine?" Uzziah seemed a bit mystified by his newly discovered sobriquet.

They all went back on the porch, and this being a century in which news of any kind was considered personal and not public domain, no one said a word about the letter till Beckwourth got called away by his fifth wife and Leah called out to Willet. It wasn't that everyone didn't want to know, it was just considered rude to ask. Your news was *your* news.

"I ain't gonna be nice 'bout this," Immanuel said. He had hit the bottle a couple of times, but not like the old days.

"'Bout what?"

"Read me that letter," Immanuel demanded.

"Uh-uh," Uzziah grunted.

Immanuel reached over and grabbed at Uzziah's vest, and Uzziah grabbed the older man's hand and twisted it till Immanuel howled!

"Y'all okay?" Standing Bear said in English when she stuck her head out.

"He hurt hisself," Uzziah said.

"Can I get ya something for it?" she asked in Crow.

"'Bout a hundred pounds ought to do it," Uzziah said in English, and Standing Bear didn't know what he was talking about, so she went back in.

The two of them sat there for another pipe's full.

"Ya think ya can take me, huh?" Immanuel asked.

"In yer condition"—he snorted—"no doubt," Uzziah said confidently.

"Ya bastard, ya take candy from a baby, wouldn't ya?"

"Ya ain't no baby, old man."

"That does it!" Immanuel said and leaped from his rocker to Uzziah's, and the combined weight shattered the rocker, and the two men went to rolling around on the porch. There were punches thrown, eyes poked, arms bit, and stomachs kicked. The noise was deafening. The children came out and watched with wonder, the older ones taking sides, some shouting for the Wolverine to win and some for Immanuel. The younger ones were crying when Standing Bear brought a rifle out and fired it into the air, which stopped the proceedings. Both men were covered in scratches and some blood here and there. Uzziah's vest was almost torn from his body as Immanuel had tried desperately to get the letter.

"What's this all about!?!" Standing Bear asked in Crow.

"Nothing," they both answered, Uzziah in Crow and Immanuel in English.

"So," Standing Bear said in English, "ya teach our children to fight and ya think that's nothing?"

They both looked at her, but Uzziah was ashamed. She had a point, for those youngins to see two grown men, who were supposed to be the best of friends, rolling around on the porch, breaking furniture and biting, kicking, and tearing at each other. Well, it was an unwholesome sight, that's for sure!

They both stood up, and Immanuel noticed that the letter was hanging from a torn pocket in Uzziah's vest.

"We're sorry," Uzziah said.

"Yeah, like he said," Immanuel said, then quick as a wink, he snatched the letter from Uzziah's torn pocket and they were off. Uzziah weighed more than Immanuel since Immanuel's health had deteriorated, and Immanuel wasn't having any trouble keeping away from his partner.

"I got it, I got it, I got it!" he yelled as he ran toward the pond, and Uzziah was on his tail.

"Give it back, ya bastard!" Uzziah screamed in English, as Immanuel continued to taunt him.

"Y'all never catch me, fat boy! Y'all never catch me!" Immanuel said, and then he grabbed at his chest and bent over with his hands on his knees, and the fun was over.

The letter was forgotten as Uzziah came up and grabbed Immanuel, and they both sat on the wet ground.

"Ya okay, partner?"

"This damn heart!" Immanuel cursed.

"Ya better take care of it, the only one ya got," Uzziah reminded him.

They sat there a bit, their butts getting wetter, but their breath coming back.

"God, I missed ya," Immanuel finally said, there were tears in his eyes, then he added, "Even ifn ya do think yer bulletproof."

They both sat there chuckling.

"Sorry 'bout George," Immanuel spoke softly, wiping the snot from his dribbling nose.

"I know yer are, hell, it seems anybody else gets

involved with us, they might as well head fer cover," Uzziah said.

"Ifn it hadn't been for the slightly broke ticker, I'd have run yer fat ass into the ground."

"Where's the letter?"

"Dropped it on the porch soon as I took it, figured ya missed that part."

"Ya old skunk! Let's go see what it says," Uzziah said, standing up and putting out his hand so Immanuel could grab it and pull himself up. It was an easy task for Uzziah, Immanuel weighed about as much as a woman.

They walked back to the porch and looked at the chaos they made—a broken rocker chair scattered about, a broken table leg. It was all fixable, but not now. Uzziah offered the only rocker that wasn't broken to his partner, and he sat in it with a harrumph. Uzziah pulled up a milking stool that had made its way out on the porch and sat down beside his partner. He started to look for his light benders, his cheaters, but they must have fallen out during the chase.

"Read it to me, will ya?" Uzziah asked Immanuel, who held it at arm's distance and started silently reading.

"Out loud, ifn ya don't mind," Uzziah requested.

"It's from yer bulletproof partner—"

"Can't ya just read it!"

"I'm havin' difficulties in this lack of light, says he wants us—me, too! Hey, ya told him 'bout me?"

"Course I did, fool!"

"Wants us to come to Omaha in the Nebraskie territories."

"What fer?"

"Scouts to help 'em find the promised land,"

Immanuel said and laughed out loud. "The Promise Land." He chuckled again. "Like we was Moses and Arron." Immanuel chuckled some more.

"I'm gonna go," Uzziah said, and Immanuel stopped laughing.

"When are we leavin'?" Immanuel asked.

"Soon, it says, they're leavin' soon!"

4

They made preparations without telling anyone at first. They rode to Vrain's and got supplies, well, Uzziah did, seeing how Immanuel hadn't ridden that far in a while, Uzziah didn't want him having to backtrack as they went east.

Uzziah got back in less than two days, he must have ridden poor Shadow into the ground, but then again, he did take an extra horse, and when he was at Vrain's, he took the air rifle that had been so handy on his trip along and from the Missouri back. Who knew? Such a rifle, and the myth about the death stick was probably still circulating.

They said their goodbyes, and Standing Bear wanted to go along with them, but someone needed to stay and care for all the children, and she wasn't sure Leah and Willet were up to it. It was a tearful goodbye for Standing Bear, and when they finally left and were on the trail, Immanuel spoke up.

"Ya notice Standing Bear?" He said as he made sure

the extra horse he'd brought along was still tied to the D-ring on his saddle.

"Yeah, I seen her," Uzziah said, puzzled why Immanuel was bringing her up. "What 'bout her?"

"She don't usually cry like that, I mean, not since her conversion experience."

"Her what?" Uzziah asked, scanning the horizon for hostiles or just about anything.

"Ya know, when she went from Ophelia to Standing Bear."

"What are ya really askin' me?" Uzziah was getting impatient with Immanuel's beating around the bush.

"Do ya think she knows somethin' we don't?" he asked.

"Like what?" Uzziah asked.

"Like maybes I's gonna die?"

"Ya done yer best to do that out by the pond, didn't ya?"

"Ya was watchin'?" Immanuel asked, insulted.

"I thought some animal was in trouble the ways ya was breathin'!"

"Yeah, it took a powerful lotta air," Immanuel remembered.

"Well, ya didn't die then, did ya?"

"Nah, didn't, and she can ride ya hard and put ya up wet!" Immanuel said with a smile, then he saw something on a ridgeline. "Hey lookie there!" he motioned with his head toward the southern horizon.

"They's just watchin', that's all," Uzziah said.

"Like ya was the other night?"

"Don't make so much noise and people won't wonder," Uzziah said.

"Yeah, they still watchin' us!"

"Till they start something, I am not putting these horses through their paces with just three Injuns on the crest of a hill," Uzziah said.

"So, ya think she thinks I'm gonna die?" Immanuel asked Uzziah.

"Is that why yer being so jumpy?"

"I ain't jumpy, why ya sayin' I'm jumpy?"

"Yer gettin' excited 'bout three Injuns, that's why?"

"They could be hostiles."

"And?"

"They might attack us," Immanuel said, his head on a swivel, looking for more Injuns.

"Oh, my God, Immanuel, who's the old lady now?" Uzziah said as he pulled the Girandoni from the extra scabbard he'd installed on Shadow.

"What the hell's that?"

"It's the Italian air rifle I told ya 'bout."

"It looks weird, like a stick of some kind," Immanuel said.

"It's a death stick and is well known among the tribes," Uzziah said.

"Uh-huh."

"Watch," Uzziah said as he held the death stick over his head and pumped it up and down several times.

As Immanuel watched, the three Injuns and their horses were kicked into action and they disappeared off the ridgeline.

"See?" Uzziah said.

"It were just time fer them to leave, coincidence."

"Okay," Uzziah said and put the Girandoni back in the scabbard.

They rode along, they were following a direct course east, going through the plains where the

Comanche and the Arapaho liked to think of themselves as kings and princes of that territory.

"Yer gonna git a crik in yer neck ifn ya keep doin' that!," Uzziah said.

"What am I doin'?"

Uzziah just looked at Immanuel and shook his head, as if his partner didn't know he was nervous as a cat in a room full of rockers.

"What am I doin'!?!" Immanuel demanded, then he saw what he'd been looking for over the past two hours, "Here they come, and there's a bunch more than three!" he said, and he kicked up Stygian into a fast trot.

"Where ya goin?" Uzziah asked him.

"The hell outta here, that's where. Ya gonna stay and greet the savages?"

"I am," Uzziah said as he stopped Shadow and took the Girandoni from the scabbard again.

"Hey," Immanuel said, "let me shake it at 'em!"

"Sure," Uzziah said as he handed the strange Italian air rifle to Immanuel.

He took it and as he raised it over his head, the half dozen or so Arapaho, Uzziah recognized them now, clicked up their horses and started yelling as they rode toward them. Immanuel pumped the Girandoni above his head, but the Arapaho riders just shouted louder and kept charging.

"What am I doin' wrong?" Immanuel asked as he pumped the air rifle again and again above his head to no avail.

"Hand it to me," Uzziah said, and he checked the air pressure, which was fine, and, aiming the rather cumbersome-looking rifle, got off a shot, which could barely be heard by the two mountain men and made no smoke at all.

Immanuel winced when the first of the Arapaho riders grabbed at his beaded chest plate and fell from his horse. All the others wheeled around to take a look at the dying man, and when they turned back, Uzziah pumped the air rifle above his head.

They were a bit undecided, but circled the dying man and then took off away from the two mountain men.

"There," was all Uzziah said.

"How come they didn't leave when I pumped the death stick?"

"Ya didn't pump it with authority," Uzziah said as he put it back into its scabbard.

"I pumped it just as ya did!"

"Maybe they know ya don't know how to shoot the damn thing, I don't know."

"Show me, show me, now!" Immanuel demanded.

Uzziah took the Girandoni and passed it to his partner.

"Ya just point it and shoot, right?"

"Yep, go ahead, see ifn ya can hit that bunch of rocks over there," Uzziah suggested, pointing to some boulders about fifty yards away.

Immanuel took it and placed the rather bulbous stock against his arm. "Feels weird, don't it?"

"A little," Uzziah said and made a motion with his hand for Immanuel to shoot the thing.

He pulled the trigger, and a moment later, the spherical ball ricocheted off the boulders and Immanuel jumped in the saddle.

"It didn't even feel like it shot!" he exclaimed.

"No recoil."

"And no sound, I mean yeah, sure, the faint plunk, and no smoke, man, this thing is scary," Immanuel said.

"That's why they flee when ya pump it just right."

Immanuel just looked at his partner and started to hand the Girandoni back to Uzziah.

"Nah, pump it again, partner," Uzziah said.

Immanuel pumped the air rifle again, but this time there was a slight difference, a sort of awe in the way he did it.

"Betcha next time ya pump that sucker fer some Injuns, they run," Uzziah said, and taking the Girandoni, he put it back in the scabbard.

It took them nearly two weeks to get across the Great Plains, and then the short grasses turned into the tall grasses, which the horses dearly loved.

"This chere's Pawnee country," Immanuel said.

"Yeah, do 'member ya spillin' yer guts when ya thought we was stuck with no water and the Pawnee had us tied down," Uzziah said.

"I'd hold that agin ya ifn it hadn't led to me meeting my true family again. It seems sometimes that the Almighty puts things in our paths which seem bad at the time, then turn toward the good," Immanuel said, smiling.

"Well, lookie here who's in a philosophical mood," Uzziah remarked.

"Young son, we done been through some shite together, and somehow it all seems to have made us stronger."

"'Cept you, yer weak as a kitten," Uzziah said.

"I am not!"

"Ya never finish yer supper, ya push yer breakfast around like it was manure. I can 'member when ya used to eat a half dozen biscuits every morning," Uzziah complained.

"Ah, yer actin' like the wife I never had, Uzziah."

"There's a reason ya never had one."

"Uh-huh, I'll bite," Immanuel said, still grinning. "Ya ain't gonna git my goat, 'cause there's no goat to git!"

"Now, I have to tell ya, if ya really wants ya a wife, yer 'bout to come on some powerful strong and beautiful womens," Uzziah said.

"The Morons?"

"Don't call 'em that, okay, it ain't fair," Uzziah said, and his goat had just been let out, and if he wasn't careful, Immanuel would have it.

"Okay, okay, I see ya still dressin' like 'em and I'm sure as fer as yer concerned I'm a Gentile, right?"

"Well, yeah, but yer my Gentile, old son," Uzziah said, getting his goat under control.

"Well, these powerfully beautiful womens ain't gonna be interested in no old goat Gentile, are they?"

"Why ya think the mens got so many wives?"

"'Cause they're horny bastards?"

"No, 'cause there ain't that many men as there are womens," Uzziah said.

"So, what's the ratio?"

"'Bout five to one, I'd say."

"Five women to every one man, well, yeah, then it kinda makes sense, don't it?"

Uzziah could see Immanuel's mind working,

figuring on if he became a Mormon, how many wives could he satisfy, and it made Uzziah smile.

"What ya smilin' 'bout?"

"Thinkin' of ya dressed up like me."

"Oh, hell no, my deerskins are stayin' on, young son," Immanuel said, then added, "Let's camp yonder, what say?"

Uzziah had more stamina than his partner and he knew it. They could have traveled until dark as far as he was concerned, but he agreed and they camped on the Medicine Creek River. Uzziah figured correctly that they were halfway to Omaha and wondered if they would get there without any more troubles.

But for the White man to understand the Pawnee he would have to know that for nearly 800 years the Pawnee, or his immediate relatives, had existed along the rivers of the Nebraska territory, and their subjection to being made into nothing but farmers, and such, and accepting the ways of the whites, did nothing but rankle the Pawnee mind, and Spirit.

Uzziah and Immanuel were passing through the Pawnee territory just at the time in their history when they were about to be disposed of, and the land which their ancestors had claimed as their own would be farmland, White man's farmland.

The rest of the way to Omaha was uneventful as far as the Pawnee, or any other tribes, were concerned. The two mountain men rose with the sun, ate a good breakfast, and Uzziah could already see that his cooking was putting weight back on Immanuel, weight that he would need in the event of troubles, or certainly need in the cold, especially the cold of the mountains in deep winter. Last winter, they had had it easy, but they both swore that they weren't going to rely on Max and Frederick any longer. They had been good to them, but if the winter had been harder, they all would have run out of wood. It was essential then that they got these Latter-day Saints to wherever it was they wanted to go, and get back so they could prepare for the winter.

The verdant hills rolled out to meet them each morning, the tall prairie grasses deep as their horses' bellies. Both Stygian and Shadow had gained some weight, which was the Injun way—in the summers the horses got fat, and winters brought them to bones and their sides looking like barrel staves.

It was a laconic time. They rode without talking, mostly, which meant they rode without arguing. An agreement grew up between them, not a new one, but an agreement which had started back in St. Louis when they both loved the one whose name they would not speak, and over the years, that agreement, that bond had grown. The last few years of them not being together had strained the bond, but it was like the bond between father and son. They may be apart, but it did nothing to decrease the natural understanding that they had between them. They made changes in course almost unperceptively, but both made them at the same time. They knew when it was time to water animals, and so far, they really hadn't used the spare horses much.

Uzziah figured that when they got to Omaha, they would either sell the extra horses they'd gotten from Jean Baptiste or keep them, whatever the time and chances warranted. Maybe the Latter-day Saints would need them?

You could have said that this was the time of their healing. The time that had passed between them, their time apart, was being washed away by simple gestures and thoughtless actions. It wasn't unusual for them to go a whole day without saying two words. And it was an easy non-verbal time. Words had little to do with the souls of these men who had accepted the great outdoors as their home, men who knew their strengths and hoped to God that their weaknesses wouldn't get them killed. And more importantly, it was a time without whiskey. Oh, Uzziah had his requisite bottles, but Immanuel seemed to be doing fine without the taste of the spirits, and that was fine by Uzziah.

As if the thoughts had communicated themselves to Immanuel, he spoke up, then coughed, and cleared his throat. "Say, them Mormons don't imbibe, does they?"

"Why ya ask?"

"Well, "Immanuel continued, "I was just thinkin', ifn they don't, then maybe we should–that is–before we get there."

"The prettiest saloon I ever saw was in Nauvoo, just down the street from the Nauvoo Temple," Uzziah said.

"Nah, really!?"

"Yeah, it looked like somebody's home. It was open in the front, and had porches on the front and back, and in the back, there was a duck pond. Ya could sit back there and drink, and I don't know ifn it were the drink, or the general atmosphere of the place, but a couple was usually all ya wanted. Nobody was even in there swearing and using the Lord's name in vain, no gambling, no loose women–"

"Whoa, whoa, whoa! No doves atall?" Immanuel asked.

"Oh, they was doves there, but no soiled ones."

"Well, I'm havin' a hard time imaginin' this chere saloon."

"To me, it was like what a saloon would be like in heaven," Uzziah shyly admitted.

"Really, ya thought that, did ya?"

"Yeah, I did," Uzziah admitted.

"Young son, truly, ya have the strangest mind that I ever encountered—a saloon in heaven, no doves! Well, what ya think a saloon in hell would be like?"

"'Bout like every other one I ever been in," Uzziah admitted.

"Humph," Immanuel grunted, then added, "Well, there's some truth in that, I don'ts walk in a saloon unless I know who's at my back, and I certainly don't sit with my back to the door."

"See?" Uzziah encouraged his thought.

"Wished I'd seen it, fer myself, understand, but I's believes ya."

They rode on, the afternoon sun was at their backs, making the shadows of their horses and the men sitting them look like they were ten feet tall. The breeze came up out of the north, and looking that way, they saw the beginning of what might be a thunderstorm later on in the night, or maybe before the sunset.

They rode, then, with a bit more purpose, and when they saw cliffs along the far back of whatever river was running east and west that they were traveling along, they rode their horses into the river, which had depth to it, and let them drink as they surveyed the cliffs and the surrounding territory. They decided to ford the river, which turned out to be the North Platte, and instead of going directly to the caves, which would have afforded them shelter from the almost certain coming storm, they rode to the heights of the area and saw that they were on a huge island. Well, they couldn't see as far as the end of the easternmost part, but they could see the western edge of the island where the river divided and streamed eastward toward the Mississippi or perhaps the Missouri, they weren't sure.

The wind picked up significantly on the little knoll on which they sat, the manes of their horses blew to one side, and their hats, if not secured by stampeded stings, would have flown away. Naturally, the horses put their butts into the wind, but Uzziah and Immanuel both turned to look at the coming storm. It was raging in the not-so-far distance, and strikes of lightning could be seen, multiple strikes before the sound of the rolling thunder slapped past them and made the horses beneath them jerk and tremble.

"Let's get someplace safe," Uzziah said, thinking that it wouldn't be good for Immanuel to be drenched in a downpour, and it certainly wouldn't make fixing supper any easier, and he was hungry.

On the way back downhill, a small deer scared up out of its hiding place, unluckily crossed their path, and as Uzziah admired the creature, Immanuel's pistol roared, and it fell dead. Well, now Uzziah knew it wouldn't be just bacon, beans, and johnnycakes.

Uzziah lassoed the horns of the young buck, which still had felt on them, and dragged him back down to the caves.

Immanuel didn't like the idea of taking a puma or bear's cave, so he made a torch and went through the biggest of them. There were bats in that one, so he chose the other.

They made a fire back from the entrance, and the horses had a little trickle off a stalactite, which supplied them with a constant source of water. Also, it was good water for cooking.

The storm raged, and Uzziah got busy cooking, and as he cooked, he remembered the words of the Old Testament.

The Lord said, 'Go out and stand on the mountain in the presence of the Lord, for the Lord is about to pass by.' Then a great and powerful wind tore the mountain part and shattered the rocks before the Lord, but the Lord was not in the wind. After the wind, there was an earthquake, but the Lord was not in the earthquake. After the earthquake came a fire, but the Lord was not in the fire. And after the fire came a gentle whisper.

And there, stood Immanuel, his cloak swirling about him, his hat blown off his head, and hanging on his back, his long hair, swishing this way and that. He was standing perfectly still, unaffected by the wind, the earthquake, or the fire of the lightning as it flashed and tore around him. Somehow, this stalwart figure of his best friend reminded him of what he loved most about the man. He was able to exist in a world that was hostile to him without holding the world accountable. He could take the so-called slings and arrows of outrageous fortune, and still look, just look upon it all as if this, too, shall pass. It was this unshakable stance in the world, not against it, which had grown in Uzziah's mind as the way a man should, if he were able, be in the world. Complaining, bitterness, revenge, all the passions were useless in the face of the might which the world, or God for that matter, could throw against you.

And after the wind, the earthquake, the fire, what was there to be perceived but the still small voice which arose from the silence, arose to advise each and every one of us, that just to be here was somehow special, just to stand and not fall was maybe even enough. Then there was always redemption, which came when the words passed away and the thoughts shrank, and the arguments settled, and you were left with you, and the feeling that something, something was out there that supported you.

Immanuel walked over to where Uzziah was dishing up supper. He took the plate, set it on a flat rock, and poured himself some coffee.

"Had the weirdest feelin' standin' there," Immanuel said as he sipped at the coffee, then put it down and picked up the plate.

"Oh yeah?"

"Yeah, couldn't explain it even if I tried, but ya know what?"

"What?"

"Think I know why Abooksigun is sitting by those bubbling paint pots every day," Immanuel said, taking a bite of the roasted young deer, which was tender and juicy.

"Why?"

"'Cause it brings him peace," Immanuel said and washed down the venison with the hot, scalding coffee.

There was no need for a sentry to watch, they were safe in the cave, and neither the fire nor its reflection could be seen down by the river. Uzziah had walked down there and checked.

As he rolled into his bedroll, he realized one of the things he liked most about having Immanuel with him. The two of them acted like mirrors for each other. It was one thing to be in the wild, but to see your counterpart there, struggling, eating, riding, fighting, and just being, gave you the satisfaction that you were for them the same as they were for you. Both reflecting the life they led, both echoing what was happening, both reverberating the pandemonium of the world, the babel about the high tower reduced to silence that allowed the space for the things that mattered. Or something like that.

5

The next four days were uneventful, though they did keep seeing Pawnee, who sat on the ridges off in the faraway hills that they didn't bother even paying them much attention. They did think, well, at least Uzziah did, about when they were coming back that way. One death stick wasn't going to do the trick if there were multiple wagons, which there would be, and many prizes for the Pawnee to steal.

There was developing the old ease that the partners had a few years earlier. Their talk was easy, and the arguing had gotten a bit more erudite. Well, maybe not erudite, but at least they'd pretty much stopped arguing over the stupid stuff. This was Uzziah's thinking and Uzziah's thinking alone, which he was about to find out.

"Ya think yer better than me, don't ya?" Immanuel was riding abreast with Uzziah, who had been having different thoughts than this, surely.

Uzziah just looked at Immanuel. This wasn't true, but how best to express it?

"Not sayin' anythin' says a lot more than ya think."

"What brought this on?" Uzziah asked sincerely.

"Ya carry that Bible around like it was a token of yer holiness, ya dress different than me, ya always finding the good in folks, yer a master at making me feel like I don't know what's good and what ain't." All this spilled from Immanuel in a torrent of words.

"First off, the Good Book is just that, it is the living, breathing book of the Lord. In the Gospel of John, it says, 'In the beginning was the Word, and the Word was with God, and the Word *was* God—'"

"Yeah, God Almighty, how many times ya gonna tell me that?!?"

"But I don't think ya understand, Immanuel, this book"—and he reached back and got the Bible from his saddlebags—"this book is Jesus!"

"What! Have ya lost yer mind?"

"No, the Word of God is Jesus, this is the Word of God, so they are the same thing!"

"So, ifn I shoot a hole in that book, then I will be shooting a hole in Jesus!?!"

"Why does everything come down to ya pullin' yer pistola, huh? What would putting a hole in my Bible accomplish other than putting a hole in my Bible?"

"Ya said the Word was God, so, ifn Jesus is the Word, then that there book is Jesus, no?"

"Yeah."

Immanuel drew his pistol, and Uzziah held the Bible against his chest.

"Is this more of that *I'm bullet and blade proof*, Uzziah?"

"No, no, this is me, saying this book is so precious to me that ifn ya shoot it, ya might as well be shootin' me!"

Immanuel reached over and knocked the Bible from

Uzziah's hands. It fell between the two horses, and as Immanuel was aiming down at it, Stygian, for some reason, reared up, and the shot went wild, and Immanuel came off the back of Stygian, hitting his head on a rock.

Uzziah was impressed that one man could continue to be so stupid. His partner of all these years, his partner who had never not revered the Good Book, and had Uzziah read it to him numerous times, had knocked it to the ground, and actually taken a shot at it!

Why Stygian reared up was no mystery. Uzziah had tapped him hard in the breast with the barrel of his Hawken, and horses move away from pressure, and since the pressure was coming from the front and he couldn't see anything there, he reared up to get away from it.

"Ohhh," Immanuel moaned from where he had been placed in his bedroll and covered. The fire was going nicely, and when he looked around, they seemed to be camped in a nice copse of trees which was close to the river, "What happened?" he asked, holding his head.

Uzziah looked up from where he was cooking supper. There wasn't any meat besides bacon, so bacon, beans, and johnnycakes it would be.

"Ya don't remember?" Uzziah asked, hoping that maybe Immanuel didn't remember and that would be a blessing, because if he did, then they would probably get into it all over again.

Immanuel got up on one elbow and gently touched the back of his head. "Did ya wallop me?"

"No, ya hit yer head on a rock," Uzziah said, stirring the beans so they wouldn't burn. The coffee began to boil and Uzziah moved it off the hottest part of the fire.

"I'll take some of that," Immanuel said, then he saw the Bible, which was sitting on top of Uzziah's saddlebags. "Ah ha!" he almost yelled as he pointed at the Good Book.

Instinctively, Uzziah brushed it off and placed it back in his saddlebags, and out of harm's way.

"I shot a hole in it, didn't I?" Immanuel said with a great deal of guilt.

"No."

"I did, I know I did, that's why Stygian reared and I fell, ain't it?"

"Ya did come unseated, that's a fer sure, and then ya hit yer head."

"Let me see the Bible."

"Nah, ya just rest, and we'll have supper in a bit."

"Give me the Bible!" Immanuel asserted!

Uzziah looked at his partner and wondered if this was where it would all unravel. Would Immanuel, who wasn't drunk, continue with this folly and blow a hole in the Bible his mother, Rahab, had given him?

"Uzziah Ferguson O'Bannon!"

Immanuel only said his full name like that, much like his beloved mother, when he was really mad at him. He reached into the saddlebags and pulled out the precious book, and could not contain himself, he kissed its cover before handing it to him.

Immanuel took the book and turned it over several times, then looked at Uzziah.

"My God," Immanuel whispered, then a bit louder said, "Partner, young son, ya know I don't miss, so how in God's name does this book remain without a hole in it?"

Uzziah was about to explain about poking Stygian in the breast with his Hawken, when Immanuel placed the Bible close to his face and kissed it.

You could have knocked Uzziah over with a turkey feather, that's what you could have done. The last thing he expected was Immanuel kissing the Holy Word of God.

"This chere Bible is bulletproof, just like yerself, ain't it?"

Uzziah reeled. What could he say? "Nah, ya just missed."

"From less than five feet away, young son, this mountain man does not miss at that range. That there book is protected just like yerself," he said as he crawled over on his knees and embraced Uzziah, "Uzziah, please fergive this old mountain man, please!" he pleaded, and his voice broke as his emotions took over.

What could Uzziah say? The truth? What was the truth? That he'd poked Stygian, or that Immanuel thought the book bulletproof? Could both be true at the same time?

"Immanuel," Uzziah began as he pulled away from the kneeling hug.

"Yeah?"

"The beans are burnin', old son."

———

They ate supper in a sort of religious quietness, and every once in a while, Uzziah saw his partner of over ten years look toward the Bible, which had been placed back on Uzziah's saddlebags. When they were almost done, Immanuel spoke up. "I'll take the pot and tin plates, everything down to the creek to wash 'em."

"Nah, yer head still needs tendin', I'll git it."

Uzziah went down to the creek and washed up supper dishes. He left the tin cups and coffee, because they generally finished that old coffee before they went to bed. He could see Immanuel sitting there, and the man was like a statue. He had taken the Bible from Uzziah's saddlebags and was holding it in his hands.

It was a good thing he looked about because coming down the trail they'd been on, there were two Pawnee, and they hadn't seen the fire because Uzziah had dug deep into the ground and circled it with rocks, one of the rocks being the one that knocked sense into Immanuel. Both Hawkens were uncharacteristically leaning against a tree just off from the fire. Uzziah was unsure whether to risk moving, since it was always the movements, especially the quick ones, that were picked up by the eye of the predator. He got low and started crawling back toward their camp when both Injuns saw Immanuel at the same time. They literally sluffed off their ponies, who immediately began eating the tall grasses, and they circled around toward the campsite.

It was then that Uzziah began to wonder if Immanuel had gone asleep sitting up, but surely, he would have tipped over, and been more lying down than sitting up.

The Pawnee, both of them, would have been seen by Immanuel if he were looking!

Finally, he looked up and saw the drawn bow of one of the Pawnee and the war club of the other held back, ready to strike.

Immanuel held up the Bible in front of his face and closed his eyes.

He heard the arrow hit and thought surely, he was about to die, then immediately following that sound, a thunk, as if someone had thrown a tomahawk.

Immanuel opened his eyes, and the arrow was stuck in the Bible, and lying beside him was the body of the other Pawnee with a tomahawk in the side of his head.

Immanuel lowered the Bible, and the Pawnee who had shot it was transfixed. He hadn't moved a step when he saw the blade of Immanuel's Bowie. He turned and was thrown forward in his journey of escape by the knife in his back reaching all the way to his heart.

You have to remember that all this took approximately three seconds to take place.

Uzziah ran up and, putting his boot on the Pawnee's head, pulled the tomahawk from it, then he put his index finger to his lips. Thinking quickly, he walked briskly over to the two ponies and, taking their war bridles, brought them down to the creek where they drank, great boluses of water one after the other, following each other to their stomachs.

Immanuel had already brushed dirt over the fire, and the two mountain men lay down beside the two dead Pawnee as a bigger party of mounted Pawnee traveled silently down the trail.

Both men tried not to breathe, but then one of the Pawnee dead started to groan till Uzziah pulled him toward him and smothered him with his big hand. His legs jerked a bit, then he was still.

They waited a good ten minutes before either of them moved, and they gathered their belongings and, tightening the cinches on their horses, took off slowly in a perpendicular direction away from the larger Pawnee party. They traveled like that till sunup and then found a place to stop and make more coffee.

Uzziah looked over and Immanuel pulled something from his saddlebags. It was Uzziah's Bible, and it had something sticking out of it. Immanuel passed it to Uzziah, who was waiting for the coffee to perk.

What stuck from the Bible was a broken-off arrow. The feathers were missing, but the flint arrowhead was embedded in the book.

"The Bible saved my life," Immanuel said reverently.

Uzziah opened the book from the back, so that just the flint arrowhead was pointing toward one verse. It had indented itself beside that verse in the Gospel according to St. Luke. Uzziah read it aloud to Immanuel, "'*Who touched me?' Jesus asked.*"

It was a moment, shall we say, for both the boys. Earlier, before the attack, they had been discussing whether or not the Holy Bible, the Word of God, was essentially Jesus Himself. And now, a flint arrowhead had traversed the entire book until it came to the 8th Chapter and 45th verse of the book of Luke. And there beside the verse was the indentation of the point of the arrowhead, where Jesus asked if he had been touched.

"Oh my God!" Immanuel whispered and got on his knees. "That book *is* Jesus!"

Uzziah looked at Immanuel and wondered how such a thing could have happened. The arrowhead stopping right there, pointing to the verse concerning Jesus being touched.

"Yer gonna hafta watch out fer arrows, Uzziah," Immanuel said.

"Whatcha talkin' 'bout?"

"Ya may be immune to bullets and blades, but arrowheads will kill ya."

6

Quite frankly, after Immanuel had inadvertently shot and killed the Mohawk George Henry Martin by shooting at Uzziah's breast and the Mohawk jumping in front of the shot and dying for his brother, well, Uzziah never really thought that Immanuel would bother with the whole bullet and blade proof blessing which had been given to him by Porter Rockwell. Uzziah himself had doubted it until he was ambushed on the courthouse steps in Jefferson City. That encounter had emboldened him enough to imagine that he might have a protection which was not earthly. And yet. And yet, he was willing to let the whole thing go until he prodded Stygian in the breast and caused Immanuel's horse to rear and throw him when Immanuel had thrown Uzziah's Bible to the ground and was about to shoot it.

He hadn't told Immanuel of his prodding the stallion, and now, the arrow had become lodged in such a place that it pointed to the Holy Bible speaking directly to both mountain men. Quite frankly, Uzziah didn't know what to do, he really didn't.

As they got close to what would later be known as Omaha, Nebraska, and they could see the crude mud, tent, and board huts which had been built into the hills as the Mormons weathered their winter before taking off for the promised land, Uzziah thought he'd just let the subject go and leave it at that. And yet, there was the person of Porter Rockwell, the one who had delivered the blade and bullet blessing to Uzziah, and they would see him, and the subject was bound to be broached once again.

"Halt, who goes there!" a man had challenged them as they rode upon the winter headquarters.

Immanuel was moving his loaded Hawken toward the man.

"Don't," Uzziah whispered, then louder he said, "It's Uzziah Ferguson O'Bannon."

"Uzziah, is it really you!?" the man asked as he stepped more into the road and could easily be seen. He was a youngster of less than twenty years, but he was holding a big, powerful flintlock rifle which was just about as tall as he was.

"Sorry, son, I don't recognize ya," Uzziah said apologetically.

"We never met, but I sure as heck know ya. I'm Hiram McKenzie, the husband of Hannah's younger sister!" he said proudly.

Uzziah rode forward and stuck out his hand. "Well, the saints have been good to ya, Hiram!"

"As they have to you, Brother Uzziah," Hiram said. "I can't wait to tell Galilee that yer here!"

"This is my partner and good friend, Immanuel James Jones," Uzziah introduced them.

Immanuel reached down and shook the boy's hand. "Any friend of Uzziah's is a friend of mine," he said, and the boy smiled like he was meeting royalty.

"Porter will be at the council house, ya see the big building in the middle of all this mess, that's the one," Hiram said.

Uzziah looked, and he could see the well-made structure that had been made from hewn logs. It wasn't a temple, but for a winter headquarters in the middle of nowhere, it was good enough.

They rode through the hodgepodge of tents, mud huts, and hastily put-together buildings. Children were playing in the streets, women were hanging up laundry, and men were chopping wood for warmth and cooking. As they got closer, Uzziah thought he recognized one of the men who had just exited the council house. He clicked up Shadow and trotted toward the man.

The man put his hand on the top of his pistol, one of his two 36 caliber Navy Colts. Then, when he saw who it was, he yelled out, "Uzziah!"

Uzziah was down off Shadow, and the two men were fiercely embracing, and saying things to one another which Immanuel could not hear.

Then, they leaned back in their embrace and looked at each other.

"The years have been good to ya!" Porter said, and then laughed, looking at the other man on horse. "And this has to be Immanuel," he said, even though he had imagined Uzziah's partner stockier and more filled out.

Immanuel put his hand down for a shake, but Porter would have nothing of that.

"Ya must get down, I've got whiskey at the hut, ya must have one with me and Uzziah," Porter said.

Immanuel liked this Porter Rockwell right off, and for whiskey, he would have hugged the man himself!

They led their two horses through the confusion of structures, then Porter opened the door to one mud hut and shouted, "Y'all never guess who's here!"

They entered the hut expecting to see—well, they didn't know exactly what they'd see. Instead of a mess, Luana, Porter's wife, had managed, as just about all good women do, to put order and structure into the hut. Porter had obviously put boarded walls up inside, and it was big enough that, sectioned off by blankets, there were various rooms.

"Uzziah!" Emily came running from the other side of the hut and grabbed him. She had only been seven when Uzziah had first met her, and now she looked as if she were a little lady.

"Papa, did ya know he was coming?"

"Well, writin' letters and havin' those letters get to people can sometimes be a problem," he said.

"And, is this yer pa, Uzziah?" she asked, referring to Immanuel, whose face dropped like a lead weight under such scrutiny.

"No, no, no, this is Immanuel James Jones, my partner, ya 'member me tellin' ya 'bout him?"

"That's Immanuel!?!" she asked as only young people can, thinking they have a vision of someone in their minds, then they're confronted by the actual person.

"I can assure ya, young lassie, that I am older than

Uzziah as ya expected, but ifn he were my boy, I, well, I don't know what to say!" Immanuel was lost for words, and everyone was rescued by Luana.

"I've got supper almost ready, the two of you will stay, and I won't take *no* for an answer. Now go do what men do, and be back in here in half an hour, but make sure you wash your hands before we eat," she said, kissing Porter on the mouth and pushing him toward the door of the hut.

Porter, Uzziah, and Immanuel walked from the hut toward a wooden barn where Porter had his roan mare, Ludean, and standing beside her, as if they couldn't be separated, was a dark-maned and tailed buckskin, who couldn't have been very old.

"Is that?" Uzziah asked.

"Yes, I've named her Umbra, sort of a token compliment to yer Shadow."

"That's Shadow's filly?" Immanuel asked as he stroked his hand down her flanks and she moved a bit away from him. He was amazed that the friendship of the two men had extended as far as breeding their horses.

Uzziah could see he was going to have to do some damage control here.

"Porter, do ya have what I think ya have?"

"Do I? Was Joseph Smith a prophet?" he asked as he pulled a bottle of bonded whiskey from his hiding place in the barn.

"It isn't Jameson, but look where we are!" Porter said and laughed. "Please do the honor," he said as he passed the bottle to Uzziah, who passed it to Immanuel.

"Well, ifn ya insist," he said, cut off the tin around

the cork, then pulled the cork with his teeth, and took a pull, "Ahhh!"

The bottle was passed around and each had a pull or two. Uzziah was amazed at how prudent—if it could be called that—Immanuel was being. His pulls were actually gentlemanly, and when the bottle was put away by Porter, he wasn't looking after it as if he wanted more.

About that time, a boy of six years came to the barndoor.

"Pa, Mama wants ya fer supper," he said and walked away.

"Is that Orin, Jr.?" Uzziah asked.

"Yeah, sure is, just imagine..." Porter said, then trailed off.

"I know, I already have, it's impossible not to," Uzziah said, and Immanuel was totally clueless about what they were talking about.

They went back inside smelling of whiskey, which Luana and Emily could have cared less about.

They sat around the big table that Porter must have brought from Nauvoo, and when they dished, they were served family-style like most folks. Immanuel spoke up. "I know it's not my place, but I'd like to say the grace."

Uzziah looked at Porter, who had already folded his hands, but graciously said, "Please."

"Heavenly Father, as we gather in your abundance, I pray that y'all bless this food, and the wonderful people who have provided it. Bless these two little girls" —Caroline, who was almost eight years old, had joined them—"and the strapping young man, Orin, Jr. Thank you, Father, that along his way back to the Mountains, Uzziah found hisself a spiritual home from which I do not believe he has wandered. We pray this in our brother Jesus's name, Amen." And an *Amen* went around the table.

Caroline, who had always, in Uzziah's experience, been the most bashful of Porter's girls, spoke up immediately.

"You're the one with our Savior's name, ain't ya?" she asked Immanuel, who was sitting next to her.

"Not sure what ya mean?" he queried as he helped himself to mashed potatoes and passed them on.

"Ya know, Immanuel, *God with us*," she said.

"Yeah, well, I sure am Immanuel."

"I like that name, it makes me feel safe," she said.

"That's why Uzziah and I are chere, to help ya'll get safe to wherever it is yer goin'," he said.

She leaned against his arm in an endearing way, while Porter and Luana looked on, but Emily had to speak up.

"Caroline, you're making a nuisance of yourself," she scolded her younger sister.

"I don't mind," Immanuel said as he moved his arm around the young Caroline. "Yer welcomed to hug me any time ya like," he said, and she smiled up at him.

"Well, I think our youngest girl just came of age, mother. She ain't ever been like this with anyone," Porter said.

"Praise be to God," Luana said, and everyone laughed, everyone but Emily, who probably didn't like sharing the limelight.

Porter leaned into Uzziah and whispered so no one

else heard, "After supper I gots to show ya somethin'," he said, and Uzziah nodded.

The meal was wonderful, and there was plenty to go around. Uzziah only ate one helping, he imagined the winter had been hard on all the Latter-day Saints, and he didn't want to be eating more than his share.

The men went outside to smoke, and after they'd all lit their pipes, Porter said, "Let's go fer a wee ride."

They rode up through the shanties, tents, and mud huts toward a hill. The sun was setting, and its ambers, reds, and oranges were resplendent among the hills. The clouds were reflecting the magnificent colors, but when the sun popped out, they could see the hill was dotted with at least 400 graves. The shadows the sun made the grave markers look like small, round-shouldered men who were in military formation.

They sat their horses at the entrance to the cemetery.

"Who are these dead?" Uzziah asked.

"Those we lost this winter, and a few more," Porter said.

"A few more?" Uzziah said, looking at Porter with a questioning glance.

"Follow me," Porter said as he rode along the outside of where the graves were laid, and getting off his horse, he began walking between the headstones toward one larger and made of granite. Uzziah and Immanuel followed him.

Porter stopped at the grandest marker there among the 400 hundred and bowed his head.

Uzziah walked up and looked at the inscription on the marker, and he gasped.

Immanuel looked and there on the marker were the names:

Hannah Larue O'Bannon
Son O'Bannon

"Ya moved her from the grave, her place of eternal rest?" Uzziah asked.

"Yeah, but ya couldn't know what it was like in the last days in Nauvoo, the Gentiles were pressing hard, and after the assassination of Joseph and his brother Hyrum, well, no one knew what to expect."

"So ya dug her up, and what about the prophet and his brother?"

"No, they remained where they was laid, we felt sure no one would bother their graves," Porter said.

"But the bodies—"

"I know what yer thinkin', but they were embalmed."

"When? After ya dug 'em up!?!"

"No, 'member when ya left 'em in the cabin afore we dressed them, the two of us?"

"Yeah, sure."

"The Mormon embalmers went down and did what was necessary to preserve their bodies."

"Even little George?"

"That's what yer callin' him, I like it, yes, even the tiny baby. At the time, I wasn't sure ya were gonna stick around, and when all was said and done, ya didn't. And I thought ya just might wanna take 'em with ya."

Uzziah kneeled in front of the grave of his wife and

infant son. His lips were moving, but the words of prayer that issued from his mouth were soft enough to be unintelligible.

Immanuel put his hand on Uzziah's shoulder, and Porter followed suit as the two big men bowed their heads and said whatever it was they had to say to Father. Finally, Uzziah stood.

"I'm gonna take her back to the high meadow," Uzziah said.

"I figured as much," Immanuel said, putting an arm over Uzziah's shoulder.

"Do ya think I done wrong by this?" Porter asked, pointing to the grave.

Uzziah looked at him with tears in his eyes. "Not as long as ya don't mind me taking her home. Besides, what else could ya have done?"

The three of them stood looking out toward the Missouri, and it became quite evident as the low clouds drifted out of the way that the winter camp wasn't a hodgepodge of buildings. The place had actually been laid out in geometrical form. Then Porter spoke up.

"Ya see how the city, well, we like to think of it as that, is divided in sections. Well, each section is called a block, which measures 380 feet by 660 feet."

"My God," Uzziah said, counting the blocks.

"Don't bother, there were originally goin' to be forty-one blocks, sixteen named streets, with 594 lots, each seventy-two feet by 165 feet. There was gonna be twenty houses in each block, which would support between 150-300 people, with garden areas in the middle. But we've had so much stealing and attacks by the local Injuns that we had to abandon some of the southern blocks and take them away from the trouble."

"Is that a wall built down there?" Immanuel asked, pointing toward the south end.

"Yeah, good, ya see that." Porter also pointed to where Immanuel had pointed. "We repositioned cabins and formed a solid wall of them growing from the Missouri west to the bluffs, and ifn ya look, there's a tall picket fence along the top."

Immanuel got out his spyglass and glassed the area. "It's genius, people are botherin' ya so ya block 'em off so they can't!"

"Exactly," Porter said as Uzziah took the glass from Immanuel.

"Look down close to the river and run west toward the bluffs," Immanuel suggested.

"Yeah, yeah, I see," Uzziah said as he glassed the entire area.

They rode back down out of the hills. There were some folks higher up than the city who were living in their wagons, they had fires burning in them, and the glow on the canvas gave each of the wagons a homey feel. As they rode downhill, the magnificent design of the winter headquarters evaporated into the details and minutiae of daily living. In fact, Porter had to lead the way to his mud hut, and Uzziah and Immanuel pitched a camp right outside the door of the Rockwells. Orin, Jr. and Caroline wanted to camp out with the two mountain men, but were not allowed. Sometime in the night, when Uzziah awakened, the two smallest children of the Porters were sleeping close to the fire and spooning together, covered by a horse blanket.

Immanuel was sitting up and it was false dawn.

"When did this happen?"

"Don't rightly know, just found 'em out chere when I woke up," Immanuel said.

"I think that Caroline got it fer ya," Uzziah said.

"Ain't the first time," Immanuel said, remembering little Sarah with the wagon train going west to Oregon. *God*, he wondered, *how old would she be, now?*

They could hear the sounds of the winter camp awakening, and Uzziah looked up toward the hill where his wife and son lay with a multitude of the Mormon dead. He said a silent prayer, or was he talking to the dead? He wasn't sure. But he wanted her to know that he and she would never be separated again. He had already thought where in the highland meadow he would place their grave, and how he would plant perennials around it, and when he died, he'd have already made himself a headstone to go with theirs.

He wondered how far into the future people would be coming upon their graves and wondering who they were, and how they died. Well, how the mother and child had died would be evident, seeing that their death dates were identical, but he knew that no matter what people thought about the years which intervened between their deaths and his own, he knew there would never be another for him. They had a celestial marriage, and he would join her in the presence of the Lord, and that's all there was to it.

7

The Rockwells and the mountain men had breakfast together, but this time it was Uzziah's turn to treat. He'd found a woman in a shanty who had chickens and bought a dozen eggs from her, and he'd made biscuits in the Dutch oven, and fried potatoes with onions—also from the chicken woman—and bacon. He decided to do all the eggs together and added some sharp cheddar cheese, which Luana offered, and even though the meal was prepared outdoors, they ate around the big table.

There was a squabble before the meal was served in which Emily and Caroline argued about who was sitting beside Immanuel.

"You girls! Cut it out! What will Mr. O'Bannon and Mr. James think!?! We are not raising up savages here in the house of Rockwell, ya understand?" That was Porter, and they knew he meant business.

"Let 'em each have a seat on either side of him," Luana said, and Porter realized that for the first time, since Emily was little, her fascination was about another man besides her father. He was saddened a bit, but knew better. It was the nature of things, and soon, probably sooner than he was willing to admit, his little Emily would be courted by a good Mormon boy, and having him grandbabies. This world just kept throwing it at you, didn't it?

After breakfast, Luana spoke. "Both of you for showing such preferences as ya have, will do all the dishes by yerselves and the pots and pans which Uzziah cooked in also."

They groaned, but one look from Luana and they got to it. Luana had chores to do, and she left, taking Orin, Jr. with her as she left. She had him balanced on her right hip as all women did back then. They could hear her talking to someone outside the hut, and before the door was closed, an older man entered. It was Elder Larue, Hannah's father.

"Ephrem!" Uzziah said and got up and went and hugged the man.

"Yer still dressed as one of us," Ephrem said.

"That's acause I am one of ya," Uzziah said. "I wanna introduce ya to my partner from the mountains, this chere is Immanuel James Jones."

Immanuel had already gotten on his feet and shook hands with Ephrem.

"Pleased to meet ya, sir," Immanuel said.

"And I, you," Ephrem said.

"Won't ya join us? I's 'bout to fill 'em in on who's gonna be in the council meeting this afternoon?" Porter asked.

"Nah, I just wanted to say something in private to this young man," Ephrem said as he drew Uzziah to the outdoors.

"Is everything all right?" Uzziah asked his former father-in-law, well, if marriages were celestial, Uzziah imagined so were the in-laws!

"Never better. We had a hard winter, and many went to join the prophet and the Savior, but the Larues did well. Which brings me to why I came by here. You remember Galilee, Hannah's younger sister?"

"'Course I do."

"Well, she got married not long after you left to a good Mormon boy, Hiram McKenzie, like the prophet's brother but spelled differently. Anyway, they are so very much in love, and...well..."

"I understand, Ephrem, I do, no more needs to be said."

"Galilee is pregnant, and her mother and I are very happy," Ephrem said, once again extending his hand to Uzziah. "You were wiser than I was in this, and I am honestly eternally grateful."

They shook hands and Ephrem left. Uzziah went back into the mud hut.

"What was that all 'bout?" Immanuel asked.

"It's a Larue family matter, right, Uzziah?" Porter asked.

"Yeah, everythin's fine."

"Okay, there will be some mucky-mucks chere at this meeting, and I want ya to know who's who so no toes get stepped on, especially yerins," Porter said.

"The first one ya need to know is Father Pierre-Jean De Smet. He's a Society of Jesus priest and a good and hard man. He helped organize the Mohawks in the Council Bluff area, where so many of them were dying of the whiskey trade, then got himself involved with the Salish Injuns out of the Washington territory, even establishin' the Mission of Saint Mary in the Bitterroot Valley. It said he's traveled over 180,000 miles in his missions, and some on horseback and some on foot. He's one tough nut!"

"Is he gonna go with us on this trip?" Uzziah asked.

"No, no, I think not, he's got other concerns, besides, he's a famous Catholic priest and these people are Latter-day Saints. I just think it's God's will that his knowledge of the territories we're gonna be going through will be able to be shared with the next man that ya need to know afore ya meet him."

"Who's that?" Immanuel asked.

"Brigham Young."

"Did I meet him when I was in Nauvoo?" Uzziah asked.

"No, no, he wasn't expected to be a leader any time soon, but when both the prophet and his brother Hyrum got themselves shot and killed in Carthage, well, Young's number came up."

"So, he's the new leader?" Immanuel asked.

"Of us, he is," Porter said.

"What's that mean?" Uzziah asked.

"The church split after the prophet's death."

"Why?" Uzziah asked.

"It had to do with the prophet's revelations about having more than one wife," Porter said.

"Oh boy," Immanuel said, "just how many did he have?"

"We're not quite sure, but at the moment of his untimely death, over forty."

Immanuel whistled.

"How did this Brigham come down on the issue?" Uzziah asked.

"Well, I ain't sure."

"Because?" Uzziah asked.

"He's letting that particular controversy go fer now in favor of finding us a new home."

"Where?" Immanuel asked.

"Well, he thinks he knows, but ain't sure," Porter said. "When we was all settling in here, he and a bunch of others went along the Missouri, then cut south and they found a big ole salty lake in the middle of nowhere. Well, it's in the middle of the Mexican territories that's where it's at, but nobody lives there. Anyways, he ain't sure he can find it goin' straight from chere, and that's the reason we gathered some of ya mountain men to help us."

"There are other mountain men?" Uzziah asked.

"Well, we made a call fer 'em, but so far, yer the onliest ones who've showed."

"So, he don't know no mountain men personally?" Immanuel asked.

"Oh, when he went with that smaller band of Mormons, he met Jim Bridger in the mountains of the southwest of the Wyoming territory. It was there that Bridger had built a fort, well, really a trading post of three buildings which were supposed to make money supplying those on the way to California and Oregon. When Young asked Bridger about the great, salty lake basin, Bridger told Young, 'Ifn ya can raise corn there, I'll pay a $1,000 a bushel fer it!' Bridger went on to tell Young that it was imprudent to bring a large population to the basin, that it would never support it."

"What Young say?" Uzziah asked.

"He told Bridger, 'Wait a little and we will show you the bushels of corn.'"

"So, he's a thinkin' old Jim Bridger is gonna come out chere and show 'em how to get to the great salty lake basin from Omaha?"

"Well, that's his hope. Have ya ever seen this chere salty lake basin?"

Uzziah and Immanuel looked at each other, they had not, and knew they'd have to say it, then Immanuel spoke up.

"Look. It's on the other side, the western side, of the Rockies, so we wouldn't had no chance to see it," Immanuel said.

"We did take the Oregon Trail with a wagon train, though, 'member Immanuel?" Uzziah said.

"Yeah, yeah, shoulda 'membered that, it was with those kids," Immanuel said, remembering.

"So, ya been as fer as Oregon?" Porter asked.

"Yep, but took the Oregon Trail, I mean, ya gots to understand, we took South Pass, but then we cut northwest toward the Columbia River," Immanuel explained.

"How big this chere salty lake supposed to be?" Uzziah asked.

"Bridger said it covers over a million acres," Porter said.

"Well, hell, 'cuse my French. Ifn we take the South Pass, then the odds of hittin' that there lake are greater than the odds of not hittin' it. I am a gambling man, and ifn we can't find it, then we ain't mountain men," Immanuel said.

"Okay, here's the thing, when Brigham was there, he took his walking stick, his cane, and he sank into the alkali soil, and he said, 'This is where we will build the temple which shall replace the one in Nauvoo.'"

"So, but wait, there's the million-acre lake nearby, right?" Immanuel asked.

"Yeah, a'course," Porter said.

"Then, I'll wager ya right now that I will pull the cane from the desert floor myself," Immanuel said, and Uzziah and Porter looked at each other and smiled.

The meeting was set for the next afternoon, in hopes that Jim Bridger would show by then. They all had supper with Porter, Luana, Emily, Caroline, and Orin, Jr., and the children were perfect angels, no arguing at the table about who was going to sit beside whom. In fact, when Immanuel and Uzziah came in after washing their hands in the bucket outside the house, there were only two seats, and both of those were at opposite ends of the long table. They sat down, and Uzziah was asked to say the grace.

He thanked this family of pioneer Latter-day Saints for their spirit of adventure, and never looking back, the spirit of those who were making this great nation what God the Father intended it to be. He praised the father and mother of this house as the good parents they were, and he extolled the beauty of their daughters and the wit and comeliness of their only son. Then he blessed the amazing food, which would nourish their bodies and send them all on this amazing trip to the promised land. He called Brigham Young the Mormon Moses, and these people who were escaping the persecution of the modern-day Egyptians, the new Israelites who would establish themselves in the land which God had promised, then he closed, naturally, in the name of Jesus, the Lord of us all.

The meal was delicious, with laughter and jokes tasteful and funny, and when Uzziah and Immanuel were rolled up in their bedrolls beside the fire that would take the chill off their bodies in the night, Immanuel spoke up.

"That were quite a prayer ya prayed in there, brother."

"Ya liked it?"

"It were liked by all the Latter-Night Saints," Immanuel said.

"They aren't called that," Uzziah instructed Immanuel.

"I knows, just wanted to know ifn yer goat was out and about?"

"Okay."

"Ya believe all that stuff?"

"The Holy Ghost led me to say what I said."

"Ya reckon the Holy Ghost is LDS?"

"Who knows?"

"Exactly."

"What ya gettin' at, Immanuel?"

"The Mormon Moses, the new Israelites persecuted by the modern-day Egyptians?!?"

"Like I said, was led by the Holy Ghost," Uzziah said and rolled away from the fire and Immanuel.

"That Ghost, who's Holy gonna scare a whole bunch of folks," Immanuel said in passing.

"Maybe they need to be scared, people get scared by less," Uzziah said, still facing away from his partner of ten years or more.

"Guess. Well, sleep well."

"You, also."

8

It was the day of the meeting. Uzziah and Immanuel carried out their normal morning routines. They ate with the family, Luana cooked, and it was ham steaks, eggs, and hominy grits. Uzziah felt right at home, the usual fare for Virginians. Immanuel didn't care for grits, and as a custom, Uzziah rarely fixed them, although they carried a supply of them at the cabins.

Porter Rockwell seemed a bit nervous for some reason, and Uzziah wasn't quite sure why.

"Porter, ya okay?" Uzziah asked his Mormon friend.

"Yeah, sure, why do ya ask?"

"Don't know, yer dressed up a bit and yer appetite seems like it's taken a blow," Uzziah said.

"Don't much care for grits, they seem bland and tasteless," Rockwell said.

"Know what ya mean," Immanuel chimed in.

"The children like them, so you adults will just have to bear with it," Luana said.

They finished the breakfast, the men stepped out to smoke, and Rockwell spoke up.

"I am nervous," he admitted.

"What's up, the big meeting?" Uzziah asked.

"Well, there is that, no, it's not really the meeting. It's this thing between Brigham and myself. Ya know I was the prophet's personal bodyguard?"

Immanuel, knowing what happened in Carthage, would have said something if he had known Rockwell better, such as, 'How'd that work out for the prophet?' but decided to keep his colorful comments to himself. Besides, Uzziah was burning a hole in the side of his face, and he wasn't going to let his partner think he was censoring himself just because of him, although he probably was.

"Yeah," Uzziah said, looking at Immanuel, whom he knew had something snide to say.

"Well, because Brigham took over as the new president of the church and probably the new prophet, he thinks I'm gonna just step into that same role with him," Porter said.

"Personal bodyguard?" Uzziah asked.

"Yeah, just like with Joseph."

"And ya don't feel like it?" Immanuel asked, thinking he could add something to the conversation that wasn't negative.

"Well, Immanuel," Porter began, "it's not exactly that neither, but I don't like it when someone makes assumptions about what I will do. Joseph and I grew up together, and it pains me that I wasn't there to protect him, but he was in jail, who'd have thought they come fer him in the goad!?! I will go to my death knowing that I failed my brother, Joseph. And I ain't too sure I'll be able to keep Brigham safe. Ya know how it goes, ifn there's a man who's willin' to trade his life for the new prophet, then, all I'd be able to do, is kill the killer. What do you guys think?"

Immanuel looked at Uzziah, who looked like he was going to think on that, so he spoke up. "It's been ten years since Uzziah and I have had each other's backs. I tell ya it feels a whole lot better to know someone's watchin' yer backtrail than not. Here's the question I gots to ask ya, will Brigham have yer back, when and if the time comes?"

Porter Rockwell seemed genuinely shaken by that aspect of the arrangement which he and Brigham were about to have, maybe.

"Ya know, Immanuel, that's the best way I ever heard that spoke. With Joseph, I knew, there was something unspoken between us. He would have died for me," Porter said, then teared up a bit. "Hell, guess he did die fer me."

They walked to the barn, got their horses, saddled them, and then mounted up. They rode the streets of the Winter encampment, and now that Uzziah had seen what the layout of the streets was like, being up at the graveyard, well, he was appreciating the fact that, amid the mud and hovels, there was an order to the place.

They followed Porter because he knew where he was going, and as they traversed the different streets, making a right here, a left there, they finally pulled up in front of a cabin that was larger than most, but as the other cabins were 12 x12, this one was maybe 24 x12.

Not exactly what Uzziah would have thought was the home of the council of twelve for the Latter-day Saints.

There were other horses tied up outside, and when they went in, Brigham Young was already seated at the head of a longish table, Father Pierre-Jean De Smet was seated to his right, and there was the chair next to Brigham that was leaned forward against the table, as if it were saved. The three men who had just entered remained standing as the men at the table stood.

"Father," Porter said, tipping his hat to the priest, then he turned to Brigham Young. "Sir, these are the two mountain men I was telling ya 'bout. This chere's Uzziah O'Bannon and the other'n is Immanuel Jones," Porter said.

The two partners shook hands with Brigham Young as he had offered it to shake. His handshake was firm and he gave a good pump or two before he went to the next man. Young sat down at that point, physically saying that he was more important than a Catholic priest, but Father Pierre-Jean wasn't in the least bit offended. He smiled at both partners from the mountains and stuck out his hand even before Porter introduced him.

"And this is Father Pierre-Jean De Smet, who had, as ya might know, vast knowledge of the Salish people and the valleys beyond, such as the bitterroot in the Washington territory."

The Father spoke with a heavy French accent. "It is wonderful to meet men from the mountains, we, who have been there and have seen wonders, haven't we?"

It was then that Immanuel, who must have picked up a little French when he was in New Orleans, let out a string of the foreign language to the Father, who smiled, and retorted with his own string of French, and it was settled, those two men had very common ground.

"You sound Creole when you speak French," Pierre-Jean said to Immanuel in English.

Immanuel said more in his Creole French and the Father laughed loudly. "Oh, please excuse me, but the Creoles have such a bawdy sense of humor!"

All three men, Uzziah, Immanuel, and Porter, were hoping the good Father would not translate a phrase which Immanuel had learned from a whore in the French Quarter, as it was now being called.

"Where's Bridger?" Porter asked as much to cover the embarrassment of what was being said right under the new president of the LDS church as it was to really inquire.

"Not so much as a note," Young said, acting every bit as disappointed as if someone had died.

"Well, I can assure you, Brigham, that these two know those Rockies as well as Bridger," Porter said.

Immanuel did want to tell Brigham Young that Uzziah had once posed as Jim Bridger and done a very credible job.

Brigham Young touched the *reserved chair* and it fell back. "Please, gentlemen, sit."

Porter Rockwell sat next to Brigham, with Immanuel sitting around the table next to Father de Smet, and Uzziah sitting opposite Brigham at the other end of the longish table.

"So, have you two led wagon trains before?" Young asked, his first question out of the box being expected.

"Yes," Immanuel said, he and Uzziah agreeing on who should take which anticipated questions, "we led a group of wagons—"

"The size of that wagon train?" Young interrupted, he seemed an impatient man, but they both supposed he had many things on his plate.

"'Round thirty wagons, weren't it, Uzziah?"

Uzziah knew the number was less, but why mess up a good story by sticking to the facts, a phrase which was very popular among the truth-stretching mountain men.

"Yes, something like that," Uzziah said.

"Well, I know how you mountain people love to stretch the truth, why Jim Bridger once told me he would give me $1,000 for a bushel of corn if I could grow it where we're going."

"The important thing is, we made it to the Columbia River, and those people got to where they were goin'!" Immanuel said, his dander up a bit with this self-righteous prig.

"Yes, you, not-so-young man, have you been ill recently, haven't you?" Brigham asked.

Immanuel just looked at the leader of the Mormons, he wasn't going to answer that question unless he was tortured.

"He had what they're callin' a heart attack, but it was over a year ago," Uzziah offered.

"That ain't none of his business!" Immanuel said in a stern voice.

"But you're wrong, old man. It is precisely my business. If I hire you two roughnecks who claim to be from the Rockies to take our people to the Promised Land, then I need to know if you will, indeed, make it."

Uzziah looked at Immanuel who was about to stand and bolt from the cabin, but unseen by anyone but Uzziah, Father De Smet had placed a hand on Immanuel's arm.

"What the leader of this Mormon group is trying to say is, he wants his money's worth, am I right?" De Smet asked, looking at Brigham Young.

"That's part of it, but Porter don't really know these two, yeah, the younger one came into Nauvoo and made quite a splash, but he bolted after a while."

"My wife, whom you knew, Hannah Larue O'Bannon, and I were married by the Prophet Joseph Smith. She died in childbirth, and I buried her and my boy, George, in the cemetery next to the temple in Nauvoo. I left because, being celestial married, I did not want to take on another wife, as many of you have done," Uzziah said, looking directly at Brigham.

"Well, well, there's no need to get self-righteous!"

"I believe it was you who was casting aspersions, Mr. Young!" Uzziah said.

Immanuel was beaming from his side of the table, and if Uzziah had gotten up and spat in the man's face, he would have left with him gladly, and not missed a single beat. And yet, Immanuel knew there were bigger fish to fry here. It certainly wasn't about the money, and both of them could have cared less about this new leader's insecurities leading the Mormons. Uzziah's tie to this was Porter Rockwell, the man who had passed on the blade and bullet blessing from the Prophet Joseph Smith, to Uzziah, and where one partner goes in the mountains, the other partner follows and has his back. It was as simple as that!

Brigham Young looked around the table. These were the men they needed. De Smet, a despicable Catholic, who believed in transubstantiation, the turning of the bread and wine into the literal body and blood of Christ, that cannibal knew more about the mountains west of the Rockies than any White man alive, and that included Bridger. If Porter had vouched for the mountain men, and yes, he knew Hannah Larue and her father Ephrem, and he was greatly saddened with her death.

He knew Uzziah, and was being this way—why? He wasn't sure, but it had something to do with being touted in the press as the American Moses, and would this great experiment in social migration into the deserts of the Great Basin turn into a starving of those involved? Would the Utes Indian, the Sioux, the Apache, and the Pawnee take it to this band of brothers in Christ and reduce their numbers and sacrifice some to their pagan gods?

Young was tormented with dreams about such things, stupid dreams in which he was arm wrestling with savages for the safety of his new Israelites. He would either go down as the American Moses or he would be relegated to the annals of history as one who had misled their followers into a spiritual and physical oblivion, and at this point, if he had been a gambling man, the odds were easy to access—50/50. He would either succeed or fail! Hero or goat. Period.

"Gentlemen, I have not been sleeping well, and one of the reasons is that I can't get this man, Porter Rockwell, to agree to be my personal bodyguard. He had nothing whatsoever to do with what happened to brothers Joseph and Hyrum, and his guilt, I believe, is keeping him from being at my side. If he were my bodyguard, I do not believe that I would be in this much mental anguish," Young said, and he looked directly at Porter.

"All right, consider it done," Porter said, and you

could see the new leader of the movement relax, perhaps for the first time since the prophet's death.

Uzziah knew about double-binding communications. His mother had been a star of such behavior. "*Yes, go on into town with yer friends, don't worry 'bout me and my sickness, I'll be fine, just have a good time,*" Rahab had said many times. But he did not like that Porter had acquiesced so easily to such devious pressure. Perhaps Porter had done it for them, himself and Immanuel, who knew?

"Apology accepted," Uzziah said, and Immanuel looked at his partner of all these years and decided if it was okay with Uzziah, then it was okay with him.

Young blanched as if what he had said hadn't been meant as an apology to the mountain men, whom he considered rough-edged to say the least. But before he could talk, Uzziah stood, and turning the map on the table toward Brigham, began in.

"It is our opinion that the worst of the trip will be what we just came through, the Nebraskie territory, as I believe it's been called. Them Pawnee are devils of the first degree." Brigham held up a finger here as if he were going to say something, but Uzziah ignored him. "They have a ceremony called the Morning Star ceremony which is like unto what Jesus called hisself in Revelation, *I, Jesus have sent my angel to testify unto you these things in the churches. I am the root and the offspring of David, and the bright and morning star.*

"This ceremony takes place at this time of the year, and ifn they catch one of us, they will tie a young woman, say one of yer daughters, spread eagle on the ground, and she will be naked, and all the men and boys of the tribe will as the sun rises that day shoot arrows into her so that she, the evening star, can join with her husband the morning star which is rising and then all the field will be fertile and the crops will be abundant.

"I ain't sayin' this is gonna happen, but ifn it does, how will ya take back that captive without having the whole village down yer backs, well, my partner and I have a—for lack of a better word—a trick which the Pawnee would call big medicine which might not only get the young girl back, but keep the other warriors from follerin' us to kill us all," Uzziah said and Brigham Young just looked at Porter as if to ask, who are these charlatans.

"Ifn they say they got this big medicine, then I believe 'em," Porter said, and he knew what was coming next.

"Show us this big medicine, or devil's trick, or whatever you have to show me, and then, I believe this idea of you particular mountain men leading my people will be canceled completely! You have spoken without purpose to put in my heart fear, which God the Father has chosen to strike from me."

They all rode, the priest, Brigham, Porter, Uzziah, and Immanuel, up past the cemetery into a large copse of trees where there was a lot of downed limbs and such, a horrible place to ride a horse.

"You don't expect us to ride into there, do you?" Young asked, aghast that these men were about to basically bring all the horses to harm.

"No, sir, ya rest yerself chere, and gander at that there tree," Immanuel said.

There was a big seasonal oak tree that was a mere ten yards from where Young sat. Immanuel took a playing card, an ace of spades, from the pack of cards he carried and forced it between the bark of the oak.

"Just watch the playing card," Immanuel said, and he and Uzziah started off into the thickets.

"I do not approve of gambling," Young shouted after them.

"A horrible habit," De Smet agreed.

As they walked about a hundred feet from where Young sat, Immanuel spoke up.

"Ya think ya can hit the spade in the middle of the card?"

"At a hundred feet, he could have been holding the card," Uzziah said.

"Why am I looking at the devil's card for?" Young asked Porter.

"Just watch, sir, just watch," Porter said. He'd seen that air rifle in operation in Jefferson City and thought it only a novelty and wondered what these two would make of it.

Uzziah took the Girandoni from its leather case and checked the air pressure. It was fine for a demonstration, but before they left, it would have to be pumped up to full capacity.

"Is he aiming that rifle at us?" Young asked, rising and getting behind a tree.

"I think he's aiming it at the playing card, sir," the priest said.

"Just watch the playing card, Brigham," Porter said.

"Ready?" Immanuel screamed.

Porter raised his arm and then let it drop. There was no smoke, no sound from the Girandoni, but the card forced into the bark of the tree then fluttered down to the forest floor.

"A wind must have blown it down," Young said.

De Smet walked over, picked up the card, and whistled. He came over and handed it to Brigham.

"There's a hole in the black spade, Mr. Young," the priest said as Brigham looked at it, then he looked back down toward where Immanuel and Uzziah were walking toward them.

"You switched the card once you'd shown it to me!" Young protested as they walked up.

"No, sir, this chere weapon don't make a recognizable sound and no smoke, it's driven by air!" Immanuel said.

"Impossible!"

"No, I mean, yes," the priest said. "It seems impossible, but I heard a fable from the Salish that Lewis and Clark had such a weapon, and it was regarded with trepidation," De Smet said.

"So, this is what's going to keep us safe, not the Lord!?!" Young asked.

"The Lord helps those who help themselves!" Immanuel said.

"That is not scriptural, and it smacks of disregarding God's precious grace!"

"It's Sophocles, Brigham, a learned man like yerself must recognize good words even if they was wrote 400 years afore Christ, *No good e'er comes of leisure purposeless. And Heaven ne'er helps the men who will not act*," Immanuel said.

"That's an ancient tragedy, *Philoctetes*," Young said. "Tell me, how does a man such as yourself know about such things?"

"*Isn't this the carpenter's son? Isn't his mother's name Mary, and aren't his brothers James, Joseph,*

Simon, and Judas? Aren't all his sisters with us? Where then did this man get all these things?" Uzziah quoted Matthew's gospel.

Brigham Young reached out and took the Girandoni from Uzziah and examined it. He put it to his shoulder and pretended to aim it.

"I would like you to show this to Brother Jonathan Browning in Council Bluffs, if you do not mind?"

"Who's he?"

"He's a gunsmith and an arms manufacturer," Young said.

"That'd be fine by me, if it's okay with Uzziah?" Immanuel said, and Uzziah nodded and smiled, knowing they'd won the Mormon leader over.

When they rode back to Porter Rockwell's mud hut, they dismounted.

"I hate to say this, and if ya repeat it, I swear I'll deny it, but I like the Prophet Joseph Smith much better than the man we just met," Uzziah said as he looked around at the people going about their business. He knew he and Immanuel would be leading the wagons, and he didn't want any bad feelings between Young and either one of them.

"Let's put the horses up," Porter said, and they followed him into the barn. As they began to loosen cinches and take bridles out of the horses' mouths, Porter turned to the two mountain men.

"Yeah, know what ya mean about that one." Porter didn't even want to say his name. "Ya see the way he pressured me into becomin' his bodyguard right in front of all of ya?"

"Yeah, nobody likes that sorta thing," Immanuel said.

"He's an organizer though, he's already met with the Quorum of the Twelve Apostles. They brought money from the British mason to help us buy supplies. He's organizing this thing like an army campaign."

"That's good, but there's always something nobody accounted fer," Immanuel said.

"Yeah, so true, and to tell the truth, I think that's why he's hiring you guys, you're his ace in the hole, although I don't think Brother Young would like that reference, though he did like the card trick."

"So, when are we leaving, exactly?" Uzziah asked.

"April the fifth," Porter said.

"Well, take us over to see Brother Browning this afternoon, we gots some monies to spend on newish firearms," Immanuel said.

9

They forded the river on the Mormon ferry, which was a crude raft-like structure that had a V-rope allowing for east–west transit. It cost them twenty-five cents for a man and horse. Immanuel sprung for all three and paid $1.50 for them to get the round-trip. When Uzziah saw Council Bluffs, he was sorry he'd let the Mohawk, George, talk him out of landing there when they were steaming their way up the Missouri on the paddle wheeler.

They rode the street along the river up to the street where Porter said Jonathan Browning had his gun shop and home.

"There it is," Porter said as he pointed to an elongated brick business with a two-story home on the far end. They reined in their horses and tied them up outside the gun shop. Over the big double doors, there was a sign which read *Jonathan Browning, Gunsmith*, and beneath that it read *Blacksmith & Ferrier*. The single-story extension that connected the gun shop had its own door.

They stepped into the shop, closing the doors behind them. The amazing smell of gun oil filled their nostrils, and it was a welcoming one.

"John!" Porter yelled. A door that went into the middle one-story section opened, and they could see there were several men and boys back in there working on several guns.

"Porter, how good to see you. Who are your friends?" Johnathan Browning spoke with no accent at all, but also, he spoke perfect English, rather an oddity in those days.

Introductions were made and hands shook all around, and both Immanuel and Uzziah commented later to each other how strong his grip was. It was probably from the metalwork he did with his guns. Browning could see that the eyes of Porter's two friends were glued to the back wall of the saleroom, where various models of his guns were displayed.

"See something you like, gentlemen?"

"I'll take one of each," Immanuel joked.

"What is that weapon?" Uzziah asked, pointing to a peculiar rifle that had something sticking out of the place where bullets were chambered.

"That is my invention, it's called, well, I call it the Slide-Bar Repeating Rifle, but others have called it the Harmonica Rifle. Would you like to see it?"

"Please," Uzziah and Immanuel said at exactly the same time. Browning took two of them down and handed them to the boys.

"Now, you want to know how they work, right?"

"Yeah, sure!"

"Follow me," Browning said.

The boys followed him out back, where Jonathan had a large berm that had target setups.

"Let me show you first how they load," he said as he pressed a lever and took out the slide bar, which had five chambers.

"You see, on this side where the hammer comes down, we have five percussion cap reservoirs, and on the other side"—he turned it over—"there's five chambers which you load. See here, on the right side is the mechanism that I pulled up to allow the slide to come out. Well, once the chambers are loaded, you push that back down, and it pushes the slide against the barrel, essentially making a seal which does not allow any gases to escape."

"So, once ya shoot the first round, what do ya do?" Uzziah asked.

"You push the mechanism up, it releases the vacuum on the barrel, and you move to the next chamber, push the lever down, and you're ready to fire once again. There is no half-cock on this weapon, once you've moved it, sealed it, and raised the hammer, it's ready to go. Want to try it out?"

The boys didn't need an engraved invitation, they got busy with their own powder and shot, loaded the chambers, put the percussion caps on, and were ready to go.

Meantime, Browning had run down to the berm and put paper targets on two ranges.

"You go first, brother," Uzziah said, handing his rifle to Porter.

"No, I've fired that particular weapon, ya try it out, Uzziah," Porter said.

Before they had finished, Immanuel was banging

away at the target downrange, getting used to pushing the lever up, then sliding the bar down, securing it with the lever, firing, and repeating the process. Both rifles were banging away now, and Browning had his hands over his ears.

When they'd emptied both rifles, they stopped and looked at each other.

"We'll take both," Uzziah said.

"Can ya make other slides that could be loaded beforehand?"

"As many slides as you prefer," Browning said, then added, "We also have this as a five-shot pistol."

"We'll take two of those also, and make us both four extra slides for both. We want the pistols in 44 caliber and the rifles in 54 caliber, can ya do that?"

"I can have my boys and myself start today, and by the day after tomorrow, you'll have your order."

"How much?" Uzziah was always the practical one among the two mountain men.

"Twenty-five dollars apiece and an extra twenty dollars for all the slides," Browning said.

Uzziah was still spending the money he'd taken off the dead bad hombres back at Gongloe's mansion when he and Porter had taken down the half-Chinese bandit boss in Jefferson City.

He handed Browning the money, who counted it immediately.

"You've given me too much," Browning said.

"We believe in tipping," Uzziah said. "By the way, Brigham Young wanted us to show you this rather peculiar rifle," Uzziah said as he pulled the Girandoni from its soft deerskin sheath.

Browning took the rifle and turned it every way imaginable, then he looked at Uzziah.

"This is the Italian air rifle, isn't it?"

"The Girandoni, yes," Uzziah said.

"Is it charged?"

"Fully."

"Back to the firing range," Browning said as they went out the back door and set up new targets.

Browning loved the feel of the air rifle and was amazed at the lack of sound and smoke. He fired about twenty rounds, then went downrange and checked out his target.

"It's as accurate as any good rifle, but it has an element of surprise, doesn't it," he said, smiling and handing the rifle back to Uzziah.

The ferry ride back was windy, and they held onto their hats. The horses tried to turn their butts into the oncoming wind. Horses were smart and never took the wind in their faces if they could help it.

As soon as they got off the ferry, they could hear the clarion call of a big bell.

"What in God's name is that?" Uzziah asked.

"That's the bell from the bell tower in Nauvoo," Porter said.

"It don't sound the same," Uzziah complained.

"It's on the ground, hanging off a bell post. Brigham has it rung when there's a meeting of everyone, we'd better get over there."

They rode among the throngs and multitudes that had left their cabins, their mud huts, their wagons, their dugouts into the surrounding mountains and were headed toward the meeting. It was the first time Uzziah realized just how many people were going on this exodus. It truly was biblical. There was Brigham Young, standing on a stump near the Nauvoo Bell. He had been the one ringing it. When enough people had arrived, he spoke in an orator's voice.

"This Saturday, we will leave. You know who you are because you have already been chosen. There will be approximately thirty wagons with from 150-200 men, women, and children on this wagon train. Every five wagons will have a captain, and every ten wagons a colonel, and of course, I will be the general in charge. No quarter will be given to anyone who disobeys a direct order. I have studied the Donner Party about which such reckless and gruesome stories have been written. They failed because they were not organized and they split the party into separate groups. We—all thirty wagons of us—will stay together at all times.

"The wagon train will be headed up by the lead wagon." He gestured toward what could only be described as a skiff or boat. There was a cannon tied down in the back of the boat, and a bell pole ready for the Nauvoo Bell to be installed there.

"That wagon will be manned by some of the Nauvoo Legion, and I, myself, will be riding in the wagon directly behind it. We have two capable mountain men who will see us to and through the Rocky Mountains. We will not be taking the Oregon Trail exactly because we have had our fill of encounters with the Gentiles. We will be traveling the north bank of the Platte River, while the Oregon Trail takes the south bank.

"The going here will be easier, but once we're deep into the Wyoming territory, we must travel through some rough territory, but in the process, we will see sights which only the Lord and some savages have beheld. This will be our trek through the wilderness, and thanks be to God our Father on high, we will not wander in this wilderness for forty years, but a scant three months before we will stand and look down upon the New Zion, the place where we will be the only people related to God, and that country shall be our New Jerusalem from this time forth until forevermore!" With that, he raised his arms, and the crowd that had gathered around him, having heard this oratory before about the New Zion, the New Jerusalem, finally realized that within a few days, they would be leaving.

They could think back three months to January, when they had been in the grip of winter's cruel hand, and so many had taken sick and died, the survey getting the majority of them. They had witnessed the fingers of the winter inching their way into their habitats and seen the children shivering in their beds, but now, just three months hence—a scant ninety days—they would behold with their own eyes the place where no other White people lived, where no Gentile had already laid claim, made provision, or held authority. They, the Latter-day Saints, would be a governing body unto themselves, to run things the way the prophets of the church had wished, and hallelujah, it was as if the Kingdom of God had descended upon this earth.

The day of the Great Exodus had arrived, and it wasn't like everyone was going this first time. Young had a vision of Mormon settlers continuing to come for as long as they wanted to, and the three months of travel would be cut after the Civil War to a mere three days by rail.

But someone had to be the first, and this was the group. Uzziah and Immanuel had gone over to Council Bluffs and met with Johnathan Browning one last time, and gathered up the superior weapons that he and his workers had put together, plus picking up the Girandoni air rifle.

"Will ya make some like it?" Immanuel asked.

"I may, it all depends on what Brigham wants for the later trips. But I did make all the measurements, and had one of our talented workers make drawings of it," Jonathan Browning said.

They bought the requisite amount of powder and shot to prime their weapons, and thanking Browning once again, they took the ferry back and were waiting that afternoon at two p.m. when the Nauvoo Bell was rung, and the pilgrims started their journey.

They only got three miles the first day, and yet, all this could be seen as practicing time, where the wagons were pulled into a big circle, the oxen—most of the teams for travel were oxen, studier and better suited to extreme climes—were taken from their yokes, and they were allowed to graze within the safety of the circle, fenced in as it were by the wagons.

The morning of the next day at five a.m., a trumpet blew—another of Brigham's tipping his hat toward a military operation—and the Nauvoo Bell rung, and the men opened up the way for the oxen to graze outside the wagon circle, breakfasts were prepared, the oxen hooked back up and when the Nauvoo Bell rang at eight a.m., the wagons unraveled the circle into a new day's journey.

The monotony of this routine day in and day out—six days a week—they did not travel on the Sabbath, but took that time to improve trail conditions, build ferries if necessary, and make the trail that much easier for those to come.

———

Before they left, Uzziah and Immanuel had gone up to the cemetery above the Winter Quarters and taken with them the wagon which they had bought. Everyone assumed that this wagon was for their supplies and a warm and dry place for them to sleep when trail conditions got bad, but it was less than that, but also more.

Uzziah drove the wagon as close as he could get to the grave where Hannah and their son George were buried. They were alone up there, the morning of the leaving day. Uzziah wasn't worried about the bodies, the coffin was sealed and Porter assured them that both the newborn baby and its mother had been embalmed. It took them the better part of three hours between the two of them to dig beneath the permafrost and then take out the soil that sat on top of the coffin. They had brought ropes, and those ropes were placed under the coffin. Then, both men climbed out and, securing one end of both ropes to a sturdy tree, they pulled the coffin from the ground.

Once unearthed and wiped down, Uzziah couldn't help but think of some of the books that Rahab, his mother, had had in the big house in Virginia. In one of the books, there were tales of Romanian mythology, and the one that he and his brothers and sisters like the most was the story of the

Strigoi. These Strigoi were troubled spirits who had died unexpectedly, then rose from the grave. They had the ability to become invisible, transform themselves into various animals, much like the shape-shifting mythology of the American Indians, and they regained their strength every night by drinking the blood of their victims. If they liked their victims or were related to them, then they only drained a little blood, just enough for them to stay alive until the next night, but if they did not like or were not related to their victims, they drained all the blood and left the victim dead.

Now, Uzziah was a believing Christian, and even a newly made Latter-Day Saint, and he did not believe these folktales, but still, standing in the early morning mist on a mountainside in the Nebraska territory, he couldn't help but think of his wife just on the other side of that wood. Lying there looking just as good as she did the day he and Porter laid her in her grave. And the little boy, George, dressed in clothes borrowed from Saints, lying in her arms, Strigoi never aged, so George would always be a newborn, and Hannah would always be just as young and beautiful as she was when she bled out.

"Hey, what's goin' on!?" It was Immanuel, and he was looking at Uzziah funny.

"What do you mean?" Uzziah asked as if he had not been standing staring at the top of the coffin for the past ten minutes.

"Are we gonna load this up, or are ya gonna stare a hole in the thing?"

"No, no, let's go," Uzziah said as they lifted the surprisingly light coffin. Well, the oak used for the coffin was thick, and thinking that a mother and her baby were in there, made Uzziah wonder.

They placed a tarp over the coffin, and really, the wagon was a good-sized one, and there was plenty of room left over.

"Ya know, ifn we encounter some bad rains, we could sleep on either side of this," Uzziah said.

Immanuel looked at Uzziah for a bit before he answered.

"No offense, partner, but ifn ya want to sleep next to yer dead wife and child, well, I certainly wouldn't care, but ya can count on me, not being there. Now, let's fill in the grave, gather up some rocks to fill in the missing mass of the coffin, so it will look like it did when she was buried here."

They filled in the bottom of the grave with some rather large rocks that lined the borders of the cemetery, probably dug out when graves were excavated. Then, they shoveled in the dirt that had lain on top of the coffin, and there in the dirt with the false dawn coming on, Uzziah thought he saw a glimmer of something in the dirt.

"Stop!" he said, probably too loud for the time of the morning and what they were doing.

"What?" Immanuel whispered, hoping to ensure his partner's quietness.

Uzziah jumped down into the partially filled grave and, reaching to where he saw the glimmer, he pulled up some dirt. As the aromatic humus fell from between his fingers, a silver bracelet was exposed. It was Hannah's! He had given it to her on the day of their wedding.

"What is it?" Immanuel whispered as Uzziah put the bracelet in his vest pocket.

Just then, Uzziah saw a toad among the dirt from the grave, he picked it up and held it high.

"Just a toad," Uzziah said.

"Kiss it, see if it turns into a princess," Immanuel joked.

"Yeah, right," Uzziah said as he placed the toad on the side of the grave and it hopped away. Uzziah struggled out of the grave with a hand from Immanuel and they finished shoveling in the dirt.

"So, there any other critters down there, ya'd like to save?" Immanuel mocked.

"No, just the one," he said, thinking not of the toad, but of his beautiful wife who lay dead in the coffin.

10

Both Uzziah and Immanuel had imagined the trek west with the Latter-day Saints to be a bit more exciting than it was turning out to be. They had been on the trail for two months now, and all they felt was that somehow, they had inadvertently joined the US Army. The discipline was tight and strict. If anyone was caught staying up too late or even remotely looking like they might be having some fun that did not include singing hymns or reading their Book of Mormon, well, you'd better pray that the new leader, their American Moses, didn't catch you, or else!

The Pawnee hadn't bothered them at all, and all that talk about the Rising Star ceremony and ritual cannibalism must have been seen by Brigham Young to be so much smoke in order to have the two mountain men hired. Young knew where the next water hole was, where the trail veered off, he knew just about everything about where they were going. Both Uzziah and Immanuel wondered, really, why they were there?

The worst thing that had happened was one

morning when the Nauvoo Bell rang at five a.m., and the young boys who were assigned to their grazing had taken the tongues of the wagon down and led them out into the prairie. That same grazing ritual had happened a hundred times by then, and no one could have guessed what would happen next.

Uzziah was sleeping under the wagon where Hannah and George were resting when he heard the high screams of young girls. He wondered what in the world young girls would be doing up at that hour, and why would they be screaming. It wasn't the pleasurable screams of excitement, but the horrific screams that connote something bad is going on. He grabbed his Hawken which was to him, an extension of his right arm, and as he walked away from his wagon, he saw quick movement out on the prairie. It was one of the young boys who had taken out the oxen and stock for grazing.

Then there was quicker movement as three or four wolves jumped the boy, who was trying desperately to run away from them. His screams pierced the morning air as more men were coming from their wagons and pointing at the tragedy.

The boy must have gone after a stray ox because he was way too far out. The rifles that the men were shooting at the wolves were ineffectual at that range.

The boy was still screaming when Uzziah was joined by Immanuel, both of them lined up their shots.

"Which one ya takin'?" Uzziah asked.

"I'm takin' the boy," Immanuel said, and Uzziah cut his eyes toward his partner.

"Can't ya see, they done tore him up so much, his face, and everythin', truly it's the Christian thing to do!"

Immanuel said, and his Hawken barked, and the shot artfully went through the head of the wolf that was chewing the face off the boy, but also passed through the head of the boy and killed him.

Someone in the party had binoculars and they came running over right after the shot.

Another boy was screaming, and he was running as fast as he could from four wolves who were about to take him down.

Uzziah's Hawken belched fire, and the lead wolf tumbled in his death, but it was too little, too late. The next wolf grabbed the boy by the throat and shook him, breaking his neck and severing his carotid artery. They dragged him off amid the screams of the women in the wagon train.

"That's my boy! That's my boy! Do something!" she screamed as she ran up on the two mountain men.

"Them mountain men, they kilt the other boy!" the man with the binocs yelled in Immanuel's face.

Immanuel pushed the man down and, tightening up Stygian's cinch, mounted up and rode for the boy who was being dragged away. Uzziah was on Shadow right behind him. When the two partners were neck to neck in the gallop, Uzziah yelled over, "That boy's dead!"

"I know, but we're gonna give his ma and pa something to bury," Immanuel said as he pulled one of the slide pistols from his belt and rode faster.

The wolves had pulled what remained of the boy behind some boulders, and there was growling and fighting back there reminiscent of the hounds of hell itself when the two men rode up.

They both had their slide revolvers out, and ten

shots were fired as fast as they could slide the rounds into place. The bodies of five wolves lay about. One of the boy's arms had been pulled off and taken somewhere. His face was unharmed, miraculously, but his groin area and his buttocks had been feasted on.

It was then that Uzziah recognized Hiram McKenzie, the young husband of Hannah's younger sister, Galilee.

"Ya recognize the boy?" Uzziah asked.

"Might ifn he were whole."

"It's the boy with the big flintlock who was sentry when we first got to the winter headquarters."

"The husband of yer wife's sister?" Immanuel asked, the tragedy and horror of it striking home as it always does when it's somebody you know.

"That's the one."

Immanuel pulled his rain slicker from the back of his saddle and rolled what remained of the boy into it. Stygian did not want that bundle on him, and he fought to keep it off. Finally, Uzziah convinced Shadow, who had been in the mountains longer and around a lot more blood, to let him put the boy's remains on the back of the saddle.

On the way in, they saw that the man with the binocs was carrying from the prairie the mutilated remains of his son.

Uzziah would have to go and find Hannah's sister, she should hear it from him, and not just have the body dumped by her wagon.

There was a man who made coffins, when they were needed. Uzziah walked Shadow over to his wagon, and when he saw the blood dripping from Immanuel's slicker, he knew.

"One of the boys?"

"Yeah, Hiram McKenzie," Uzziah whispered, not wanting the word to get out, then he heard a horrible screaming. It was coming from the Larue wagon. He left the remains, and that's exactly what they were, with the carpenter, and rode over to where the screaming was going on.

Hannah's father, Ephrem Larue, was holding Galilee, she was trembling, and when she saw Uzziah, she broke from her father's arms and ran to him.

"I have to see Hiram's body," she said.

Uzziah took her in his arms, and she pushed him back.

"No, you don't understand, I have to!" she pleaded with Uzziah.

"He was a good-looking boy, and ya loved him."

"His body, Uzziah!"

"There are some things ya can't unsee, dear one," he said softly. "'Member him as he was, the way he looked at ya, when he held ya tight. He's gone on to his Maker, and what's left is a poor excuse," Uzziah said.

It looked like she would protest, then it seemed she did remember Hiram, her young husband, and smiled, then the smile faded. "A remnant?" she asked.

"Yes, ma'am, just a remnant," Uzziah said, realizing he was old enough to be her pa, but the respect in his voice was due a young widow.

That morning started with a funeral for the two boys. It was decided then and there that no one younger than eighteen years of age would take the stock out in the morning and that two other *armed men* would accompany them at all times.

The graves were dug in the hard scrapple and the families threw dirt, but mostly rock and dust, down on the boys' coffins where they were laid to rest. Stones were gathered mostly by the families of the departed and put on top to keep the wolves from getting what remained. Galilee looked like a true grown woman when she walked away from the graves.

The whole wagon train attended their funerals, and Brigham Young himself preached their eulogies.

Way in the back, Porter, Uzziah, and Immanuel stood, still armed to the teeth.

"Them rocks ain't gonna keep no wolf from eating those boys," Porter said.

"Yep, onliest way would be six feet down, and I ain't seen any wolf use no shovel," Immanuel quipped.

A woman in front of them turned. "Have ya no respect fer the dead!?" she asked, not knowing that without those two men there wouldn't have been any funeral, just missing young men scattered all over the prairie in wolf scat!

About halfway through the third month, when they entered Lords of the Plains territory—the Comanches were called that because of their prowess in riding and fighting from the horse—everyone kept watching to see if they would be attacked. The Comanche were able, much like trick riders, to do things upon horses that confounded those who saw it, and it never seemed to be able to be duplicated by anyone else.

The thirty wagons had their usual problems—broken axles, broken wheels, water shortages, arguments among the saints, a couple of fistfights which Brigham Young broke up with his cane, beating the two boys fighting much worse than if they had been allowed to simply finish the fight themselves!

They had pushed with much dust and choking, bandanas tied about their faces, into the high desert, camped in the shadow of Chimney Rock, gone through the devil's gorge, and then ascended into the territory that led up into the Rockies, then through South Pass, which would take them to the other side of the Continental Divide. It was there that Uzziah had figured he would take the coffin south to the high meadow above their cabins and rebuild. He and Immanuel went to see Brigham to get permission to leave for a week, then rejoin the group as they got close to the salty lake basin.

"You want to do what!?!" Young was angry, he had what they called mountain fever, and he was lying in his bed in the back of his wagon. He did not look good.

"Well, we's got this cabin a three days ride from chere, we thought—"

Brigham leaned to the side of the wagon wall, pushed back the canvas covering, and vomited. It was mostly bile.

"Why aren't you two sick? A lot of people are sick, but it hadn't affected either of you, why!?"

"Lucky, I guess," Uzziah offered.

"Luck is the atheist's blessing, there is no such thing as luck. Tell me, how do you keep from getting this fever, these chills, and the inability to keep anything down, how?"

"He meant blessed, that's what Uzziah meant, he

don't ever talk of luck. Besides, Mr. Young, we been in these chere mountains for nigh onto ten years, and that don't count the twenty I was chere afore Uzziah."

"So, you're immune, is that it?"

"Most likely, whatever that means?" Immanuel said.

"About the request—" Uzziah put in, hoping to bury Hannah now rather than later.

"No, you may not go! We have been unencumbered by savage attacks, but we are entering Comanche territory and will not leave it for some time. You and all the expensive guns that you purchased from Brother Browning will be needed, it's not time to quit just yet!" he said, then vomited over the side of the wagon board again.

"Well, it ain't like she's goin' nowheres," Immanuel said as they walked away, referring to Uzziah's dead wife.

"Yeah, got that right."

Game had been sparse, and Uzziah and Immanuel knew that between the wolves, the coyotes, and the Comanche that whatever game there was had been harvested. They figured the Injuns were eating lizards and maybe even chewing on their buffalo robes.

They went out, nonetheless, and there simply wasn't anything to shoot. Then, there came the strangest sound from the south. It sounded almost like the northern lights, the green ones, which Immanuel had heard twice since moving to the mountains. When Uzziah and Immanuel looked up, the sky was blackened by a migration of birds that stretched the far horizon onward for miles. The sun was literally darkened by them. By the sounds they made, they had to have been mourning doves because, as they flew, they were making their calls that had earned them their names.

As they watched, a dove fell down beside Shadow, and the horse literally jumped off the desert floor and caught Uzziah off balance. He tried to stay aboard, but landed on his arse, and Immanuel thought that was the funniest thing he'd ever seen. Just as he was whooping it up, birds started falling from the sky all around them, and Stygian took off running with Immanuel holding on for dear life. He was able to keep his seat, and while the birds were still descending in a mass, he rode back to where Uzziah was standing, watching the bird rain.

"Ya ever see anythin' like it!?!" Uzziah asked.

"Hell, son, it's rainin' manna!" Immanuel said as he reached down and pulled Uzziah up behind him, and they rode to where Shadow was standing in the outcutting of a big rock. No birds were falling on him.

"Seems to me," Immanuel said as they both dismounted and watched the *showers*, "that the only sane one is Shadow."

When it stopped raining doves, they rode back to the wagon train and were not even noticed by those who had already plucked a dozen or so birds and were having a barbecue.

No preacher ever misses an opportunity to preach, and when doves, the symbol of peace, are falling from the skies, it wouldn't have mattered to Brigham Young that migrating birds lose half their weight when in transit. Old Brigham Young, the preacher, gave it his best.

He brought up the Israelites in the desert and Moses asking God for food and the manna, which then fell from heaven. The food of angels, he called it, as the people tried to listen as they stuffed their faces on partially cooked fowl.

Uzziah had seen something similar when he was a young boy. He and his pa had gone into town to get grain for the horses, and coming back, the birds just kept falling from the sky. His pa explained it, they were out of water, hadn't stopped either because the land was dry, or their usuals haunts for water were used up, whatever the reason, it didn't necessarily mean that God had smote them and delivered them into the hands of the Latter-day Saints, but Uzziah kept his mouth shut and secretly would be glad when it would be just he and Immanuel and they could have their arguments about the difference between what the world offered and what we mortals wanted.

On the third day in Comanche territory, the warriors came out of the sun, literally riding their ponies from the center of the rising orb, which, of course, blinded everyone to their arrival. The cliffs and chimney rocks that shot up from the high desert witnessed the bands of Comanche as they rode their fleet-footed ponies right for the wagon train, not veering, not doing anything but shooting into the boat, which was the first wagon. The Nauvoo Bell ringing with each slap of a slug hitting it, calling all the saints to battle. They rode like the wind, with their long hair flowing back gracefully and they screamed so loud that Uzziah was sure several of the women in the party probably peed their pantaloons.

The confusion of the wagon train was obvious and complete. Yes, they had practiced for such an occasion, but perhaps the fact that there had been no trouble till this very moment was what made it so unfortunate and disorganized. The men who knew what to do forgot everything in the face of their impending deaths, the capture and raping of their wives, and the slaughter of their children. The Lord's name was being taken in vain as those who worshipped him wondered why this band of Satan's army was now descending upon them.

Uzziah's wagon was the last one. Well, there were two reasons for that. They were the rearguard assuring that no one snuck up on the wagon train, and they had done their jobs to this very moment. The other reason they had taken the rearguard was to keep others from seeing exactly what they carried in the back of their wagon.

Uzziah's wagon was always the last one that would finish the neat circle of safety, but the Comanches were everywhere, like swarming locusts or yellow jackets, stinging, buzzing, biting! Immanuel had stuck around long enough to get the wasps off their arses. He'd killed several with his Harmonica Rifle and now had reloaded and was killing more, but when he abandoned the wagon and left Uzziah driving in order to ride Stygian up and away—and had thoughtfully, unhitched Shadow from the back of the wagon, as Uzziah prepared to pull it into place completing the circle—Immanuel did not see the Comanche Brave as he whipped his pony up alongside the wagon and jumped Uzziah.

The two men struggled. Uzziah was trying to push

the Comanche off the buckboard, but then Uzziah got whacked upside his head with a war club, and he fell back into the box, lying unconscious beside his dead wife and child.

The Comanche who had commandeered the wagon violently shook the reins of the oxen and got them into a run. Immanuel took several snapshots at the wagon as the Comanche, unscathed, took his coop and plunder away from the rest of the wagons.

Immanuel saw the whole thing, but when he was about to jump the wagon tongues that completed the wagon roundup, he knew it was too late. Considering there were at least a hundred or more braves circling the wagons, hanging on the far side of their horses, shooting arrows and rifles from beneath the ponies' bellies, there wasn't anything he could do but stay and help the pioneers. So, stay is what he did. But he never, ever forgot for one moment that his partner, Uzziah was being taken somewhere away from the safety of their company, and no blade and bullet blessing was going to matter to any savage as he bludgeoned Uzziah's head into a pulp and then cut out his heart and ate it, only to finally take Uzziah's topknot in memory of this glorious day. Immanuel was sick with grief, then all of a sudden it was over, the circling Comanche strung their line out straight and rode away, whooping and yipping in their retreat.

How long had it been, Immanuel wondered. He hadn't looked at his chronometer when the attack began—twenty minutes, half an hour, forty-five minutes? All he knew was he had fired many times at the Comanche and also taken out many horses, which now lay out there around the circled wagons, screaming their whinnied cries in the agony of their deaths.

Immanuel stepped over a wagon tongue and walked with a certain amount of deliberation out to where the horses were struggling. Horses were horses, and they didn't take sides, no matter what Samuel Colt had drawn on his pistols, they just got rode by whoever had them, and what those folks did while they were being ridden had nothing to do with what horses wanted.

Shouts were coming from the wagons, people wanted him to come back and not risk his life. They had no idea what they were talking about.

Women and children were crying, there were some dead, but more who had simply been struck with arrows, and Immanuel was sure they didn't know what to do with those wounds. He would go back and tend to them as soon as he finished this mission of mercy.

"Get back to the wagons, they may come back!" Young ordered as he ran up, his face scarlet with the fever. The attack had gotten his gumption up.

Immanuel looked at the American Moses and fired a slug through the brain of the first Comanche pony.

"What are you doing, but wasting ammunition!? You're needed elsewhere, now do as I say and stop this nonsense, immediately! Killing horses, really, who cares?"

"They do," Immanuel said as he continued to walk the circle that circumscribed the outer ring where the Comanche had glorified their art of battle with such splendid riding. He came upon a Brave who was raising a firearm at Brigham Young. Immanuel fetched his tomahawk and whacked the Brave, sending a string of blood on the new prophet, marking his face.

"Stop this senseless killing!" Young shouted, trying desperately to wipe away the blood of the enemy. That was the difference between them and the Comanche, who reveled in the blood of their enemies, who lived to drink it and finish off the bastard whites who had entered their lands.

Immanuel continued walking the outer circle, killing wounded horses and dying Comanche. Brigham walked with him now, not speaking, but watching with an eye that spoke more than simple curiosity.

"They deserve this mercy," Immanuel said to Brigham, and the prophet-to-be looked at Immanuel and started to say something, but didn't. He threw his hand at Immanuel as if he were throwing something away, perhaps the mountain man's notion of what God's mercy could look like. As he walked back, Immanuel kept shooting, and with each shot, the new prophet jerked as if someone were shooting at him.

When Immanuel got back within the circle, he figured rightly that the Saints would probably not risk another mile, but stay right there tending to the wounded, and this would be where they took off in the morning. He was good with that. He would, after attending to them, ride off to find what was left of his partner.

"They got him, didn't they! Those bastards!" Porter screamed, and several people looked at him accusingly.

"Mind yer mouth!" one man shouted at him.

"Mind yer wounded!" he yelled back at him.

Between Porter and Immanuel, they took care of most of the arrow-wounded. There were ten of them.

One man had the arrow too close to his heart to push it all the way through, and the only doctor on the train took him to his wagon, where he would be tended to till morning, then die.

As they were pushing arrows through less vital spots in men's bodies, Porter said, "We need to go after Uzziah, we gots to!"

"I understand that's what ya want to do, but the general," he said, referring to Young, "ain't 'bout to let us. We'll wait till night, then we'll go get 'im," he whispered to Porter.

That night, there were extra guards put out, and it was going to be interesting trying to get by them. Immanuel knew that Young would think it a waste of manpower and resources for them to go after Uzziah, but he didn't give a shite what the man thought.

The Comanche Brave who stole the wagon was the hero of the hour, and they had pulled the wagon as far as they wanted to before they stopped it and slaughtered the oxen while they were still in their traces.

There was an old saying that a man wanted to die while he was still in his traces, but seeing the team slaughtered like that, with each of them knowing what was happening, did not instill anything but disgust in Uzziah, who had been tied to a mesquite bush. His head was aching, and an arrow stuck out from his arm. Uzziah wondered what they would do with the casket that was still in the back of the wagon. They had already split up everything else of value from the wagon —the blankets, the flour, the bacon, the cans of beans, and other foodstuffs. They took Uzziah's Dutch oven out and liked the way it sounded when they beat it with a tomahawk, but then it broke and they threw the pieces away and yelled after it, as if the oven were at fault.

"I'm gonna kill 'em fer doing that," Uzziah said to himself. The Comanche closest to him swung a warclub and knocked him out again.

When he awakened, he was buried up to his neck in the desert sand. The sun was setting, and the Comanche were sitting around a campfire. They laughed and were acting crazy, then Uzziah realized they must have discovered the Jameson that he'd hidden under the floorboards of the wagon. The bottle was being passed around, and there was a lot of yelling going on—typical Injun behavior surrounding whiskey. Hell, typical human behavior surrounding whiskey!

It looked like they had tried to open the coffin, there were marks all over it. He wondered why they just didn't tear it apart to see what was inside, but was glad that that didn't seem to be part of the bargain.

He knew what they had in store for him. His eyelids, which were still intact, would be cut off in the morning as the sun came up. He was facing east, and the uncompromising light from the sun would blind him since he would neither be able to turn his head away nor shut his eyes. Even if Immanuel and Porter came for him, which he was sure they would, he, Uzziah, would be blinded when they found him. Not much use for a blind mountain man, although he could see Immanuel taking him back up to the cabins, burying the coffin if the stupid Comanche hadn't decided to burn it since they couldn't get it open. He was so glad now that the Mormon mortician had insisted on sturdy mahogany and a double lock for the casket.

Anyway, he'd sit up there with Immanuel, and probably turn into a drunk, then one afternoon when Immanuel was gone hunting, a grizzly bear would wander into the camp, and tear him limb from limb—well, at least he had that to look forward to.

They, the Comanche, had probably planned on getting the coffin open after they had a drink or two, but Injuns could never handle their liquor, and soon all of them were sleeping around the campfire, and the light from the fire was kept from him by the shadow of the coffin.

He must have slept because he didn't remember anything before he heard his whispered name, "Uzziah." It wasn't Immanuel or Porter or anybody else he knew. Well, it was someone he knew. He had to have been dreaming because it was Hannah's voice. She was calling to him, and unfortunately, it was impossible for him to look around and see her. The voice was coming from behind him.

"Where are we?" she asked softly.

"Captured by Comanches," he whispered back.

"Where is your body?" she asked him, fearing the worst.

"Buried up to the neck," he said, and he thought he heard her softly laughing.

"It ain't funny, I can tell ya that," he said in way of explaining.

It was then that one of the Comanche had gotten up to relieve himself. After peeing, he wandered over to check on the prisoner. He laughed when he remembered how Uzziah had been buried. Perhaps he was the one who had done it?

The Comanche came closer, and Uzziah was a bit worried about what the savage might do to him, since he was defenseless. As he reached down to touch Uzziah, a terrific wind gusted from behind Uzziah, and the Brave was thrown over and over until he hit the coffin, which made a resounding booming noise, as if someone had hit a big drum with a body!

The Comanche slid off the coffin unnaturally, as if he had no spine. Uzziah was fairly sure he was dead.

The sound of his body hitting the coffin had awakened the other Comanche, and it was getting on toward false dawn, so they struggled to their feet, laughing about the great time they had that they couldn't remember. Then one of them discovered the body of the dead Comanche whose back had been broken on the coffin when it made the sound of the big drum.

There was a lot of shouting, and Uzziah supposed it was cursing in Comanche, then they turned on the only one there who could have done such a thing, the buried man with only his head sticking out.

They wanted to approach the head there in the desert sand, but something kept them back. Wasn't one of them supposed to cut the White man's eyelids off so he could stare at the rising sun, which was getting a lot closer to topping the desert horizon? A discussion ensued between the Comanche, but somewhere in there, they must have decided that the medicine the head possessed was big. How else could that Brave been killed like that?

They all took arrows, and notching them in their bowstrings were about to make his head into a porcupine. Then a strange thing happened. The light from the sun broke the horizon and cast their shadows toward where Uzziah's head was sitting and where they were aiming, then another shadow joined theirs and rose above it. It seemed to come from the coffin.

The sun was shining right into Uzziah's eyes, but one Brave turned and inadvertently blocked the light for a second, and what Uzziah saw made him tinkle in the sand.

Hannah had risen from the coffin! She was smiling, and in her arms was their baby, who was cooing and his arms were moving akimbo. Then she began speaking, *"My soul magnifies the Lord, and my spirit rejoices in God my Savior, for He had looked with favor on the lowliness of His servant. Surely from now on, all generations will call Me blessed."*

It was the Magnificat from the Gospel of Luke, where Mary, the Lord's mother, testifies to her wonder and amazement.

While the Comanche watched and did not understand a single word that Hannah spoke, she extended the moving, cooing baby, their son George, toward the Comanche. She moved toward them, not really walking, but floating. She was offering the Comanche the salvation of the baby, and a cry of helplessness escaped their combined lips as the Comanche broke into a confused escape, running away from the coffin and away from the extended and cooing babe.

It came to Uzziah that the Plains Injuns had been decimated by smallpox, and this extending of the small, newborn must have seemed to them to be the ultimate weapon that could wipe out an entire village.

The sound of their hoofbeats drowned out everything as they made their escape. Finally, all their noises faded away as Hannah knelt before him. She was translucently, magnificently beautiful as she held the baby close to Uzziah's head. He felt the little arms pattering about his head, grabbing his nose, and batting at his eyes. He closed his eyes instinctively.

When he awakened, he heard hoofbeats again, and he thought, *Oh, great, the Comanche have come back to finish me off.*

"Uzziah! Uzziah!!" he heard Immanuel screaming as he dropped down off the moving horse and started digging around his partner's head.

11

They were descending into the valley of brine. The salty lake was there, spreading its million acres across the desert to the very horizon. Both Immanuel and Uzziah were riding their wagon, to which they had hooked Stygian and Shadow, and regardless of what the Mormons had thought, the two stallions understood their job and had cooperated beautifully with each other. Immanuel had the reins in his hands and was clicking them up as the trail opened, and everyone was going a bit faster.

Uzziah turned to see if the coffin was shifting with the newly acquired speed, but it was fine. There were marks around the sturdy lock, but it had not been opened.

After Immanuel and Porter had shown up and dug him out, they put the coffin back in the wagon and rejoined the wagon train. Uzziah had ample opportunity to tell both men what he'd seen. But all they wanted to talk about was the arrow that had been broken off in his arm before the Comanche buried him.

"Well," Porter said, "Guessin' yer blessin' is over," and when Uzziah looked at Immanuel, he could tell that his partner was relieved that it was so. He was all patched up, a bandage encircling his arm, and the valley of brine lay before them. Brigham was yelling something from the Book of Mormon, or was it from the Old Testament? Didn't matter, the man, the American Moses, had made it finally to his New Jerusalem with his Israelites, and he wouldn't be going back.

They were there when he pulled his cane—the one he wasn't using—from the middle of the ten-acre plot, the place where the new temple would be built by the salty lake. They were there when they hung the Nauvoo Bell from a bell post, which was also eventually used as a whipping post for thieves. Yes, even among the citizens of the New Jerusalem, who had been brought there by the American Moses, theft rose its ugly head.

Porter had been into the surrounding Uinta Mountains and brought back enough lumber to build himself a nice little three-bedroom cabin with a loft for extra guests. Immanuel and Uzziah, after he'd gotten back the use of his wounded arm, both helped as best they could. Once again, Uzziah was surprised by how much Immanuel knew about carpentry.

The last night of their stay, Caroline sat so close to Immanuel that he found it hard to eat, but he didn't care. These loving children of the Rockwells had made the trip successfully, and the joy which both their parents demonstrated by their smiles, it was evident that they were all where they were supposed to be.

Invitations had been made by many who had come with Uzziah and Immanuel for them to stay, join the church, and help build the New Jerusalem. They fended off these requests with a lot more grace than they knew they had. These were good people, and both mountain men knew it.

The day Uzziah and Immanuel were leaving the city, which had been laid out just as the one at the winter quarters, and they had said their painful goodbyes to Porter and his family, they couldn't help but notice the blood that was being whipped from the body of the man who had been caught stealing a loaf of bread for his family.

And who was throwing that black snake at the man, none other than Brigham Young himself!

As they made the rise, which just two months earlier they had come down, neither of them bothered to look back. Something about Lot's wife ran through Uzziah's mind. He was no longer dressed as one of the Latter-day Saints. He had his deerskins back on, and he and Immanuel looked the perfect picture of two mountain men going back to the mountains, which is exactly what they were doing.

When they got to the spot where the pilgrims had, their one and only time, circled their wagons and defended themselves against the army of Satan, Immanuel put his elbow into Uzziah's ribs.

"Huh?" Uzziah grunted.

"Over thar!" Immanuel said, and when Uzziah looked, there was a horde of Comanche riding like the wind coming their way.

The Comanche may have been the lords of the plains, but they had never seen a wagon pulled by two blacks that could almost pull a wagon faster than they could gallop. They didn't know what to think of it.

Finally, they fired flaming arrows at the canvas covering the wagon, and when it lit fire, they whooped it up and yipped their way closer to the fleeing mountain men.

"Should we stop and put it out?" Uzziah asked.

"Hell no, the speed we're goin' it'll burn itself out!" Immanuel said, using the reins on the two blacks as a quirt, snapping it on their butts, and sure enough, there came the extra speed.

They had to give the lords of the plains their due, several of them were catching up, and it looked like they might have to stop and fight them to the death, but when the fire totally destroyed the canopy and there was nothing left but the smoldering stays, the Comanche reined up and fled away from their prey.

Immanuel looked back almost in a scratching-head mode. "Wonder what brought that on!??" he asked Uzziah, who was looking back, but not at the Comanche, rather at the top of the tied-down coffin where his wife, Hannah, and their son, George, rested eternally—maybe?

By the time they got close to the cabins, they had to abandon the wagon. They were so grateful that there was no wagon road going to where they were going. Uzziah made a travois as Immanuel hunted, and when he brought back the two small deer, he helped Uzziah lift the coffin onto the travois, which was behind Shadow, and they were off.

They knew it was going to be another hard winter. They had spent all their time, not exactly lollygagging, but they hadn't jerked meat, or cut wood, or anything else that would have prepared them for their long winter stay. Still, God had been good to them, hadn't he? They were back together, like the old days. No magic blessing which kept Uzziah from harm, and the cabins—once they'd been cleared out from mice, spiders, and smoked out from the bugs—were as good as they ever had been.

They rode up to the high meadow and dug a nice, deep hole just across from where they'd buried the Mohawk, George Henry Martin.

When the hole was dug and the coffin was ready to be lowered into it, Uzziah took the silver bracelet he'd found when they were filling back the hole in the cemetery at winter quarters. He took his Bowie knife and gently tinkered with the mechanism of the lock and it snapped open.

"What are ya doin'?" Immanuel asked. He'd been unwinding the ropes they would use to lower the coffin.

"Not to worry," Uzziah said as Immanuel stepped around on the opening side of the coffin, and there was a mama and a baby like they were sleeping. It looked to Uzziah that he and Porter had just laid them there.

"What a beauty!" Immanuel said with awe. "And the boy looks perfect."

Uzziah took the silver bracelet and, lifting the arm that did not hold the child, he put it back on her wrist. However did it get off? Thoughts of Strigoi rushed in upon him, but he was not afraid of this one. She had come from her coffin without it being opened, and saved him and his life. No amount of dirt or grass, nothing could keep her down there unless that's where she needed to be. He reached over and put his hand on the forehead of his son, then bent over and kissed

Hannah's cold lips. Something stirred in him, he wasn't quite sure what.

When he closed the coffin and tricked the lock closed, Immanuel's head was bowed.

They put the ropes under the coffin, and gently, so gently, they lowered the coffin, then began the love act of filling the grave. There was a moment in which Uzziah wanted to take off all the dirt and hold Hannah one last time, but he knew. They were celestial married, and when it came time for his time to end, she would be there, just as she had been the morning when he needed her. She would have a small child's hand in hers, and she would, with her other hand, take his, and lead them to the real New Jerusalem.

THE GREAT NORTHERN CATTLE COMPANY

1

The winter they hadn't wanted was the winter they got. Last winter, they had relied upon Frederick and Max to help them out, but when they went up to their place, which was higher in elevation, they found a crude, very crude note nailed to the door. It was written on the skin side of a beaver pelt, and it basically said they had had enough, and anything anybody needed from their cabins was theirs for the taking. The bastards hadn't even said goodbye!

Uzziah started tearing down the big cabin and the small barn, while Immanuel thought about making a travois, but they still had the one they'd made to bring the coffin with Hannah and baby George in it, so Immanuel went back to their cabins and got it. They piled the wood Uzziah had stripped from their friends' cabins on the travois and made trips all that day, and the next.

They got a lot of wood, enough to sustain them just so winter didn't hold on till April, and that was surely what they were thinking.

When they got it all unloaded, Immanuel began swinging the axe and making the wood fit the stove that Uzziah had, plus his fireplace, and Immanuel's fireplace.

Immanuel had taken off his buffalo coat and was sweating profusely.

"Think ya better take a break, partner," Uzziah said. He'd been standing in the doorway to his cabin and watching.

"Nah, got me plenty of energy left," Immanuel protested.

"Look, yer still not up to speed, and there ain't no doctor anywheres near, so," Uzziah said as he came over and reached out his hand for the axe.

"Yeah, yeah, yer right, I knows yer right, but I do feel like I'm gettin' back into my health, don't ya think?"

Uzziah just looked at Immanuel as he put his buffalo robe back on, it was nearly impossible to swing an axe with something that big on.

"Yer not gonna say!?!" Immanuel protested.

"It ain't that, just judging how much fat ya put back on and how much muscle. Ya maybe close to the same size, but it's sorta slid down toward yer belt."

It was Immanuel's turn to stare at his partner. "Toward my belt? Is that what ya said?"

"Yeah, it's like ya was a candle and ya been melting."

Immanuel took off his buffalo robe again and reached for the axe. "Then, this is exactly what I need to be doin'!"

"'Cept it's yer ticker that's the problem, right?"

"That's what they tell me!"

"Ain't no way fer usn to know what shape that's in, right?" Uzziah asked.

"Well, that Doc down in New Orleans told me it's a dang muscle, and the longer it ticks, and the harder it ticks, the stronger it gets, right?"

"But what ifn ya get a cramp in it?" Uzziah asked.

"Guessin' that's the same as them heart attacks, huh?"

"Yeah, so put yer coat back on and I'll swing the axe fer a bit."

Uzziah started in, and immediately it was evident to both of them that Uzziah's rhythm, his swing, and his chopping abilities were simply superior to his partners. Nobody said anything for a bit. Immanuel figured, why argue over something as obvious as the fact that Uzziah was doing a better job of it.

Immanuel built a fire between their cabins, and he was sitting there enjoying the warmth and really enjoying how Uzziah was taking the work in such strides that it was going a lot faster than he had anticipated.

"Say, ya n'ver told me just exactly how ya got them Comanche to leave ya when ya was buried like that," Immanuel said.

"Nah, guess I didn't," Uzziah said in a rather normal voice, considering all the work he was doing.

"So, tell me."

"They just left."

"Bull, I don't believe that."

"Well, it's true," Uzziah protested.

"Nah, it ain't."

"Okay, guess ya caught me, I'm lyin'," Uzziah said and kept on chopping.

"Yeah, got that. But what interests me is why yer lyin'?"

Uzziah didn't say anything, he just kept chopping and sweating.

"That dead Comanche, the one by the coffin, his back were broke," Immanuel noted as he pulled his pipe out, stuffed it carefully, then lit up.

"Ya shouldn't smoke, ain't that right?"

"Don't change the subject, old woman! How'd his back get broke?"

"Hey, I was buried up to my talking box in sand and rock, how the hell should I know?"

"Well...ya was there, weren't ya?"

"Yeah, I guess, I was wounded in the arm, and by the way, it healed well with the treatment ya gave it," Uzziah said as a compliment.

Immanuel raised both his index fingers in the air about chest level and swirled them around in circles. "Wee!" he said as he made the motions.

"Don't change the damn subject. Somebody, or something, kilt that there Comanche, and it sure weren't the man buried up to his neck. Did Porter get out there first? Is that how we found ya so readily?"

"Yeah, that's it, Porter was there, kilt the Comanche, then went back fer ya in case there were more of 'em!"

"Liar, liar, liar!! Porter was with me the whole time."

"It's yourn turn," Uzziah said, holding out the axe at about shoulder level, and it was as steady as a rock.

"Nah, hate to break up yer rhythm, young son, ya just go on and keep chopping!"

Uzziah went back into his rhythm, and Immanuel

watched him like a hawk, finally, he spoke. "I been askin' ya things 'ready know the answer to," Immanuel said.

"Ain't that what ya do!?!"

"Yeah, 'tis. I know who kilt that Comanche and who drove off the other braves."

"Well, good, now we won't have to have this stupid conversation," Uzziah said.

"Hannah," was all Immanuel said.

"Hannah was dead and lying in her locked coffin, Immanuel, ya done lost yer mind?"

"That's what ya'd like me to believe, but sooner or later, I'ma gonna get the particulars, hell, it's all I'm askin' fer. Love a good story, and yer being selfish not tellin', that's all there is to it!"

"Yer gonna drop it, then?" Uzziah asked.

"Fer now, yeah, fer now."

A good thousand miles south and east, Rudley Quatrain, was standing in a bar in a saloon outside Fort Belknap, Texas. The fort was located a bit east of the center of Texas and close to the Indian Territories north. It was early in the season, not even the end of March, but Rudley, a man in his forties, and used to getting his own way, was interested in putting together a crew of ten to fifteen men, men used to long hours in the saddle, a second in command and a good cook who could load and service chow out of a church wagon and keep the crew happy while they were on the trail.

Rudley, who sported a huge mustache which drooped over the corners of his mouth and was not a small man by any means, had taken the Chisolm, the Shawnee, and the western trails with cattle in the past, and had made some handsome monies doing it, had decided that he would try a trail further west than the so-called western trail which led to the Ogallala Nebraska territory. He wanted to drive his herd right toward the Rockies, then take them along the front range and drive them toward the Montana territories. He'd make Cheyenne, then sell the cattle off. At least that was the plan as far as all the partners were concerned. They called themselves the Great Northern Cattle Company, and a lot of money had gone into all their planning.

What Rudley Quatrain didn't know was that one of the men he was working for, one of the partners, was, how could you say it, a damn crook!

Texas Brownley was not a young man, and over his 50-some years, he'd made a lot of money, and none of it honestly. But he was respected in the town of San Angelo because all his nefarious activities had been carried out in other parts of Texas, and, within the bandit community, it was known that if you did business with Ned *Texas* Brownley, you'd better just do it once and get the hell out. He was infamous for not leaving loose strings on any of the deals he did. Drawing on his contacts throughout the state of Texas and the Oklahoma territory, he had invited them by word of mouth only. Brownley knew all too well about paper trails and how they could come back to bite you in the arse, about a half a dozen men of terrible reputation, which meant they were perfect for this job.

On a stormy night in the basement of his home in San Angelo, Texas, Brownley sat in his big overstuffed chair and laid out his plan to a select group of men.

"All ya gots to do is be where this fella Rudley Quatrain will be when he's a hirin' his cowpunchers. Don't seem over anxious to get the job, in fact, since it's a newish adventure, bargain with the man, ask fer $50 a month, try to get him to pay ya more, so he'll know yer probably worth it. Now, he thinks he's just goin' up Cheyenne way, but I'm more interested in going all the way to the deep grasslands of eastern Montana, where cattle can fatten at their leisure, and maybe, just maybe, if they survived the winters that far north, me and my partners, the men who had bought the longhorns that we're going to drive, can increase the herd and drive the increase toward the southern markets of Cheyenne, Ogallala, Ellsworth and Abilene.

"The hot and potentially weight-losing drives from the heart of Texas to those markets had been done, but no one has kept herds that far north, increased their sizes and then, in the cool of the northern fall, driven them to market. The increase in cattle weight, them not losing a lot of weight on shorter drives, would mean a market that was unknown at this time, and there is the potential to fatten many wallets, yours included. The math is simple, it's half the distance from eastern Montana territory to Cheyenne as from San Angelo, Texas, to Cheyenne. Half the miles would mean a lot when it came to what the cattle would weigh in at.

"Yes, there are Injun troubles up north, too. The Blackfoot and the Crow are up there, and although mortal enemies, they all liked the taste of beef, especially since the buffalo are dying out. But hell, don't worry 'bout them none, I got me a surefire plan to take care of them Injuns. Besides, going from Texas, you got the Kiowa, the Comanche, the Apache, and the Navajo to deal with. In the southwest alone, you have nine different Apache bands, all warriors and all with families to feed. It makes more sense to eventually travel south with herds, and that's what we're goin' to do once we take the herd from Rudley Quatrain".

A hand was raised in the room. Jack Tate was taller than most men, and he was middle-aged. He had a dark, longish beard which ran down to about his navel, and his navel was a long way from his neck. He only carried one gun, but folks who had seen him shoot knew that once he drew that weapon, the person he was going up against was probably dead. His other weapons were a Winchester, which was in the boot on his saddle, even now in the rain, and a large Bowie knife. When he threw the knife, it was like a magic trick, one second it was in his hand, and the next second in the chest of the man he was aiming for.

"What is it, Jack?" Brownley asked as thunder rumbled through the house above them.

"What ifn he don't hire us at all?"

"You make sure he does, okay?" Brownley said.

Harry Gnomes was the youngest of them, and his inexperience showed.

"How much will we really make?" Gnomes asked.

The others, O.B. Thomas, Davidson Lord, Buck Krieter, and Todd Aimes, all chucked.

"What's so funny, huh?" Harry asked, his hands resting on his two revolvers, both worn low and tied down to a leg.

No one reacted at all to the kid's feistiness.

"Harry, the only reason yer here is your mother is Jack's wife's sister, ifn ya cause trouble, any one of these gentlemen could take you out, so relax, already!" Brownley said.

"I don't even know these guys," Harry said.

"That's the idea, dummkopf," Tate said. "That way, when we meet up near the fort and he's hiring, it don't look suspicious."

"What's dummkopf mean?"

"It's a German word fer good-lookin'," Buck said as the others had a good laugh at Harry's expense. Buck pushed his cowboy hat back on his head. Buck was heavy for a small man, but carried the weight well. His only weapon was the Winchester, which he had leaning against the table he was sitting next to. It wasn't about fast for Buck, it was about sleight of hand. He could roll around on the floor like a dog and was always a bit drunk, which he was sure gave him an advantage.

"Okay, ya got it. Ride up to Fort Belknap, come in at yer leisure, and none of ya know each other. Get hired on Rudley Quatrain's cattle drive, and somewhere along the way, kill all the other drovers, and take the cattle on into the Montana territory. By the time ya get there, we'll all be rich men," Ned Brownley said, but he wasn't going to tell them how that would come about, the less they knew, the better.

As the men left the basement by the storm door, they rode off in different directions.

Later that night, when the storm had passed, five of the six—they left Gnomes, the kid out—met at the Longhorn Saloon in San Angelo. The bad weather had kept just about everyone else at home, and the bartender/owner was glad for the business.

They sat around a big round table in the back. They all knew each other and had worked for Jack Tate before. From left to right around the table, they were: O.B. Thomas, a disgruntled priest who had been defrocked for praying with some of his younger parishioners while lying down. They had all been young women, and he was not sorry.

Davidson Lord, a man who had read a lot and thought his own reasoning was his God. If he couldn't figure it out, it couldn't be figured out, or so he thought. Davidson was heavyset and clean-shaven. He looked mean till he smiled, but when he smiled, he was, in fact, even meaner.

Buck Krieter was small, heavy, and a fool for whiskey, but could get amazing results in all sorts of ways when he was drunker than most men. Last, Todd Aimes had fallen asleep in his home, knocked over a lamp accidentally, and burned the house down with his wife and three daughters in it. He could still hear their screams.

The shot glasses were passed around, and the bottle right afterward. They filled their own glasses and lifted them as Jack Tate made a toast.

"Here's to easy money, easy women, and easy work!" he said, and they all drank.

2

The wood that Immanuel and Uzziah had gathered from Max and Frederick's cabin had saved their bacon, so to speak. There were nights in which they could have been warmer, but snuggled under their buffalo robes, they got by just fine. They had almost given up on beaver pelts, since the price of them was nominal. They had taken up hunting puma and bear, whose pelts seemed to draw better money, and they didn't have to spend all that time in the cold streams and ponds.

Immanuel was the one who could not stay in one place when hunting, and that might have been for lots of reasons. He was thinner than Uzziah, and he said the weather, even when it was tolerably in the 40s, was too cold to lay up waiting on some bear or cat to decide to come his way.

Uzziah had learned to hunt in the Appalachian Range, and lying quiet and still was perfect for a man who carried close to 275 pounds on him.

They had both gone out that morning to kill what

could be killed, eaten, and their hides sold down at Vrain. Immanuel had gone down the mountain, while Uzziah had gone up to the high meadow, where he stopped by his wife and son's grave before he settled into waiting on the prey. He'd seen both puma and bear track up that way but had neglected to tell Immanuel. Well, hunters and fishermen rarely disclose their spots, and that's a fact.

He sat on the ground, which was mostly dry, and looked at the fine marker he'd made over the winter. It was chiseled out of stone, granite, and he was pleased with the job he'd done. He didn't have the proper tools, but he used his Bowie and a carpenter's hammer to cut the letters into the stone. He wasn't done with it, and when he wanted to do more work, he simply pulled it out of the ground, laid it back, and went to work. So far, he had their names, the dates of life and death, and that was about it. He wanted to put scripture on it, but every time he thought he'd come up with the perfect chapter and verse, he read something else that seemed more appropriate.

Uzziah didn't talk to graves. It simply wasn't in his nature. He thought that just being this close to the mortal remains of his loved ones would serve a purpose, and it did. For some reason, he always felt more comfortable just sitting and letting his mind wander where it would.

When he saw the bear that morning as it had entered the meadow at the far end, really the farthest point from where he was sitting, he'd initially thought that it would not stay in the meadow, but look for trout in the small stream, then be on his way. He paid it little attention till, a half an hour later, it had gotten to the middle of the meadow and Uzziah was thinking that the bear was probably wondering what that enormous lump was—it was Uzziah.

He'd been thinking about when Hannah used to bring the lunches to him at the quarry when they were digging the rock out of it for the Nauvoo Temple, how sometimes, either before or after lunch, they would kiss a bit, and get so excited, he'd be thinking of her all afternoon. One such afternoon, he'd almost been killed by a swinging granite that barely missed his head.

The bear made a noise, and when Uzziah looked up, he couldn't have been any more than twenty yards from where he was sitting. Evidently, the wind had changed directions, and Uzziah's scent had been nosed by the bear.

The bear sat back on his haunches and swiped at the air alternatively with one then the other big paw. The Hawken was across Uzziah's lap, the way it nearly always was, but depending on how sleepy this particular bear was, he wasn't sure if he could get it up, aim, and shoot before the bear was on him. Damn, he'd have to stop daydreaming so much at the gravesite. Earlier, he'd been thinking of the trip he and the Mohawk George Martin had taken up the Missouri River in the small paddle wheeler. He was remembering how easily it was to fall asleep when you were listening to the little steam engine running.

The bear must have just gotten away from his cave and hibernation, it seemed a bit drowsy, just like Uzziah. It was then that Uzziah sneezed!

This type of sneezing had happened to him before, but not in such a situation. The bear rocked back on its hind legs, then threw itself forward, covering an amazing amount of ground in a short amount of time.

Uzziah didn't have time to raise and cock the Hawken, so he parried the weight of the bear by sticking the barrel of the Hawken into the bear's stomach and letting the force of the running bear push him out of harm's way. Unfortunately, the bear swiped at the Hawken, and it went end over end, too far away to be of any use. Uzziah wasn't about to outrun any bear, no matter how sleepy it seemed, so he pulled the Bowie knife out. He'd been wrapped in the bearskin with the hood up on his head, and to all intents and purposes, the attacking bear may have thought he was a bear, until he'd poked it in the belly with the Hawken.

Behind him, Shadow had seen the bear's attack and run away. You always ground-tied a horse for this very reason. That gave Uzziah just the fraction of the second he needed as the bear followed the rapid movement of the black horse and paid less attention to Uzziah's fast walk to where the Hawken had landed.

By the time the bear, and it wasn't a grizzly, just a big black bear, had seen Uzziah, he ran humped backed, the way they do, toward him. Uzziah picked up the Hawken just in time to swing it this time like a club and whack the bear in the head. If it had been baseball, it would have been a home run.

As it was, the bear was momentarily stunned, but shook its head, and that's when Uzziah was fairly sure he was done for, but then something black flashed behind the black bear. It was Shadow, who had taken advantage of the bear's being stunned and ran directly at the back of the bear.

When a horse at a gallop runs into anything, there

is an equal and opposite reaction to the force of the horse, its weight, and the speed of the horse at the time of impact.

The black bear was shot past Uzziah and took a swipe at him, which tore his buffalo robe, but then the bear was tumbling over and over and into the creek. He stood up, soaking wet, and growled just as the 54-caliber lead slug from the Hawken penetrated his head on the left side during his energetic shaking of his head. He stopped there in the creek, looked down as if he were thinking about fishing again, then toppled like a felled tree directly into the stream, water splashing up two to three feet on both sides of the banks.

When Uzziah walked over there, the water downstream from where the bear lay was traced with crimson, and Shadow gimped over to where Uzziah was looking at the bear.

Uzziah ran his hand down the left front leg of Shadow, and there was a point he reached where the horse winced. It wasn't broken, but probably badly bruised. He would be leading the horse back to the camp.

Even as he walked Shadow back down the hill from the high meadow, with each step the horse seemed better. He was a bit amazed that Shadow had come to his rescue like that and wondered if that was particular to Shadow or whether other horses would have done the same.

"What happened to yer horse?" Immanuel asked. He was sitting by an outside fire, and skinning the puma he'd shot.

"Had a run-in with a black bear," Uzziah said.

"Right?"

"No, really, damnest thing I ever seen. He saved my life, that's what he did!"

"Uh-huh," Immanuel said, then added, "Ya interested in this puma meat?"

"It's sweet, yeah, I like it."

"Where's the bear now?"

"Lying up in the high meadow."

"Ya can use Stygian ifn ya like," Immanuel offered.

Uzziah rode Stygian up there. It wasn't the first time he'd ridden the horse, both partners felt it absolutely necessary for each partner to be able to ride the other's horse. But he was reminded that there was thoroughbred blood in this black horse, and he stepped a little higher and held his head up like he was a king.

Stygian had finally gotten used to the smell of death and blood. Uzziah tied a lariat around the bear's shot-through head and dragged him back down to camp.

"Where'd he die?" Immanuel asked.

"Close to the graves."

"Yer gonna get yerself kilt mopin' round them graves."

"I wasn't mopin'," Uzziah said.

"Sure, ya was dancing around and having fun, I'm sure."

"Well, ya can't kill some creatures without lyin' in wait fer them."

"Sometime, with ya, I ain't sure who's lying in wait fer who."

Rudley had been sitting in the Sweet Grass Saloon in Fort Belknap, Texas, for the better part of the morning.

He'd had the beef stew for breakfast, and a beer, and was nursing another beer till it was just about as warm as the horrible coffee the saloon offered.

Several prospective cowpunchers had come in. They obviously didn't know each other. Well, they'd come in at different times and were drinking alone. He decided the best way to get cowpunchers was simply to announce it to everybody.

"Hey," Rudley Quatrain said as he stood up from his chair, and every eye turned his way, "that big herd, some fifteen hundred strong, that's in the stockyards when ya come into town from the south, that herd's mine. I need cowpunchers, who wants a job?"

It was almost too easy. Rudley had all the help he needed to start the drive in two afternoons. It seemed that cowpunchers were just rolling into Fort Belknap. He wanted to doubt this good luck, but his mama had always told him, *"Do not look a gift horse in the mouth."*

They were getting the chuck wagon all settled, and the men used to who the bosses were—there were only two, the boss wrangler, Rudley Quatrain, and the cook. He'd hired a man he thought would be great at the job, his name was Buck Krieter, a German from Fredericksburg who had made him the best rabbit stew, he called it, Hasenpfeffer, that Rudley had ever had.

Back in San Angelo, Ned Brownley was in his home

office talking to a young cowboy. The young man looked hungry.

"Now all ya gots to do is drive the freight wagon too fast, I'll make sure Tad Snow will be on the street at the appropriate time."

"But, Mr. Brownley, ain't this"—he looked around as if someone else might be in Brownley's home, then he continued sotto voce—"murder?"

"Ya got a loan that's about to be collected by Tad Snow, the banker. Yer wife, who's pregnant again, and yer 1-year-old daughter are gonna be on the street ifn ya can't pay. Yer pa might own the freight company, but he's barely better off than you are. He ain't gonna pay the loan, can ya pay?"

"No sir."

"Then, what yer really doin' is savin' the life of yer pregnant wife and yer baby girl, ya got to learn to think 'bout these things in the proper terms, son, ya understand?"

"Yes, sir, I do."

"Good, remember, noon he'll be crossin', do not miss the opportunity to do good fer yer family, son," Brownley said as he showed the young man out.

"Ned! Ned!" Brownley's wife, Eloise, was coming from the kitchen, and there was hatred in her eyes.

"What is it now, *L*?" Brownley said, turning to her with a contemptuous expression on his face.

"Why are you looking at me like that?"

"No reason, dear, what's wrong, why were you screamin' my name?"

"These servants that you hired are terrible, just terrible. Look at this glove," she said and held her white-gloved hand out to him. It was grimy on the fingers. "I got this from running my hand along the windowsills—top and bottom—just look at that dirt!"

"Eloise, this is not an Army base. Why do you insist on doin' these inspections?"

"I hate dirt, I just hate it!"

"Look, why don't ya join Tad Snow and I fer lunch, meet us at May's 'round noon, okay?"

Eloise liked to eat, and she forgot all about the dirt. May's had wonderful chicken and dumplings, and she was going to have a double portion.

Rudley Quatrain had never had a cattle drive begin with such ease. All the men knew what their jobs were, and amazingly, all were doing them. The fifteen men he had working the cows were getting them to move right along, and it looked very much like by the end of the day, they would be out of sight of Fort Belknap. With this kind of drive, these cattle could be in Cheyenne early enough to fatten them on prairie grass before taking them down to market.

Off the trail a bit, one of the big bulls with his danglins as large as Rudley had ever seen, was off in the bushes making more beef. He was quick about it, and the heifer ran off, and Rudley just smiled. What could go wrong with a drive that had started in such an auspicious manner?

3

San Angelo had several good cafés and other hacienda-type restaurants that served both American and Mexican food. Eloise had worn her best dress and had skipped breakfast, thinking that it was only right that Ned would have to pay for her rather abundant appetite. She knew she should lose some weight, but when a woman has a husband who can afford to feed her, then her belief was that that woman should eat, and eating was one of the things Eloise did best.

She had been told to meet her husband, Ned, and Tad Snow at May's Restaurant. Perhaps, Ned had decided to up her allowance so that she could get better help. The Mexican girls just did not know what clean meant, and the slovenly White women, who had too many babies already, thought clean meant there were no discernible spots on things. Really, what was this world coming to?

She had stopped at the mercantile and bought some hard candy, which she was sucking on her way to

May's. The restaurant was closer than she remembered from the mercantile, and she would have to swallow the candy if her gluttony was not to be discovered. Instead of eating the candy and going into May's early and waiting, she decided to go down and cross the street and meet her husband and the good-looking bank manager there at the bank.

As she walked up to the bank door, it opened, and there stood Ned and Tad. They were getting ready to go out.

"Eloise, you're joining us?" Tad Snow, the president of the bank, asked.

"Yes, didn't Ned tell you?"

Ned was looking at his watch, and it was very close to noon. In fact, the clock on the bank's wall was beginning to strike the hour.

"Come, come! We don't want them to sell out of May's special for the day," Ned said.

They were halfway across the busy street, dodging this and that traffic, when Ned saw the freight wagon going much too fast.

"I've left something on Tad's desk, I'll join you at May's," Ned said as he rushed back across the street, just in time to see the two of them, his obese wife and the president of the San Angelo Bank as they threw up their arms as if that would save them and were run over by six Shires and a freight wagon full of bricks.

There were screams up and down the street as their bodies were trounced about, and their arms and legs did things arms and legs don't usually do, as the horse hooves did the majority of the damage and the wagon wheels finished them off.

It was a good thing that everyone was watching the

horrid accident, otherwise, they might have seen the quirky little smile on Ned Brownley's face just before he rushed into the street—heedless to his own safety—as others would report—to hold his dying wife's head in his arms. It looked like she was trying to speak as he bent over her.

"Ned, you bastard!" she whispered, and he put his ear closer to her mouth so that others would not hear whatever else she might have to say. Her death rattle surprised and excited him as she jerked in his arms and was dead. Tad Snow, the president of the San Angelo Bank, had a head which had been bisected by heavy wagon wheels, his tongue was lolled out, and his eyes stared God knows where.

The first on the scene was the sheriff of San Angelo, Starr Kingsley. When he got to the victims, both of them were dead. He had seen the accident out of the corner of his eye. He had been sitting outside his office on this nice Texas afternoon in his favorite chair, tipped back and enjoying the sun when he heard a female scream—it must have been Ned's wife, or perhaps another woman who had seen the accident, or maybe the banker had screamed thusly, it was hard to tell who would do what when death came knocking.

The driver, Kelly Jones, almost twenty years old and the father of one—and his skinny wife expecting another—was sitting on the buckboard of the freight wagon he had handled for years for his pa, and never had an accident. He was bawling his eyes out when Sheriff Kingsley jumped on the box next to him.

"What have I done!? What have I done!?" Kelly was saying over and over again, rocking back and forth on the buckboard. Already, his pa, Arthur Jones, was running down the boardwalk—bad news was always the fastest traveler—he was sure his boy had been hurt, and he couldn't stand that thought. Hadn't he just two days before refused the boy a raise!? Kelly had married way too early, and his skinny wife was pregnant again, as if all it took was him passing her in the night on the path to the outhouse. He saw his boy, Kelly, sitting there, being comforted by the sheriff, then, down from that, he saw the two bodies lying in the street waiting for the coroner's wagon to pick them up. One moment you were a respected citizen, then you were refuse on the street, being picked up like so much horse shite and thrown into a wagon.

"I should have known better," was the tune Kelly Jones was singing now, and Arthur, whose business was already in over its head because of the mercantile store owned by Franklin Rivers, all Arthur could see was a civil suit in which he and his freighting company would be sued right out of San Angelo.

He jumped on the buckboard and brushed the sheriff's arm from around his son's shoulder, and leaned in close.

"Don't say another word, do ya hear me, not another word!" He was harsh, and his voice did not sound comforting, and when Kelly looked at him, he almost thought his pa was in cahoots with Ned Brownley.

"Pa?"

"Not another word!" the elder Jones said as he

pulled the boy off the freight wagon and back down the street toward the freight office.

That night, the men who were the business partners of Ned Brownley met in the sheriff's office. It was a big office, and the stove was gently warming the room.

Those there were Franklin Rivers, the owner of the biggest mercantile in town, Ned Brownley, who had conceived the idea and been brilliantly joined with the men of means in the city of San Angelo, Steve Hudley, whose idea of the railroad eventually going all the way across the county was ahead of its time, but his investments in local Texas Railroads had already made him a fortune, and then there was Starr Kingsley, the sheriff of San Angelo, who when he came to San Angelo already had quite a nest egg.

"I called this meeting," Brownley began as he stood and faced the others, "because it needs to be decided what will become of the share in this adventuresome cattle business which we have surreptitiously begun, now that Tad Snow is dead. I think, personally, that the share should be spread among all of us, which could mean that each of us would hold in this new company 1 and 1/5 a share."

"Well," started in Steve Hudley, the railroad man, "he wasn't married, does anyone know if Snow had kin anywhere else?"

"He did not," Brownley said, then added, "Tad was a bachelor, the most eligible of bachelors, and he enjoyed the company of some of the finer women in San Angelo, and that isn't speaking ill of the dead, or of those who sought out his company. It's just that what was Tad's was Tad's. It was his money, not the bank's, which he invested, and this seemed to be the only equitable way to divvy up his share."

"Unless there was foul play," Starr Kingsley said as he stood from his chair behind the desk and the star on his chest suggesting that his authority might outweigh that of money alone.

It was times like this that not only try men's souls, but also call into question their hearts. Where exactly did the matter lie? Was the money more important than the fact that a good man, a handsome bachelor man, who was also president of the San Angelo Bank, was wiped out on the streets of his beloved town in broad daylight? This mention of foul play had everyone looking at the sheriff, and none of them felt safe. An extra fifth of an interest in something as lucrative as Brownley had planned might make the difference between simply fame and generous fortune.

"I hardly think that's appropriate," Franklin Rivers said as he stood. The man was close to seven feet tall, which was freakish in the times they were living, and things that were said behind his back were sometimes not only not kind, but downright loathsome. The doorways and entrances to and within the mercantile store that he owned were made to his specifications, and made ordinary men look smallish when walking through them.

"Sir," Sheriff Kingsley said. "Murder is never appropriate in any and all circumstances."

"But are you suggesting that one of us, one of the four remaining partners of the Great Northern Cattle

Company, is actually involved in the murder of Tad Snow, and Mr. Brownley's wife!?!" Franklin asked.

"Look," Sheriff Kingsley said, "I don't want to say any of this, but I saw, granted out of the corner of my eye, one of the potential victims of that freight accident running from the scene of the accident shortly before it happened—"

"Are ya suggestin' I kilt me own wife!?!" Brownley roared as he came at the sheriff, who simply put up a hand to stop him.

"Kelly Jones, there's something he said when I first joined him on the buckboard that had me reeling. Perhaps it's nothing, but he kept saying, 'What have I done? What have I done?'"

"Why wouldn't he say that? Two people lay dead in the street behind his freight wagon, and he was driving!" Brownley nearly shouted.

"That's another thing, why was he speeding in the middle of town. I smelled his breath, there was no alcohol on it, and he doesn't have a habit of drinking. But there he was, veritably racing down Main Street at high noon!"

The cattle drive was still on track, and it looked very much to Rudley Quatrain that this might be one of the easiest drives he'd ever been on. He liked the money. He was making $175 a month on this drive, and the others were making $50 a month. It was equally attractive to the wranglers who had pushed cattle for a lot less many times.

And then there was Buck Krieter's cooking. No

man had memory of ever being fed so well on any cattle drive. He had such an inventive spirit when it came to cooking, and sometimes he could be seen drinking from a bottle of whiskey in one hand, while stirring one of his imaginative stews with the other. Sometimes, he'd add a shot of whiskey to whatever it was he was making, and he'd brought along grits, which was a favorite for all the southern cowboys.

How could things get better, Rudley wondered to himself? That night, as he got into his bedroll and had O.B. Thomas riding the night ride singing to the cattle with his glorious bass voice, Rudley had no idea that on the other side of the herd, the group of men whom he thought had just met each other, were scheming to take the lives of those honest men who had signed on.

Jack Tate sat his horse and was smoking a cigarette.

"We've gotten far enough away from Fort Belknap that it's time for some accidents to happen. Buck, somebody's got to die of food poisoning. I want ya to take care of that," Tate said.

"No problem," Buck said, thinking of the snake venom he always carried just in case of emergencies. One never knew when a foe would be too formidable, and nature's remedies would have to be enjoined.

"And Harry, the next time ya follow a cowpuncher into the brush, see to it that when ya come out, yer the only one who's alive."

"How am I to do that? I can't just shoot him, right?"

"Ya can ifn he draws on ya first. Get one of these

cowboys, more wet behind the ears than you, in a card game and cheat his socks off him," Tate said.

"Ah, yeah, then when he calls me out for cheating, I can drill him," Harry said.

"Okay, there's six of us, all we got to do is get rid of the others and leave us in charge of the herd, ya got it?"

They all nodded their heads and were glad that they were on this side of the double-cross.

San Angelo was reeling from the two deaths in the middle of their main street. The banker, Tad Snow, had been a heartbreaker within the society of women. He had been such a gentleman and taken all his lady friends to places they loved to be seen with the successful man. And yes, some of them—well, all of them—had dreamed of being Mrs. Tad Snow, but Tad had always played the field like that, even when he was in Dallas and had almost been driven from the town on a rail. There was only so much rivalry that some men could take. When the news reached Dallas that he'd been killed in a wagon accident, there were many glasses raised in honor of his passing, but not exactly.

Sheriff Starr Kingsley was keeping his eyes open. He had made an enemy with Ned Brownley, but he'd seen what he'd seen, and it sure looked to him that Brownley had run from an almost certain death before he could have known of any danger, unless, of course, he was the danger and had arranged the whole thing?

Kelly Jones was back to driving freight for his pa, but the sheriff had had a couple of talks with the boy, and it seemed that his father, Arthur, had stopped up that leak. There wasn't any more information coming that way. Of course, there was the newish house, which the boy had bought and moved into with his skinny pregnant wife and his little girl. Sheriff Kingsley thought it strange, almost like he'd been paid off for the accident, but then his father had stepped in and said the boy needed help, and since he was his only boy, he was going to see to it that the boy got along better than he had.

Then there was the drinking that Kelly Jones was doing now. He had never been a saloon man, always a man who had stuck around the house with his wife, but now, he had been seen with various soiled doves and staying out all hours. Finally, the sheriff had had enough, and he went to talk to his pa.

"Say, Arthur," the sheriff said as he walked into the freight office.

"Yeah," Arthur said, and he immediately became busy.

"Got a moment?" the sheriff asked.

"Got these invoices to get out, and I'm a bit short-handed this morning."

"I'll wait," the sheriff said and hung out by the front windows looking down the street where two people had recently lost their lives, and he still had this niggling feeling that it wasn't any accident.

"What can I do for ya?" Arthur asked.

"Can ya step out for a second?" the sheriff asked.

The two men stepped out on the porch to the freight office, and both took the chairs that were leaning up against the wall there.

"What is it, Sheriff?"

"Yer boy," was all the sheriff said.

"What 'bout him?"

"Ya know he's been drinkin' and hangin' out with some of the doves from both saloons," the sheriff mentioned, knowing that it was common knowledge.

"Yeah, so?"

"So, I know the town is giving the boy lots of rein because he's essentially kilt two of our prominent citizens, but he never done anything like his afore has he?"

"Okay, I'll come clean," Arthur said, and the sheriff sat forward on his chair and tipped his hat back.

"I told him to," Arthur said.

"You told him to run those two citizens over?!?" the sheriff asked, almost standing up.

"Hell no! I told him to take up with the doves," Arthur said, smiling.

"Why would a father do that?"

"He ain't made of money and times are lean, ifn that Franklin Rivers gets any richer, it might be the end of this freighting company."

"I didn't know it was that bad, but that don't make any sense, ya told yer son to waste his money on doves and whiskey?!?"

"Doves and whiskey are cheaper than more kids," Arthur said, making a face like he was the wisest man who had ever walked the earth.

Sheriff Starr Kingsley stood up and looked at a father who may have been dumber than his dumb son. Didn't Arthur know that once a woman is with child, she can't get with child again, till the present load is dumped?

"Well, just want ya to know, I'm watchin' the boy," Sheriff Kingsley said.

"Watch away," Arthur said, "And have a good day."

4

All the men from the drive were standing around one particular bedroll. The man in that bedroll was writhing in pain and screaming from time to time. This had been going on for the better part of three hours. Nobody was getting any sleep.

Several of the men were trying to comfort the trail boss, Rudley Quatrain, but nothing they were doing was making any difference.

Off behind the chuck wagon, Jack Tate was berating Buck Krieter.

"Ya stupid son of a bitch, he's the boss, he's the onliest one who knows where the watering holes are up this way. Without him, we are all dead," Tate whispered violently.

"It weren't him I was trying to poison, it weren't!"

"Then how did he get the poison?"

"I made that rabbit stew he likes, but the bowl I put the rattlesnake venom in was meant fer the young kid."

"And?"

"He rode drag and was late gettin' back, and afore I

knew what was happening, Rudley took his bowl and was finishing it off!"

"Why didn't ya stop him?!?"

"He were wiping the bottom of the bowl with a biskie when I saw him! I didn't mean fer him to die," Buck said, almost sorry, then added, "But what the hell, one less is one less, right!"

Tate rapped the barrel of his gun across Buck's face, and he went down hard.

"If this goes to shite, y'all be the first to go of the new crew," Tate said, and Buck made plans right then and there to save the rest of the venom for Tate in case things went south.

On his way back to lock up the sheriff's office that night, Kingsley noticed that the door to the office wasn't quite closed. He took his pistol out and cocked it. He wasn't going to be the next one to go in the partnership. He had invested every cent he had in this Great Northern Cattle Company or whatever the hell they were calling it. He'd tried in the past to make some honest money, but the only real money he'd ever made was with a gambler up in Fort Worth who had a crooked roulette wheel, and when he was sheriff up there, he looked the other way for a percentage of the winnings.

He pushed the door opened and pointed his gun at a one-year-old toddler who was struggling to make it from his desk to the chair. Kelly's wife, the skinny pregnant one, was sitting behind his desk, talking softly with the little girl.

When she saw him, she stood up and immediately

grabbed her tremendous belly, which looked very much like it wanted to bounce off the floor and be done with this world.

"Sorry, Sheriff, this looked like the most comfortable chair here," she said apologetically.

He looked at her, and for the life of him, he could not remember her name. Maybe if he stalled long enough, it would come to him.

"Mama," the one-year-old said, well, that was one of her names, but not the handle he was looking for.

"Nah, ya go ahead and keep that seat, how can I help ya, darlin'," he hated to use a term of endearment with a pregnant woman, but hell, he couldn't remember her name. Wait, now it came to him. Nelly, that was her name.

"Nelly, when's that baby due?" he asked, so proud that he'd remembered.

"Doc says in a week, but hell, it feels like I been pregnant forever, ifn ya know what I mean?"

"Thankfully, I do not," he said and sat in the chair that the toddler was using to stand up with, and when she came back from the door, she started crying, realizing that her prop had been taken. Now, she'd have no place to hold on to as she made her way around the room.

"It's okay, sugar pie, it's okay," Nelly said in the most soothing voice. The sheriff wished he had a woman who could, would talk to him like that.

The toddler, he couldn't remember her name either, damn, he must be getting old.

"Sally, ya just stop yer cryin'" her mother said.

So, now he knew everybody's name except for the one in the oven, and that would be here soon enough.

"Kelly talks in his sleep," Nelly said.

Nelly and Kelly, now why hadn't he been able to remember that combination?!?

"Did ya hear me?" Nelly asked.

"Yeah, yer man talks when he's a sleepin', lots of folks do, so?"

"He kilt them people on purpose," she spat out, and it felt like a knife had been thrust into the heart of the sheriff. Why the hell didn't he trust his instincts?

"How do ya know?" Sheriff Kingsley asked softly.

"He said as much in his sleep, and not just once. He's a tortured soul and I feel he will continue to be until he atones fer this grievous sin. It's the first of them, don't ya know—Thou shalt not kill!" she said, and he realized that he did not know that Nelly of Kelly and Nelly was a righteous woman. Well, good for her. Righteousness just might pay off for the law. But why would Kelly want Mrs. Brownley dead, or the banker, Snow, for that matter?

"That ain't exactly evidence, sugar," he said, and there he was talking to her in terms of endearment, what the hell!

"No, but ifn ya get him in here, and sweat him a little," she suggested.

Good God, was the woman serious? "He's yer husband, Nelly, and ya can't be forced to testify agin him!" the sheriff said softly.

"Yeah, well, I will 'cause he's a cheatin' no good son of a bitch! And that's one of the ten, also, don't covet yer neighbor's wife, or another man's soiled dove!"

Well, there it was. *No fury like a woman scorned*—he thought the Bard had said that, but he was not a learned man. He had seen one of the Bard's plays when he was in Fort Worth, and slept with the woman who had played Macbeth's wife. She was weird, they just put a crazy person in a crazy play, and it seemed to work for the traveling theater company.

"What ya gonna do, Sheriff Kingsley?"

"Well, what do ya suggest?" he asked, knowing that if she had thought it through this much, then she probably had an idea.

"Come by my house, come in after he's slept off the whiskey and the smell of the whores has dissipated, and I'll let ya in, and ya can sit by the bed and hear the whole mess. What ya say, Sheriff Kingsley?"

He was impressed. She probably had a notion about how his hanging would go, too, but he certainly wasn't going to ask her.

They buried Rudley Quatrain the next day. Two of the wranglers who weren't on the dirty crew did the work, as well they should. Buck felt bad, but Jack Tate was really worried. To hear Rudley tell it, you had to know exactly where the watering holes were going north, and if you missed just one, it meant the cattle would start dropping like flies.

Two more days passed, and there were no other deaths. That night, as they sat around the campfire, several men, four in all, started a poker game, and Harry Gnomes started cheating openly. The three other men, regular wranglers who could tell right off that Gnomes was cheating, took into account that Gnomes had those two low-slung revolvers tied down, and even though he was young, he looked like a killer. Two of the men bowed out, but the last of the real wranglers, an older man who wasn't keen on cards and probably hadn't caught on to Gnomes's cheating, stayed in the game.

The game went on and on, and the older man was losing his shirt. Finally when Gnomes disappeared to relieve himself, one of the other players who had dropped out whispered something to the older man. His eyebrows went up, and he looked at the other man who knew his cards, and all he did was agree by shaking his head.

Gnomes came back and, while he was gone, had taken the circles of wang leather off his revolvers. Surely, this old goat would eventually call him out for cheating.

Jack Tate had seen it all and knew that the two poker players who had already folded out of the game knew Gnomes was cheating, and after the whispering had gone on, he figured the older man could be trusted to call Harry out.

The cards were dealt by Gnomes, and obviously, he'd dealt from the bottom for himself, where he'd kept an ace.

Without calling Harry Gnomes out or anything, the older man drew from his sitting position and drilled Harry twice in the chest! His expression was priceless. He'd fancied himself a gunslinger, but when the old man drew unannounced, he'd just sat there, not even reaching for his guns!

As Harry flew back against one of the chuck wagon's wheels, his hands, which had always imagined themselves the hands of a gunfighter, managed to pull both revolvers from their holsters, and he began firing. They were double-action Colts, and there was no need to cock and shoot. All you had to do was keep pulling the trigger, which it seemed Harry was able to do until the hammers clicked down on empty cartridges. One of the regular wranglers had taken a shot in the head. His eyes were open, but he was dead.

Another bullet grazed across the back of O.B. Thomas's head and took out his vision as he was turning away from the action. The bullet that did that found Todd Aimes, the man who had fallen asleep and burned down his house with his wife and three daughters in it. He was smiling, really grinning it up, as he looked down at the hole in his shirt, which was directly over his heart. The errant slug had passed through the pumping organ, which was destroyed by the lead, but Aimes smiled a genuine smile for the first time in years, like since he'd been responsible for the total loss of his family. He slumped over dead. There was nobody home as blood stained his shirt and vest.

"What just happened chere?" Tate asked, looking around, his hand on his pistol.

"That man will not cheat in another card game," the older man said as he took the winnings from Gnomes's pockets and passed them out between himself and the other player who was still alive.

"He was a cheater, that a fer sure!" someone whispered.

Tate just stood there. The best laid plans, he thought. Now, two of his gang were dead, and they had the tallest blind man in the territory, of that, he was sure. That left him with two men, plus himself, to ride the big herd!

Sheriff Kingsley had sat in Nelly and Kelly's bedroom for the past two nights, and what his wife had said were confessions were nothing more than the mumblings of a drunken young man. The last night there, she had encouraged him to lie on the bed next to her husband so he could more easily hear what the man was saying.

The disturbing thing about Nelly was that she might have been a skinny woman, but she sported some big tatas, and evidently, they had not been like that till she was pregnant with her little girl Sally, and wanting to keep them big, she had continued to nurse the girl.

Sheriff Kingsley crawled up in the bed beside the young man as he mumbled, and Sally awakened and crawled in with her mama.

The drunken Kelly kept mumbling, and Nelly kept nodding as if this were the real confession. She smiled as she lay there, her tongue licking her lips with a wicked look in her eye.

Sally was placed by her ma on the side where Sheriff Kingsley had laid, and the sheriff came over behind her and massaged Nelly's breasts as he entered her from behind. He wasn't worried, and evidently, neither was she, about her getting pregnant as he unloaded his jissum into her.

The motion in the bed encouraged Kelly to speak up, and it was plain as day what he said. "I kilt 'em and I'll go to hell fer it!" Then he began to snore.

Well, the sheriff left Nelly and Kelly's house, and she followed him out on the porch like nothing had happened. He looked at her, but she started right in on what Kelly had said.

"Ya heard, didn't ya?" she asked. She had pulled the nightgown down, and it was dragging on the porch floor, but there were stains of milk on the front of it where she was still leaking. The sheriff was trying to wrap his mind around what had just happened back there in the couple's bedroom.

"Yeah, yeah, I heard all right," he said.

"And the reward, it still stands, right?"

The town of San Angelo had offered a $100 apiece reward for information leading to any information which might lead to a conviction in the two deaths. The coroner had been convinced to leave the cause of death blank until a further investigation could be conducted.

"Yeah, yeah, it's still good. Nelly," Sheriff Kingsley started in, but she put a finger to his lips.

"It was a one-time thing only, he's gettin' some, why shouldn't I?" she said and turned and walked back into the house, the screen shutting softly.

5

The rustlers under Jack Tate were down as much as the true wranglers. And to boot, it had been nearly three days since they had found water. The longhorns' intake would have been between three and thirty gallons a day, and this lack of water had almost brought the herd to a standstill. They had trouble getting the cattle up the past few mornings, and as they drove them, some had simply collapsed and not been able to rise.

"What are we gonna do?" Buck asked.

Tate looked down at the cow that was obviously dying.

"I ain't got a clue," Tate said, then looked at Buck.

"I told ya, it tweren't my fault, the bowl was meant fer another."

"Ya just might have to take the rest of that snake venom yerself to even things out," Tate said, and Buck's hand went to his rifle.

"The first thing people lose when things go south is

their sense of humor," Tate said, slapping Buck on the shoulder. "Now, climb back up onto that chuckwagon and let's see if we can find some water."

San Angelo was abuzz! Kelly Jones had been arrested for the willful—or negligent—homicides of the banker Tad Snow and Mrs. Eloise Brownley. The sheriff had shown up on the morning after he'd slept with the suspect's wife, not so much to make the arrest as to keep Nelly Jones from crowing to her husband about getting some on the side. Stranger things had happened, and the sheriff was covering his bases. If Nelly agreed to testify against her husband, Kelly, then there might be a good chance of getting a conviction, but the next thing that had to happen was Kelly giving up who had put him up to the killing of those two people.

There was a banging on the sheriff's door, which was usually unlocked, but since he brought the boy in, it was always locked. Starr Kingsley didn't need to look out the curtains and see who it was, the man was screaming through the door.

"Starr, ya sorry son of a bitch, let me in." It was Arthur Jones, Kelly's father and the owner of the freight company.

Sheriff Kingsley went to the door and flipped the curtain back. Arthur Jones was indeed alone. He unlocked the door and hurriedly locked it back once the man was inside.

"How'd ya know he was here?" Kingsley asked.

"His pregnant wife, ya know, Nelly, she done come

runnin' to me this mornin' tellin' me ya showed yerself earlier than a rooster and picked the boy up."

Sheriff Kingsley started to say something, but Jones continued.

"What is the meanin' of this?!? Hasn't the boy had enough trouble already?"

"Well, what 'bout the trouble that old Tad Snow and Mrs. Brownley went through?"

"They were victims in an awful accident, and we need to leave it at that?"

"I got evidence to the contrary," Kingsley said.

"What evidence!? Hell, yer runnin' fer reelection this chere year and a conviction on this would make ya look awful good."

"I ain't through 'vestigatin', Arthur, and I can't tell ya no more."

"I wanna talk to my son, now!"

"No."

"Whatcha mean *no*?"

"Ya can't talk to him till I get a whack at him, now it's time ya got outta my office, ya hear!" the sheriff said as he guided Arthur Jones toward the door.

"Don't say nothin', son. Nothin', ya hear me!" Jones yelled as the sheriff pushed him from the office and locked the door behind him.

The weather had been uncommonly dry. There was plenty of water flowing down from the mountain's yearly snowpack, but the storms that sometimes were a part of the unsettled weather along the front range were simply nonexistent.

And, of course, right in the middle of this drought of sorts, Immanuel had decided to make him and Uzziah a shower. They'd both used one at the Wolverine Hotel in Chicago after they got off the charges of murder on the Pinkerton Agent Robert Spells, and the memory of how refreshing it felt to stand and bathe, to stand and rinse with clean water instead of getting out of a bathtub with the soap scum on one's body still was a vivid memory for Immanuel. He knew Uzziah felt the same way, and he hadn't done anything particularly nice for his partner in a long time. At least this project would be around the cabins, they wouldn't be going out amid the throngs and multitudes and getting invariably into some sort of trouble.

Immanuel's version was going to be cruder than the indoor plumbing of the Wolverine Hotel, but possibly just as effective.

While Uzziah was still having his morning coffee and reading, Immanuel jumped on Stygian's back and rode up to Frederick and Max's cabin. They had said to use what they needed, and he felt sure that, amid all the junk they'd left, he had remembered a storage tank. He thought he remembered they had had plans to make their own whiskey, and when it fell through, just like all their other projects, they had abandoned the tank.

The morning was glorious, and the sun felt good on an old man's back, not that he was going to admit to anyone that he was approaching old manhood!

He rode Stygian around the rubble that was those lazy mountain men's habitats, and the horse seemed glad to be out, just as he was. Wow! There was a lot of junk, then he spied it. He rode over to where a bunch of lumber had been discarded, and there was something jutting out from the pile that wasn't wood. He jumped down off the tall horse and almost lost his footing, then, turning back some of the board, there it lay!

It was tin, and rusted somewhat, but other than that, it was good-sized and looked just the thing. But he hadn't ridden a saddle over there and didn't have a rope, so he rode back to where they'd left the wagon when they brought back the bodies of Hannah O'Bannon and their son, George. He found it without any problem whatsoever, but evidently so had someone else. The things that they'd left in the back of the wagon were not scattered around like they should have been. An entire winter had come and gone, winds had blown, drifts had been made, shifted, then melted. And yet, the few items, there weren't many—a blanket, a tarp, some ropes—they had all been neatly arranged in the wagon.

Well, Immanuel guessed that Uzziah just couldn't stay away. He'd come to see if there was anything else of value, and folded the blanket? Nah, he wouldn't do that, would he? Well, he'd ask Uzziah later. Now he had use of the ropes, which were neatly wound up and stacked in the corner of the wagon. He gathered them up and rode back to Max and Fredericks's place.

Once there, he tied the rope around the—it wasn't a stock tank—the vessel, and then, tying two rope ends together, he had enough rope to tie about himself and jump up on Stygian. The horse wouldn't feel the weight at all, since it would be pulling against Immanuel's body, but what Immanuel hadn't counted on was the noise the tank would make. First, when it broke from its bonds in the rubble, throwing planks and other trash about.

Stygian was startled and made a bit of a run from

the noise, but the noise was connected to Immanuel now, and whenever the tank hit a tree or tumbled over rocks, Stygian was sure the devil himself was after him and his rider.

By the time they made it to the clearing where their cabins were, Immanuel had to pull the rope off his body so that the noise would stop. And he had to admit, it had been quite noisy.

"What in God's name are ya doin'?" Uzziah asked. He was leaning in the doorway to his cabin. The heat was getting out, but it was a beautiful morning, and really, the only reason he'd stepped out was the noise which he couldn't place at all!

"Ya'll see," was all Immanuel was willing to commit to.

"Ya need help?" Uzziah asked, seeing the tank, which was fairly dented up now that it had been dragged for a good three miles.

"I was sick, but I'm over all that. I'm gettin' more and more healthier every day, and no, yer help is not needed, but thanks," Immanuel said.

"Okay, got it, yer in tiptop condition and don't need any help with whatever that is," he said, motioning toward the dented tank. "Weren't that up at the lazy's place?" Uzziah continued.

"Yep," Immanuel said, being noncommittal.

"Let me guess, yer gonna run whiskey through that to yer cabin?"

"Ha! Ha!" Immanuel made his mocking laughter.

"Want some coffee?"

"Yeah, yeah, that would be good," Immanuel said as he looked back at the tank and wondered if dragging it had put holes in it. That wouldn't be good.

Uzziah disappeared and came back with a tin cup of steaming coffee. Immanuel was busy straightening out the holding tank, or whatever it was, and so Uzziah walked over to where Immanuel was reshaping the tank.

"Oh! Oh!" Immanuel said, seeing that his partner had come over, he took the cup from him. "I need this, partner," he said, taking a gigantic sip and burning his mouth. "Damn, that's hot!"

"Thought that was the way ya liked it?"

"Yeah, yeah, but not hot as hell, good grief."

"Yer gonna make me guess, ain't ya?" Uzziah said, sipping his cup while Immanuel rubbed his burned lips.

"Ya always got the best coffee." Immanuel finally said after taking another cautious sip.

"Beans are always greener."

"Huh?" Immanuel asked, still staring at the tank.

"Water, yer gonna put water in it, right?" Uzziah asked.

"Uh-huh."

"So, the horses and Jenny can drink from it instead of the streams?"

"Nah, ain't fer the horses, nor Jenny."

"Well, I ain't drinkin' from that rusty old thing," Uzziah noted.

"Me, neither," Immanuel said as he dragged it toward the cabins.

"Where ya takin' it?"

"Y'all see," Immanuel said as he laid it down halfway between the cabin that Uzziah liked with the potbellied stove, and his own cabin.

"Uh-huh," Uzziah mused, drinking more coffee as Immanuel disappeared into the barn.

In a moment, Immanuel emerged with the ladder.

"Oh, this just keeps gettin' better and better," Uzziah said.

"Y'all never guess."

"Yer right, never in a million."

"Think, Wolverine, think!" Immanuel said.

"My nickname?"

"Nah, besides, that's a stupid nickname."

"Thought ya liked it?" Uzziah asked.

"Well, I wouldn't want it. *Wolverine*," Immanuel said, elongating the syllables as he said the word.

"The hotel in Chicago?"

"Yer gettin' hotter."

"No, I'm not, I'm totally lost now."

"What did we do the minute we got released from jail?" Immanuel asked.

"Yer gonna make whiskey in it?"

"An idea, but not the right one—'member the minute we got to the hotel—what'd we do?"

"We ate lunch."

"Afore that."

"Immanuel, are you okay?" Uzziah asked.

"I'm fine. My body is fine. My mind is fine."

"Okay, okay."

"We took a shower," Immanuel said, trying to jog Uzziah's memory.

"Not together, we didn't!" Uzziah insisted.

"Well, acourse not, we ain't that kinda partners, jeez, Uzziah!"

"So, we took a shower, so what?"

"So, what! So, what?!?" Immanuel looked at Uzziah and knew he wasn't getting the idea.

Immanuel placed the ladder on the edge of Uzziah's cabin and climbed a bit up.

"Hand me the holding tank," he asked Uzziah too politely.

"Here ya go, kind sir," Uzziah said, mimicking his politeness.

"Now, foller me up this chere ladder, young son."

The two men walked up the ladder, and Immanuel placed the tank on Uzziah's roof, while Uzziah just looked at his partner strangely.

"I gots better things to do than watch ya go crazy," Uzziah said as he turned and went back down the ladder.

"Get my coffee, will ya?"

Uzziah grabbed Immanuel's coffee and came back up the ladder.

"I done forgot how far ya can see up chere," Immanuel said as he sipped the coffee.

"Tastes good, don't it?" Uzziah asked.

"Yes, dear, it's wonderful!" Immanuel mocked, "I wasn't too hard on ya last night, was I?"

Uzziah chuckled and turned on the roof to look out at the view. He looked out and realized that because the cabins were built on a rise, they could almost see over the plains. Uzziah turned again and looked up the mountain.

"Look there, the ponderosas have caught the setting moon," he said, and Immanuel turned around and looked.

The moon was full, and the way the early morning light, which was mostly pink from the rising sun, was catching the sky and the clouds, and reflecting off the full moon, it was breathtaking.

"Couldn't see this in no citified arrangement," Immanuel said.

"Sometimes, I wonder if God is waiting for compliments on his creation. I mean, he made everything, and so this, too, this setting moon amid the blushing skies, the way the wind is playing with the tops of the ponderosas," Uzziah said.

Both mountain men were standing on the roof of Uzziah's cabin, and the wind was whispering through the leaning pine tops.

"Abooksigun could probably understand them whispers," Immanuel said softly, not wanting to disturb a really magical moment.

Uzziah turned away. It was simply too much, all God had done for him, for them, over the years, keeping them safe from harm, warning them when danger was near, seeing to their supplies, so much help. He was looking east now, and something caught his eye. Before Immanuel could say anything, Uzziah was scrambling down the ladder like only a younger person could do, using it almost like steps in a stairwell. Now you've got to remember this is a man of 275 pounds, and he's scrambling around like he was a six-year-old!

"What's up?" Immanuel asked.

Before Uzziah said anything, he was back up the ladder and had Immanuel's binocs from New Orleans in his hand.

"Lookie there, right over the last Pondie on the right," Uzziah said.

Immanuel put the binocs to his eyes and focused in as each person has to do since their vision is different.

"What the!?" was all Immanuel said, then he took them down and turned to Uzziah. "Thems circling harpies, ain't they?" he said as he put the binocs back up to his eyes.

"They is!" he said and handed them back to Uzziah, who quickly placed them over his eyes.

"There must be a load of carrion out there to draw that crowd of hooked-nose buzzards!"

6

The San Angelo Standard had picked up fairly quickly on the arrest of Kelly Jones and his possible involvement with the deaths of two prominent citizens. After all, regular folks don't like to imagine that walking across the street can end your life right before lunch. Most people like to think that their time is down the road, not sneaking up on them from just down the street.

The writer who had published the article really wasn't saying that Kelly Jones was guilty, but he wasn't saying he wasn't guilty, either.

The sheriff had made sure that a copy of that article made its way to the cell where Kelly was sweating it out. It wasn't only the fact that he might be guilty of murder that he was sweating out, but also the enormous amount of alcohol that he had consumed since the *accident*. The sheriff, being a wise lawman, took advantage of the boy's delirium tremors and questioned him while he was down.

They were sitting in the cell, and Sheriff Kingsley,

besides feeling guilty about humping the boy's pregnant wife, wanted a confession so that at least that time spent in their bedroom wasn't really just a preamble to adultery.

"Boy, ya gots to come clean," the sheriff said.

"I know, too much whiskey has made me sick."

"No, I'm talkin' 'bout the murder of those two innocent citizens, ya knew 'em both."

"That twere an accident, Sheriff, and ya know it."

"I do not know that, and I suspect ya don't know it neither. The parson gonna come over and hopefully cleanse yer soul."

"What's Parson Olson comin' chere fer?"

"Ya sinned, Kelly Jones, and as I was reminded recently, it's the first in a list of ten," the sheriff said.

It was about that time that the front door to the sheriff's office opened and closed.

"We're back chere, Parson," the sheriff yelled, and he could see the look on the Jones boy's face. He was being caught between the rock of ages and a hard place.

Parson Olson was always smiling, and most people believed that it was his general good nature that caused the smile to perennially be on his face. But what they did not know was that he'd married young, and his wife was a terrible cook, but everyone assured him she would get better, but she hadn't. He'd never complained about her cooking, he let his stomach do that for him. He was in constant stomach pain, and imagined rightly, that someday that pain would grow into a tumor and take his life, so much for a woman's good cooking.

He waddled down the short hall that led to the jail cell because he wasn't about to let his wife's terrible cooking keep him from enjoying meals whenever he could, wherever he could. If he visited a parishioner, he knew and they did, too, that no matter what time of the day it was, you could feed the parson. He ate two breakfasts, two lunches, and usually two dinners, if he could cram it in.

He was weighing in at around 300 pounds, and none of it was muscle. Many a hog farmer wished his hogs had the weight—gaining ability and sustainability of the parson's heft. When he talked, his thick lips flapped a bit, reminding one of pancakes and syrup. He walked slowly and with a great deal of effort since he was, in fact, almost always out of breath.

He sort of turned sideways so his bulk could squeeze through the bars, and looking at the tiny chair which was at the table where the sheriff and the Jones boy sat, he took the better part of valor, and sat on the cot. He knew he'd need help up from the chair, but the possibility of an accident and ramming splinters from a broken chair into his arse was not on his agenda today.

"Parson, good to see ya," the sheriff said.

"I'm happy to be here," the parson said and then panted.

"I was reminding the Jones boy here that what he is accused of doin' is the first of all the rules, right?"

The parson looked around the cell as if he were looking for the answer to the sheriff's question. What in God's name was the sheriff referring to? Then it came to him, the Ten Commandments!

"Well, they are the Ten Commandments, not the ten suggestions," Olson said, and the sheriff laughed even though it was the millionth time he'd heard the so-called joke from Olson.

"Pastor Olson, I didn't do nothin'!" the boy exclaimed.

Calling him pastor reminded the good man that he was indeed the boy's shepherd, and that a good shepherd always kept the flock from the wolves, but this sheep may be a wolf? Sometimes, it was hard to tell the difference. They were all innocent, until they weren't!

"Did you know," Pastor Olson began, and had to stop to catch his breath, "that Eloise Brownley was particularly fond of you." It was a lie, but one meant to draw a confession from the boy, and save his soul, so it was an excusable lie.

"Nah, she weren't! She'd barely give me the time of day," Kelly Jones said.

The sheriff looked at the parson and thought, *It was a good try, but now, it was time for those better suited to confessions*. He'd brought a paper bag with him into the cell, and now he withdrew something from it and placed it gently on the table.

Jones's eyes bugged out of his head, and his hands immediately went to his face, where they tried to stop the flood of tears that rushed from the boy.

The two mountain men partners rode for a couple of days before they got to the plains and prairie that spread out away from the front range. The circling buzzards must have sent out buzzard messages to their relatives because the sky was almost black with the circling birds. The ones who had found carrion, and it was in abundance, fought over the carcasses of the rotting cattle, and the others circled further north.

"Whatcha reckon's up thataway?" Uzziah asked.

"Well, either there's a herd loose on its own, or there is a bunch of stupid cowpunchers up there leading a herd to their destruction," Immanuel said, kicking up his horse Stygian into a dogtrot. There was no use in working their animals into a thirst, but they wanted to get up there as soon as possible.

If Ned *Texas* Brownley had known what was going on with his herd of—at least at the start—fifteen hundred longhorns, he probably would not have bothered fishing, but simply cut bait and run.

As it was, he had read the article in the San Angelo Standard, and fear had gripped his heart even more than in the past few days. Brownley had thought that it was a stroke of genius when Eloise showed up at the bank, and he decided, well, what the heck, two birds, one stone!

But the nights since her death, and subsequent burial, he had wondered if perhaps he had overstepped.

They had both funerals at the same time, down by the Concho River. The cypress trees that adorned its banks reached right into the water of the river, and the knees were prominent as they never seemed to get too much moisture. There was a canopy of live oaks that led to the cemetery gates. It was closed at night mostly to keep kids from going down there when they couldn't find any other place to be away from adults and kiss. The cemetery was beautiful, and the stillborn children that Eloise had given Ned were buried down there. It seemed only appropriate that they should have their dead mother now to keep them company.

Tad Snow's coffin had looked better than the one Brownley had afforded for his wife, Eloise. The family plot of the Brownleys had some extra plots in it, and Ned figured, what the hell, just bury them next to each other, friends in dying, friends in death. He hadn't thought much about it, but the community of San Angelo was impressed that someone could be so selfless. Tad Snow had come from upstate and had no family, and putting him to rest beside Brownley's wife seemed tasteful and appropriate. You see, Ned Brownley hadn't been bad, well, this evil, all his life. No, he had wanted badly to make a fortune when he was younger, but time was racing past him, and in his anxiety to not be cheated by father time, his avarice and ability to run the truth over roughshod had grown in him till he wasn't certain just who he was anymore.

And so, the old house that Brownley lived in was creaking and shifting now more than ever. Or was it? He imagined he'd seen his wife standing in the shadows in the kitchen when he got up in the morning, and had nearly fainted, well, it felt like he was going to faint. Then there were the words he kept hearing as he was falling asleep. *Ned, you bastard!*

If Brownley had heard them one time, that would be bad enough, but every night since her death. He had not believed in ghosts before this, but began to understand some of Shakespeare's plays a bit better now.

In any case, Ned found himself lurking outside the back of the jailhouse and eavesdropping on the interview that Sheriff Kingsley was having with Kelly Jones. He was sure he'd paid the boy Jones enough money to keep his mouth closed, and he wondered how the sheriff had enough evidence to arrest the boy. He also wondered how the boy would fare under pressure, since he knew the boy had been drinking way too much and consorting with the soiled doves in town. Well, he was fairly certain that any more pressure on the boy and his name—Ned Brownley—would come up, and that would be disastrous. There hadn't been a hanging in San Angelo for some time, and he didn't want his corpse dangling from a rope for all to see while idle mouths consumed popcorn and sweet treats.

It was convenient that the alley that ran behind the jail was narrow, and there were many trash receptacles to hide behind.

He heard most of what the sheriff had said, and now that that awful man, that Pastor Olson, was there. Well, who knew what men, or especially boys, would do when faced with an eternity of burning in hell? He wasn't worried about hell, the years he'd spent with the living Eloise, and now, probably, the years he'd spend with her dead spirit was hell enough for him.

From what he could hear, the boy was holding up well, and perhaps some of that had to do with both their nemesis—the idea of being strangled to death in public seemed, for now, sufficient restraint on the boy.

Finally, the obese pastor left, breathing like it was going to be the death of him, and the sheriff saw him out. This was the moment to strike.

He had thought about shooting the boy, but when you take immediate and direct action in someone's demise, there is usually an immediate and direct consequence. Instead, he stood up near the jailhouse window and whispered through the bars.

"Kelly, Kelly, can ya hear me?"

"Mr. Brownley," Kelly said, coming to the bars.

"Do not say my name, boy, understand?"

"Yes, sir," he said, trying to see where Brownley was, but could not.

"Who turned evidence on you, son? Was it your wife, Nelly?"

"She told the sheriff I admitted to the crime in my sleep," Kelly said.

"What?!?"

"Evidently, I talk in my sleep."

Brownley thought that it was just his luck to employ a murderer who talked in his sleep, then he thought about something that might help both him and the boy.

"It's 'bout the reward, ain't it?" Brownley whispered up into the bars.

"Yeah, that, too."

"Whatcha mean?"

"She got jealous of my time with the whores."

"Okay, don't say anything, I'll get ya outta this," Brownley said, then he heard someone's back door opening from one of the businesses along the alley.

"I'll be back," Brownley said, and scurried off.

Brownley was tired of sneaking around. He decided to do what he was going to do next in a more or less legitimate manner. He drove his carriage, which he'd left parked on Main Street, to the freight office of Arthur Jones. He rode right to the front, tied the horse to the hitching post, and walked brazenly into the freight office.

Arthur Jones looked up from his desk, where he was preparing orders. Ned Brownley wasn't his favorite person in the world, but the man did have money, and

Arthur's orders were about to take a nosedive if Kelly was convicted of killing those two people. He had known there was something wrong, but he couldn't put his finger on it.

"How can I help ya, Mr. Brownley?"

"It's how I can help ya and yer boy that interests me, Arthur," Brownley said, and Arthur felt a bit better about seeing Brownley.

"Well, that's good of ya, sir, but as ya know, my son was arrested this morning for, well, ya know what. Anyways, unless ya've come to help with that, I don't know what to say?"

"How would you and your daughter-in-law like to come to the hotel and have supper with me tonight?"

"What's the occasion?"

"The arrest of yer son, sir."

"I don't like sarcasm, sir, and this seems inappropriate, to say the least," Arthur said, getting a bit bowed up.

"No, really, we—the three of us—and of course darling Sally, need to talk. I've reserved the back room for us to have dinner in. It is well out of sight of those who would cast aspersions against yer family."

Arthur Jones agreed, and Brownley wasn't sure what he was going to say or do, just yet, but he had a notion. Whatever the case may be, he had to get the guilt of what had happened and the stain of what might happen thrown somewhere else besides toward himself. He knew Arthur Jones's freight business was headed downhill, and that the wife of the man who had committed the murders for him was one money-hungry young lady. What he didn't know was that she was the perfect person to approach because she had a secret weapon that she would be more than happy to use against the sheriff if that meant she could be financially rewarded and her husband, she did miss the boy's love making—could he be exonerated and they could go off somewhere that no one knew them and start over again.

By the time, Immanuel and Uzziah saw the trailing end of the herd of longhorns, they knew that they had stumbled, quite accidentally, upon a mess that wasn't going to be that easy to straighten out. What they did not know was that in an effort to fix things, they would inadvertently throw a monkey wrench into the situation and actually make things worse. No good deed goes unpunished, as Immanuel was fond of saying. The herd was literally on their last legs, and the cowpunchers, who were guiding them to hell, were no better.

In fact, both Uzziah and Immanuel knew because they had taken this very trail northward when they went on the buffalo hunt that these men were heading in exactly the wrong direction. They had pushed the cows, or perhaps the cows had wandered off by themselves, further from the front range than was safe and further away from life-saving water. Plus, there were tribes out this way that needed meat for the coming winter, and jerked beef made just as good a stew as jerked buffalo.

"How do we approach these guys, this herd, Immanuel?"

"Good question, young son. Ifn we go too quick and seem too confident, they may take us fer rustlers, or worse."

"How far are they from water? I'm guessin' it's just

back over our left shoulders, and if we can get the herd turned, it will smell the water and we won't have to lead 'em," Uzziah said.

"That gives me a bad idea, but how much worse shape can this herd be in?"

"You're not thinking of what I think yer a-thinkin', are ya?"

"Well, a stampede will only work as long as they got the energy, but ifn they smell the water, they won't need to worry 'bout the energy, right?" Immanuel said with a particular look on his face that spoke of nothing but trouble.

Jack Tate and his two partners figured they had reached the end of a most disappointing venture. The man who could have led them directly to water was dead, poisoned by Buck Krieter, the cook and second in command on the drive. Their other efforts to diminish the cowpunchers who weren't in on the double-cross had only ended with the death of two of their partners, Todd Aimes and Harry Gnomes, and the blinding of a third partner, the seven-foot-tall O.B. Thomas.

If water weren't discovered in the next day, their plans, the plans of the rustlers, was to leave the damn herd to rot and make for the mountains, and see if they could find water there, themselves.

They did not see the two horses coming from the northwest, galloping at a great rate of speed toward the dazed herd, but when the Hawken rifles exploded and then Uzziah and Immanuel pulled out their harmonica pistols and started shooting up into the sky and whooping and hollering like Injuns, it didn't take the bedraggled herd long to turn away from the pressure of the attack and run in exactly the right direction.

Neither Immanuel nor Uzziah knew how long it would take before the herd smelled the water which was not that far away, so they kept up the harassment, a few of the wranglers fired at them, but the wranglers' job was keeping the herd together, if the bond between the herd was broken and these cattle wore themselves out running, they would all be dead the next day.

That was when the rustlers' horses and the herd itself smelled the water to the southeast. Well, there was no turning them back now. Unfortunately for the rustlers, their horses were in better shape than the herd because, in an effort to save their horses, they had shared what little water they had from their canteens. Now, the horses were all outrunning the herd and were, in fact, in front of the herd. When the herd finally saw the water, the rustlers were in the most precarious of positions. They and their riders were no better than a bum standing on the railroad tracks as a runaway freight train was bearing down on him. The inevitable was nearly always irreversible.

Immanuel and Uzziah pulled up and looked at each other. Their horses were well-watered, they had just come from that watering hole, and the instinct to rush toward the water was not in them.

"Uh-oh!" Immanuel grunted.

"This ain't good," Uzziah said, "This ain't good at all!"

7

When Arthur Jones picked up his daughter-in-law, Nelly Jones, he was amazed that someone so pregnant could look so beautiful. The gown she had on was cut deep in the front like a saloon girl might wear, but the quality of the workmanship, the long sleeves and gloves, the way the material was hitched up in an empire line and almost—almost—hid the enormous belly, well, it was quite stunning. The flowing skirt was cut on the right side, and when Nelly walked, her shapely legs were momentarily revealed, then hidden, revealed, then hidden. And there was a wrap of ermine fur, which kept the decolletage from the cool of the evening and from eyes not dining in the best dining house in San Angelo. The owners had done well in Austin, mere miles away, and had opened this bistro with great success.

"Aren't ya bringin' Sally with ya?" Arthur asked.

"To a fancy dinner with the richest man in town, I think not!"

"But—"

"She's at the neighbors, she'll be fine," Nelly said as she sashayed out on the porch.

"Where did you get that dress?" Arthur asked her after they had arrived and were being led to the private dining room.

"A friend bought it for me," Nelly whispered as she was led into the room where Ned *Texas* Brownley was already seated. He immediately got up and grabbed Nelly's chair and pulled it out for her. She sat, thanking him in a whisper, and Arthur Jones knew instantly that this was the dress-buying friend. He wasn't sure how he felt about that, but he was willing to let it go, for now. What he couldn't figure out was what Brownley was up to. What angle was he working?

No one ordered, the food just started arriving shortly after they'd had a drink or two. Arthur drank whiskey, and Nelly was drinking gin with tonic and small slips of lime stuck on the glass. Arthur hated gin since it had been his wife's drink of choice, and the less he thought about her, the better. He had made up a story of her dying before they moved to San Angelo, but the death she suffered allowed her to go somewhere else and have some fun. Nelly knew the real story, Kelly had told her, and she didn't blame Arthur for lying. Sometimes, well-placed lies were a man's only friend.

The courses came, the appetizers, the salads—Waldorf—Nelly thought Brownley called it, then the Beef Wellington with its fillet steak coated in pate de foie gras and wrapped in puff pastry, then baked. Neither Nelly nor Arthur had ever tasted anything so delicious. Asparagus was steamed and served on the side, and Brownley explained to Nelly how she could bend the stalks till they broke, and only eat the tops, the most tender and delicious part.

A tres leches cake was served for dessert, and Brownley asked Nelly's permission to smoke as he handed Arthur a Cuban cigar, which topped off the meal perfectly with hot coffee and cream.

"You're probably wondering why I called this meeting?" Brownley asked in a slight British accent and with no Texas slang at all.

"Well, yes, of course," Arthur said, a bit taken aback by the way Brownley was speaking.

"In case you're wondering, I am British, but doing business in Texas makes it hard when you speak like this. It's much easier," he said, changing his accent, "to talk like the locals, and say the dernest things, ya know?"

He looked at both Nelly and Arthur, who both seemed like they had suddenly been thrust onto the stage and did not know their lines.

"Look, it's all very simple, I had Tad Snow killed, and as an extra added benefit, my wife Eloise showed up, and she was also taken care of, so to speak," he said and looked at them with the most confident and evil look.

"This must be some sort of joke, right?" Arthur asked, looking about as if those also in on the joke would come through the curtains, make themselves known, and everyone would have a good laugh!

"It is not, I'm afraid. Now, I know that you, Nelly, have said something to Sheriff Kingsley, and you need to relate to me what exactly it was that you did say, and how all of it came about, do you understand?"

"This is an outrage!" Arthur said, standing up and

throwing his napkin in his dessert plate, and it accidentally landed in his coffee.

"No, what's an outrage, is that you, Arthur Jones, and your freighting business are in a tailspin and about to go bankrupt, am I not correct?" Brownley said, looking up at Arthur and pulling on the Cuban cigar at the same time.

Arthur sat back down, pulled the dripping napkin from his coffee cup, and took a sip as he picked up the delicious cigar from the ashtray.

"Yes, it's only a matter of time, since the—"

"You don't have to relate to me anything else. I know I got Kelly to run Snow and my wife down, and as your daughter-in-law can confess, I paid him handsomely to do it!"

"It wasn't an accident?" Arthur said meekly.

"You know it wasn't, you were there when he almost confessed up on the buckboard seat."

"But why, why would you involve a young boy in murder?"

"I'll tell you why. I have a lot of money, but I want to corner the beef market in the United States. To do that, I need to have the largest herds coming the shortest distances to the slaughterhouses, and the beef that gets set on dinner tables across America will be mine. To do that, I am driving at this very moment a very large herd, 1500 head of longhorns, to the Montana territory, and when they get there and enjoy the lush grasses of the prairies, they will fatten up, and reproduce, and when some of them go to market in the fall, they will be traveling half the distance to those markets and bringing in twice the amount of cash. It's simple mathematics."

Nelly started to speak, but Brownley held up a hand. "In just a minute, I will reveal your part in this plan, which shall make you richer than Croesus, okay?"

She nodded her head, and Brownley went back to Arthur.

"You, sir, will have my backing, and with it, you shall undercut the competition and drive them all out of business, including that giant Franklin Rivers.

"Nelly, all payments on your house are gone. It is paid off. All you have to do is tell me, and this is very important, everything that happened the night you told the sheriff about Kelly's involvement."

"You, Jezebel, how could you!?!" Arthur stood again, seemingly outraged at his daughter-in-law.

"Sit down, old man, and don't get up again," Brownley said as he cocked his revolver and put it on the table next to him. "By the way," Brownley added, "every cent of Sheriff Starr Kingsley's share in the Great Northern Cattle Company will be deposited in your account, Mr. Jones."

Arthur Jones sat down and was quiet, secretly wondering just how much money that might be!

"Your daughter-in-law knows that the jig is up, as they say here in America. Your son is about to be tried and hung for those two murders, it's only a matter of time," he said.

Nelly gasped and appropriately put her hand to her mouth. *Oh, she was going to be perfect at the trial,* Brownley thought.

"Tell me everything, Nelly Jones, and if Arthur's being here is too much, then, so what, tell me anyway!"

Nelly looked between her father-in-law, whom she secretly resented for not giving Kelly a raise, and then back at Brownley, whose smile spoke of everything that she did not have. At that instant, her heart flipped, and she decided she would do whatever it took to get what she wanted, and the devil could take the hindmost.

"I was gettin' pretty tired of being ignored, ya know? Kelly was richer than he'd ever been and was drinkin' it all up! And sleepin' with every whore in town!" She looked like she might cry, then she took a deep breath, and went on, "So, I told the sheriff that Kelly was talkin' in his sleep, and he was, 'bout how'd he'd murdered those two, just run 'em down like they was vermin in the street, and I invited the sheriff over."

"To listen to your Kelly's drunken confessions?"

"Something like that. Look, women in a family way have needs just like regular gals. Kelly was humping everythin' he could, and I was home nursin' a one-year-old and gettin' ready to birth another one to nurse! What was I, some kinda cow!?! What fun was I havin' no bulls 'round? So, I'm thinkin' that Sheriff Starr Kingsley is a good-lookin' man and ifn I can get him over to the house, lying on the bed, and I nurse my Sally while he watches, well, tit would follow tat, won't it?"

The two men sat there. Arthur, stunned with disbelief. Brownley, stunned with admiration that a young Texas girl with little to no upbringing could have the mind of a Lady Macbeth. It was perfect!

"So, he raped you, isn't that right?"

"What! No," Nelly began.

"Oh yes, he did. He raped you on your marriage bed, while he was supposedly listening for evidence against your husband to send the father of your babies to the gallows, isn't that right?" Brownley said, looking directly at Nelly.

"Yeah, that's how it was, sure," she said, her eyes glistening as she got the idea of what Brownley was saying.

"I told Sheriff Kingsley Kelly talked in his sleep, then he just shows up with no invite from yers truly and lies on the bed to listen, but all the while he's ogling me with the eyes of a rapist—"

"Then, you couldn't stop him, could you? Your daughter, Sally, asleep on the bed, and so was your husband, and this evil man, Sheriff Kingsley, who, in fact, had hired your husband to do exactly as he had done—run that poor couple over in the middle of Main Street for everyone to see them sprawled in their deaths —this evil man, who orchestrated the whole thing, waltzes into your home and rapes you and tells you to come to his office and tell him what the father of your children did, and throw the blame back on anyone but himself, the sheriff, the upholder of all that is right and good."

Nelly had the look of Judas as he stood before the Sanhedrin. She saw the bag of money, the thirty pieces of silver, and she knew, well, of course she knew, just as Judas had known, that she was a betrayer, and as a betrayer, she would play her card of betrayal, the card that was always dealt in every relationship, the card which, when played, blamed others, and punished others, and left them holding the bag, and you holding the money—that's what betrayal was all about!

"That's exactly as it happened, it was almost like you were there, Mr. Brownley," Nelly said.

"I was," Brownley said, and Nelly looked at him in disbelief, "In imagination only, of course, but then again, it doesn't take much to imagine the worst of people, does it?"

They should have known better. They did know better, but their first and only thought was for the herd. Food was nothing to be disregarded. Families lived and died with and without it. In times of plenty, it was good to have more, more could always be jerked and saved. In lean times, the look of that herd, bedraggled and lean the way they were, was enough to make a grown man cry. Whatever the reason for them looking like that, whatever the circumstances that had brought these cowpunchers to this state, it had to be dealt with now, and that was the only thought of the two mountain men as they stampeded that herd toward the water source.

They probably should have thought about the horses. They did think about the horses, but like the cowboys who had let their horses drink from their meager portion of their canteens, they thought that having some water would have kept the horses at bay, would have kept them from running without regard toward the water source.

But alas, it hadn't.

The horses stared to the side at the cattle that were gaining on them, and they drew their last ounce of strength to push harder, get there faster, get there first! It didn't matter that behind them a force like that of a tornado was bearing down upon them. It didn't matter that thousands of pounds of beef would soon be shoved up their arses. It simply didn't matter. Nothing mattered except to have their dry throats slacked with the abundance of water, clean, pure water!

The train wreck that took place that afternoon was beyond belief. Horses butted into the air with riders still attached, legs broken, bowels ripped open by the thundering longhorns doing battle to get to the water. It was all about the water.

The commotion, the dust, the screaming of the horses, the roaring of the bulls, the bellowing of the female cows as injury and death came to those who stopped dead in their tracks for a drink.

Immanuel and Uzziah could only watch, and hardly then could they even see. It wasn't till the dust settled and the badly injured had succumbed to death that they got even a partial visage of what they had inadvertently done.

If God were a cow, they would never be forgiven!

The men whose horses had taken them in front of the herd and run halfway into the big pond, those men should have jumped and run at that point, but it wasn't till they turned and saw nearly 1200 longhorns heading for the water their horses were standing in, did it hit home. Boy, did it hit home.

Some of the men had been thrown completely across the pond and lay there smashed as if they'd jumped off a 1000-foot cliff, while others were trampled in the mud of the pond, as longhorn after longhorn pushed their way in, driving them further into the mud, drowning those who only wished now for a breath of air.

About a hundred longhorns lay dead, or dying. They had been the first to make it to the water, and the first to ram and trample, and then, the first to die.

There were three men who lived through this debacle—Buck Krieter, the cook, whose horse had to pull the chuckwagon to the water source. Jack Tate, who somehow got his horse to veer at the last minute, after being side-swiped by a steer and Jack's leg being broken. And then, amazingly, the blinded O.B. Thomas, the defrocked priest, even blind, or perhaps because of it, his horse took control and carried him out of harm's way. In truth, when disaster struck, there was no justice, not a stitch of it, but sometimes you could find a divine intervention or perhaps revenge. After all, *Vengeance is mine, sayeth the Lord.*

Jack looked around, dazed and confused, for sure. Who were these men dressed in deerskins, with Hawken rifles across their laps? Had they been the ones who stampeded the cattle? One thing was for certain, the regular wranglers had been taken care of. They were dead, drowned, trampled, or missing in action, and in a way, Jack Tate wanted to thank the two mystery men for doing what it seemed no one on his crew had been capable of doing.

He would have thanked them if he could have gotten up from where he'd dismounted and, putting weight on the broken leg, fallen. His mind wasn't quite right. For a moment, he suspected old Brownley had arranged this, but hell, Brownley was too far away, and this was beyond his purview, unless of course, Brownley turned out to be God, and Tate seriously doubted that—he might turn out to be the devil and a devil he was. This whole scheme had turned sour fast enough, but now it looked as if it might be saved.

They set up a camp near the watering hole. Once Immanuel saw to Tate's wounds, they took to pulling the dead wranglers, horses, cows, and bulls from the pond. Shadow did his work well and made no complaint. Stygian was a bit put off, but for a thoroughbred, he did fine. The dead bodies of the cows were feasted on by the vultures, so at least, they hadn't made their trip to the front range in vain. The pile of bovine bodies disappeared one bite at a time, but at least the stink was downwind most of the time from their camp.

They dug, even the blind O.B. helped out, a mass grave for the wranglers, well, it was better than leaving them for the vultures.

Immanuel set up a tent where Tate could be taken care of. There at that tent, O.B. was able to help Uzziah with the chores of caring for Tate, and when Immanuel showed him how, he wasn't bad at changing the bandages of Tate's compound fracture. Luckily for any cattle drive, the bedrolls and the supplies that each cowboy/wrangler carried were always packed away with the chuck.

Buck Krieter had little to say. These men had saved the herd and therefore saved his hide, that was for sure! He wasn't quite sure what would have happened to him when Jack Tate realized all had been lost because he'd poisoned the wrong man. He liked both of the mountain men and wondered why he had never considered going to the mountains himself and leaving all the bullshite behind!

"Are ya sure, yer okay?" It was Immanuel, and he was looking right at Buck.

"Could use a drink, other than that, yeah, fine," Buck said, thinking that he was the luckiest man who had ever lived.

"I think we can arrange the drink after supper,"

Immanuel said, and he went back to tending Jack Tate, who was coming around nicely. He'd set his leg and wouldn't be able to ride for some time now, but the cattle needed to be fed. There was plenty of prairie grasses beyond the pond, and they needed resting.

Immanuel and Uzziah sat around the fire that night. Jack Tate seemed more himself, if a man can be seen as more like himself, when you didn't really know the man. Buck had had a snort or two and was telling the tale of when he worked with these cowboys who rode down into the Grand Canyon. Whatever that was. Uzziah thought it an interesting story, but Immanuel later confided in his partner that no such place existed and that they should watch the tall-tale teller because he just might be a crook.

"Ya can't be a crook simply because ya stretch the truth," Uzziah said.

"Sure, ya can!" Immanuel insisted.

"Well, then I'm guessin' that makes us the biggest crooks of all!" Uzziah whispered.

"Maybe, just maybe," Immanuel said, pondering that for a bit.

O.B. Thomas didn't realize that Uzziah and Immanuel hadn't gone that far away when they left the campfire, just that they had gone. O.B. started telling Buck Krieter, thinking that he and Buck were still with a group of bad hombres, about how when he was a priest, he'd lure the young girls into the confessional, take off their clothes, and have his way with them. He probably wouldn't have said as much as he did if he hadn't had some of the whiskey in him. Buck kept giggling at the stories of the young girls who had been sullied. He'd look over at Uzziah and Immanuel, who could obviously hear, but didn't bother telling O.B. to shut up.

Immanuel and Uzziah listened, then moved their bedrolls to the other side of the big fire, hoping that the sound of the crackling fire would drown out O.B.'s stories. It didn't.

Jack Tate was sleeping in the tent, after all, he was the worst of the injured, if you didn't take into account O.B., but then again, it was obvious that the blinding had happened rather recently. The wound at the back of his head had festered up a bit, and Immanuel treated it with a poultice.

"I ain't sure of any of these fellas," Uzziah said.

"Yeah, I know, but hey, we sorta put them into the position they're in right now."

"Hell, we did, they were out here with all these longhorns and no idea atall, where the water was. I'm thinking Jack Tate wasn't the Trail Boss when they started out. And Buck was the second in command, come on! He can cook, sorta, but he don't know any more than Tate as far as this part of the country is concerned."

"Ya know as well as I do that we owe them, and we're gonna help, that's it," Immanuel said.

Uzziah just looked at him as if, just maybe, Immanuel wasn't the one in charge.

"Okay," Immanuel said, knowing exactly what Uzziah was thinking. "Ifn it's okay with ya, we'll help 'em, what do ya say?"

"But how?" Uzziah asked.

"We gotta let these cattle fatten up a bit afore we take off north, so I's thinkin' that ifn we got some of Beckwourth's Crows to come down and help, we could trade the wranglin' of the Crow for some meat for them this winter," Immanuel said.

"Yeah, but we don't own this herd, and obviously it ain't owned by Tate. We may be oversteppin' ifn we do what yer sugesttin'?"

"Well, ifn we don't do somethin' like that, the first thunderstorm that comes along will scatter this herd from here to hell and there won't be any cattle to drive no how, nowhere!"

8

It happened like a tornado. One day, Sheriff Starr Kingsley was sheriff and still questioning Kelly Jones, and the next day, a Texas Ranger rode in and the sheriff was in the cell next to Kelly Jones. Well, young Kelly Jones must have thought that was one of the funniest things he'd ever seen. One day, he was afraid of the man, the next, he was a cellmate, so to speak. Jones couldn't stop giggling as the Texas Ranger, one Lieutenant Brian Wolfe, was questioning the sheriff, and he seemed to have a lot of questions for which Sheriff Kingsley had no answers.

The San Angelo Standard ran a special edition spelling out how Sheriff Starr Kingsley had had some run-in with the law up in northern Texas, where he got paid to look the other way as a crooked roulette wheel spun him a fortune in gold. Due to sources which they could not name, the Standard knew about Nelly's unfortunate rape, and the eyes of all of San Angelo turned black when they looked upon the sheriff. If there was one thing that those in the west would not tolerate, it was the mistreatment of their women, and that was that.

The circuit judge made a special trip down from Austin to make sure justice was done and that a bad law dog would be put in his place.

Every time they questioned Kelly, he swore it was Brownley who had hired him, and that was confirmed by the ex-sheriff, but those in cahoots against the law are always telling the same story, right? Tell a lie and stick to it was their motto.

The trial was quick and furious with Nelly, looking poor and destitute as she waddled up to the witness stand, perjured herself on a Holy Bible, and then told the most amazing lies. All twelve men of the jury sat transfixed as she told about the night of horror when she was raped upon her marriage bed, with her baby girl and her future child within her.

She added everything she could remember, and some things which she had been encouraged by Brownley to make up, and the stories she spun were like the web of a black widow spider—errant and all over the place, but sticky and long enough to entangle those she incriminated. She told about the sheriff sucking her dry so that her baby wouldn't have any milk the next morning, and how he was callous to a fault, saying that she should be glad he didn't prefer the backdoor or she would be shitting blood for a month.

When she got through with her testimony, the jury of twelve men were transfixed in their chairs. Truth be told, they couldn't have stood up without revealing that each and every one of them had been aroused by the rapist's acts, which said more about mankind than the lying testimony itself. In cases like this, it is always incumbent upon those who are aroused by evil acts to throw their own guilt upon those accused and make sure they suffer the consequences of their simply being human. Always better for scapegoats to die in the wilderness than for righteous folks to croak at home.

Witnesses abounded, all paid for by Brownley, who told of the plans that the sheriff and Kelly had made before he was arrested, and how they had almost gotten away with it if the courageous young pregnant woman hadn't come forward and testified to the truth, which at that point was red-faced and standing in the back alley.

Everyone in San Angelo knew that Kelly had been a good boy before the sheriff had turned him, and that afterward, he was nothing but a drunk and a whore monger, the worst in town.

To top it all off, when Nelly was called back up by the defense and was being questioned, her water broke, and she had to be carried to the doctor's office, where she gave birth to a ten-pound baby girl. When the news was announced in court, there was a cheer for her and the baby, and it was then that the sheriff, well, the ex-sheriff, and Kelly, who were tried together, knew that they were going to swing and pay the price, no matter who would eventually be charged for the account.

Two days later, a guilty verdict was read by the head juror, then those two men—one a mere boy and the other a mature man who had served the law well until he'd met his match—walked up the gallows steps, and the nooses were put about their necks. They both were offered black hoods, both refused, and as Pastor Olson was reading to them both from the Bible, he inadvertently stepped on the trapdoor for the sheriff and fell through to the ground below. He was carried away to the doctor's, sounding like a wounded heifer with unspecified injuries.

Well, this amused the younger of the two murderers so that even after they put the black hood on his head—so they wouldn't have to see his toothy laughter—you could still hear it, and with the cloth sucking in and out furiously as he tried to catch his breath right before he fell straight through the gates of hell.

It wasn't long after that that Ned Brownley, whose real name was Neddy Farnsworth Brownley, who had made it to New York a mere ten years before and started for Texas to make his dream of being the baron of beef a reality, started out for the Montana territories. He wasn't going alone. After a meeting of the Great Northern Cattle Company, he was taking the remaining majority stockholders with him.

Franklin Rivers wanted to stay and protect his interest in the mercantile company, which had grown by leaps and bounds since the death of banker Snow and Mrs. Brownley, but Texas Ned convinced him that, since it was down to only three majority holders that it would be incumbent on Rivers to be in Montana when the cattle were driven down to market later that year. Well, that is, if he wanted his money.

Steve Hudley, the Texas railroad man, didn't need convincing. He was looking for towns in which the railroad could land once it stretched itself across the country. Hudley was a quiet man and had a reputation as a hard negotiator and businessman, but Texas Ned knew that secretly Hudley hated horses—hence his interest both emotionally and financially in trains—and that this trip would probably come down to he and the tall man to duke it out, or just maybe it would be better to have at least one partner, that way, when things went south, which it seemed they had a tendency to do, there would be somebody to take the fall. And the fall which Franklin Rivers would take would be a long one at nearly seven feet tall.

Brownley, Franklin Rivers, and Steve Hundley left on a stage the next day for Memphis. They would catch the paddle wheeler to St. Louis, then jump another one for the Montana territory.

The longhorns were getting fat and sassy. Bulls were busy doing what bulls do, and the heifers loved it. The prairie grasses and the good water from the large pond that was formed from the streams that emptied down from the Rockies were keeping the cattle fat and happy. The ones who had been near death were no longer that way. And it was time to move the herd if it was to be taken to its destination, if anyone actually knew that destination?

Buck Krieter had continued to cook for everyone there, but Immanuel didn't like his cooking.

"When ya gonna take over cookin' from that pretender?" Immanuel whispered to Uzziah.

Uzziah leaned in toward Immanuel. They were all around a fire near the chuckwagon.

"Time to be gracious, old son," Uzziah whispered.

"And this fare which is givin' me the heart fires, am I supposed to be gracious 'bout that?!?"

"It ain't our chuck, we're eatin' fer free."

"You must have the stomach of a wolf, no wait a minute, it's the stomach of a wolverine, no wonder ya can take this crap and not feel sick," Immanuel continued to complain.

O.B. Thomas had learned to listen because that's about all he could do. He was listening to most of what Uzziah and Immanuel said, and it didn't make any difference if they were whispering, besides, what those two called whispering was normal talk to most folk.

"Anybody want more?" It was Buck, he was over at the chuckwagon asking.

"Nah!" Immanuel immediately said.

"I'll take some," Uzziah spoke up, got up, and walked to the chuckwagon holding his empty tin plate.

"We all knew he weren't no cook," O.B. whispered over to Immanuel.

Immanuel looked at the blind man, then looked away.

"Did ya hear me?" O.B. asked.

"Was ya talkin' to me?"

"Ain't ya the onliest one at the fire besides me?"

"How'd ya know that?"

"I may be blind, but I ain't stupid!"

"So, what was ya sayin'?" Immanuel asked. "Sorry I ignored ya."

"It's okay, it's what everybody does now that I can't see. I was sayin', every one of us on this drive knows, or knew, as the case may be, that Buck ain't no cook."

"That a fact?" Immanuel said for lack of anything else to say.

"Yep," O.B. said and continued eating.

"Say, these cattle are 'bout to be ready to move,

where the hell ya takin' 'em anyways?" Immanuel asked, taking the opportunity to maybe find something out.

"Ya better ask Jack about that. Say, how's he doin'—his leg sure don't smell rank no more, and I knows that's a good sign."

"Yeah, yeah, no infection, well, there was a little, but some herbs took care of that. Thanks, I'll go ask Jack," Immanuel said, and started to get up.

"What ya gonna ask me?" It was Jack, and he was limping toward the fire on a crutch. Uzziah had made him a crutch from a gnarled limb.

"Where the hell is this herd headed?" Immanuel asked.

"We are headed up Wolf Point way. Ya know it?" Tate asked.

"Yeah, I know it, been by it several times as matter of fact, but there ain't nothin' but a wood station up there," Immanuel said as Uzziah came back with a plate full of the undercooked navy beans and burned bacon. Immanuel took one look at it and turned away.

"Ya want some?" Uzziah asked, smiling.

"I do not," Immanuel said, trying not to look at the dripping plate.

"Yeah, so I heard," Tate said, referring to Wolf Point, "but the steppes is a good place to raise cattle. The grasses are plentiful and go on for miles," Tate said, accepting a cup of coffee from Buck.

"Whose idea was this? Wolf Point and all?" Uzziah asked.

Jack Tate just looked at both mountain men, but did not answer, figuring his association with Brownley was his business, not theirs.

"Look," Tate said, sipping the hot, black coffee, "we appreciate all ya done." And Immanuel and Uzziah both knew that the man did not remember, or chose not to remember, their Hawkens starting the stampede, which cost most of the wranglers their lives. Then again, it's exactly what Tate meant since his own team of bad hombres were having a time with that particular chore. Tate continued, "But we'll take it from chere."

"Well, the Royal Hanneford Circus will be wantin' to get in touch with you three," Immanuel said, then he stood up and announced the last like a ringmaster. "Ladies and gentlemen, in the center ring, please take note of the death-defyin' Tate, Buck, and blind Thomas as they wrangle a thousand head of longhorns in this most amazin' of western acts!" Then he looked over to the 1000 head of longhorns and laughed like a hyena.

"That's not funny," was all Tate could offer, while Buck was chuckling it up at the wagon.

"You're either the stupidest hombre I ever met, or what happened at the watering hole has affected yer mind," Immanuel said.

Tate wanted to bow up and be angry, but the mountain man was right. There was no way, a cook, a blind man, and himself, still hobbling away on a crutch, was going to drive a herd that size anywhere, but two more wouldn't make that much difference, neither!

"So, what's yer plan, since they ain't exactly yer cattle? And besides, what the hell difference will two mountain men make, unless yer plannin' on stampedin' 'em all the way to the Montana territory!" Tate yelled.

"Ya two settle down," Uzziah said, standing up with the nearly full plate still in his hand. "Immanuel, you thinkin' what I'mma thinkin'?"

"Yeah, probably, after all these years, but it don't make it any more sense than what Tate just suggested," Immanuel said, sitting down.

Tate cooled off and also sat. He pulled his pipe from his vest, packed it, lit it, tamped it down, then got it going good.

"Okay," he said, blowing smoke over to the fire where it picked up the draft and shot skyward. "What's yer plan?"

"We know where we can get us a dozen men who will help, if we give them some beef," Immanuel said.

"A dozen men up thisaway, really?"

"Yeah, he speaks the truth. They're friends of ours and would gladly help if we asked," Uzziah chimed in.

"They's mountain mens?" Buck asked, cleaning up the chuck wagon.

"Not exactly," Immanuel said. "More like plainsmen."

Buck and Tate looked at each other and nodded, then it was decided, they could deal with these plainsmen when they got to Wolf Point. Until then, there was no reason to sit here and miss the rendezvous with Brownley.

The Mississippi River was a big, damn river. The paddle boat they jumped on in Memphis took their horses to the stable on the bottom deck and the three men wined and dined their way toward St. Louis. But Brownley knew that once they got on the Missouri, it would be harder to get rid of another partner, at least, he assumed it would be.

The fifth night on the Mississippi, Hudley had found himself a whore, well, she probably called herself a soiled dove or some such approximation of what she really was, but still, a whore, and make no mistake, she had found him, not the other way around.

Hudley was spending money like the Great Northern Cattle Company had already made them fortunes, and Brownley knew that it was all because of the woman with the big tatas that Hudley was doing a fairly good job of impressing.

The parties on the boats had been touted as something grand, and this one was no different–gambling, whoring, other games of chance, the beautiful Mississippi at night with the fingernail moon reflecting off its surface. Brownley wished he had a woman along, but they had a habit of messing things up, and besides, he'd just gotten rid of his baggage on the main street of San Angelo, hadn't he?

The whore went to use the ladies' room, and Hudley was staring after her with an air of being positively drunk.

"Let's get some fresh air," Brownley said to Hudley, who staggered up out of his chair and finished the drink that had been in front of him.

"Yeah, let's," he said as Brownley helped him out to the deck, and the refreshing air that was blowing in off the river. Brownley walked him back to where the big paddlewheel was making water noises as it churned up the waters and sent the boat upstream. They were standing right where the big paddlewheel came up and went back down again. As far as Brownley was concerned the perfect place.

"Wow! So pretty!" Hudley said, and they weren't

exactly the kind of last words that would be remembered in absentia, but they were indeed last words.

Brownley whacked Hudley across the back of the head with his Colt revolver, a heavy weapon, while pushing him into the paddlewheel. He could hear the bones in Hudley's body being broken as the wheel continued churning as if nothing had happened.

When he turned to leave, the whore was walking toward him with a smile.

"Did ya see where Stevie went?" she said, obviously being encouraged to use his partner's Christian name and a diminutive at that.

"Why yes, let me show you," Brownley said as he picked her up and gave her a kiss.

"Oh, yer forward now that Steve ain't around, eh?" Her bosoms jiggled as she talked in his arms, but her breath was just as intoxicated as the rest of her.

"Goodbye," Brownley said and flipped her into the moving paddlewheel. Her astonishment at being tossed like so much garbage from the boat was enough to silence her for a split second, then she screamed, but one arm of the paddle knocked further screams from her throat as she was incorporated into the big muddy.

9

Uzziah had stayed behind to help take care of Jack Tate, and as Immanuel rode toward the Crow village, he did so while singing. He sang *Give Me My Arrows and Give Me My Bow*, a ballad which had just become popular when Immanuel and Uzziah had been in Chicago. The irony of the tune did not escape the mountain man.

"Tempt me not, stranger, with gold from the mine,

"I have got treasure more precious than thine,

"Freedom in forest, and health in the chase,

"Where the hunter sees beauty in Nature's bright face,

"Then give me my arrows and give me my bow,

"In the wild woods to rove where the blue rapids flow."

His wasn't a voice which could be said to be in tune with anything, much less nature, but he could bellow with the best of them, and as he rode closer, he turned up the volume and fairly soon, there were a dozen or so Crow riding out with lances and bows, hollering in the Injun way that they would soon have his scalp.

He pulled Stygian to a halt and kept on with the singing, even closing his eyes when he sang the chorus. "*Then give me my arrows and give me my bow, In the wild woods to rove where the blue rapids flow*."

When he opened his eyes, they sat on their ponies all around him, and there was the one Brave that Immanuel had hoped to see, Buffalo Warrior. He had been the boy at the buffalo run who had lured the buffaloes to their untimely deaths, stumbling off the cliffs, and he, and some of his warriors, had accompanied Immanuel and Uzziah as they made their way back to face their trial in St. Louis.

"You croon like a wounded bull buffalo," Buffalo Warrior said to him in Crow.

"And you listen like a cow in heat," Immanuel said back in Crow, which got all the warriors laughing. Buffalo Warrior blushed as he looked back and forth, silencing his fellow braves.

"Surely, you did not travel this far to insult an old friend?"

"My sincerest apologies, great Buffalo Warrior, your courage at the buffalo run is still spoken of in the south, and your knowledge of your people is celebrated everywhere," Immanuel said.

Buffalo Warrior knew that Immanuel was laying it on thick, but in the presence of his braves, he appreciated the mountain man's efforts.

"Come with me to my teepee and we will smoke the sacred pipe," he said.

They rode side by side with the braves riding behind them, much as they had when they crossed the

Great Plains on their way to the confluence of the Mighty Mo and the Big Muddy. Immanuel felt someone touch his arm, and he saw riding to his left and back a little one of the young braves who had been there shortly before he and Uzziah were captured by the Pinkerton woman. The two men nodded in recognition, and the other braves were a bit jealous that they had not been there.

Stygian's reins were taken by a young boy, who would lead the horse out to the river, where he would be joined with the other Crow ponies. The boy smiled as he walked through the village, knowing what a great honor it was to be leading such a magnificent beast.

The tent flap was opened by Buffalo Warrior, and Immanuel entered, momentarily blinded by the absence of the bright sun which had been shining on him all day. He saw the small fire in front of him and took the position with his back to the opening, which was the place of the guest.

Buffalo Warrior came in and said something in Crow to someone, or someones, who were already in the teepee, but Immanuel still was blinded by the sudden darkness. The only thing he could see was the fire in front of him. They were female voices that had answered Buffalo Warrior, and he hadn't caught quite what they were saying. It didn't matter, he was in a place of peace here in the warrior's tent.

As the wooden handled pipe was loaded into the iron bowl painted red, Immanuel wondered if they would just be smoking tobacco or would it be the sacred mixture–Buffalo Warrior had said, *let us smoke the sacred pipe*, which usually meant the latter, a mixture of tobacco, sage, and peyote.

When the pipe was passed to him, and he drew in his first breath, he knew it was the sacred pipe indeed. It didn't take him long to feel like the small teepee was as large as the prairie itself, and that Buffalo Warrior and he were seated in the sacred circle of life, waiting, he wasn't quite sure for what. Then Buffalo Warrior spoke from what seemed like a great distance. He spoke in Crow.

"We have had a hard winter. No buffalo, and it is hard to be warrior of the buffalo when they are not around. Many were sick, the winter was cold, so very cold, and babies were found frozen in their papooses."

Immanuel felt he should say something, but remembered that sometimes it was better to wait than to charge ahead.

"Remembering how your courage stuck to the sticking place when you opposed the Blackfoot, I was reminded then and also now, that your presence here is a godsend. What news have you brought us, brother, from the far mountains?"

Immanuel opened his mouth and tried to speak, but the sound that came from his mouth were the sounds of lowing cattle, the sounds of the giant longhorn bulls as they humped while in heat. He kept making these sounds, and instead of Buffalo Warrior and the two women who were gathered around the fire laughing, they stared at him in great expectation.

Immanuel went on like this for a good ten minutes. It was like he was the herd of the longhorns themselves. At one point, he got on all fours and crawled about the fire, grabbing one of the women and mounting her from behind. They both still had their clothes on as Immanuel humped her in great stylistic fashion, throwing his head back, his arm flailing up like a bronc rider as he bellowed when the stream of bull sperm impregnated the female longhorn. Finally, his mouth drooling, he shut it and wiped away the spittle of the bulls.

"You have brought us great joy, brother. Your words of lowing told us many things, not the least of which is your expectation of our help. When do we leave?" Buffalo Warrior asked.

There was an investigation into the disappearance of Steve Hudley. Ned *Texas* Brownley had insisted upon it. It was discovered that a soiled dove had also disappeared off the paddle wheeler, and the authorities, the captain of the ship, decided that they had absconded together, men and women do such things from time to time.

"She wouldn't do that!" a young man shouted from the back of the salon.

"And why not?!" asked the captain.

"She were my girl," the youngish, bold man said as he stepped forward. He wore two sidearms, and his vest was golden, and his hair black.

"If she was your girl, she is your girl no longer," the captain said, and the young man attempted to speak again, but the captain held up his hand. "I have seen you on this boat before, young man, and you are always with women, which would suggest to me that you are a fancy man and have more than just one *girl*!"

"I resent that remark," the young man said as

several of the sailors took him in their arms and pulled the pistols from their holsters.

"Actually, you resemble that remark, and shall be put off at the next wood station," the captain said, and that was seemingly that.

At lunch, the very tall Mr. Franklin Rivers, his legs akimbo so he could place them under the table, spoke up. "Do you really think that's what's happened to Hudley?"

Brownley looked at Rivers with a cold eye. "Whatever do you mean by that?"

"Well, we done started out with five of us. You, Mr. Brownley, Snow, the banker, Starr Kingsley, the sheriff, Hudley, the railroad man, and myself, and now, quite unexpectantly, we are down to the two of us. What do you make of that?" Rivers asked, too upset to eat the food that he had ordered.

Brownley looked at Rivers as he continued to stuff his face with the steak and potatoes. The steak was tough, but the potatoes were warm and comforting.

"This is what I make of it, sir. We were once five who made up the Great Northern Cattle Company, and now, we are three—"

"No, two, just you and me," Rivers corrected.

"I did make Arthur Jones and his beloved daughter-in-law, Nelly, partners, didn't I tell you that?"

"No, you did not, and why on earth would you do that!?"

"They gave so much in the recent unpleasantness, you know. Arthur losing a son, hanged in public for his crime, and Nelly her husband and father of her two children, the one barely born before the hanging. Now, tell me, Mr. Rivers, would you have me take the bread from the mouths of the children so that you could be richer, is that it? Is that what you're telling me!?!" Brownley asked, his voice rising as he spoke, until at the end, all in the salon were gaping at the table.

"No, no, no, of course not," Rivers said, looking down into the cold plate of his dinner.

"I thought not, don't worry about this, I've got it," Brownley said as he motioned for the waiter to bring him the check.

The pond where Uzziah and Immanuel had stampeded the longhorn herd to was surrounded by lazy cows and bulls. The chuckwagon, which was manned by Buck Krieter, was sitting right where he'd parked it after the stampede. Buck was asleep under the chuckwagon with his hat pulled down over his eyes. He was snoring loudly.

Jack Tate, the man that Ned *Texas* Brownley had entrusted to bring the longhorn herd up to the Montana territories, was thinking he'd never see any of the monies he'd been promised besides the little bit he'd been advanced to get chuck and ammunition for the bad hombres who were going to take over the herd and drive it up there basically rustling the herd for one man and one man only—Ted Brownley.

Well, Jack hadn't been very successful at doing that. Yeah, he'd taken the herd away from Rudley Quatrain, but then, Rudley had been the only cowpuncher with the crew who actually knew where the watering holes were. He blamed Buck for that. The damned fool had placed a venom-poisoned bowl of stew out for the youngest of the authentic crew, but Rudley had shown up and taken the bowl. And instead of keeping him from eating it, Buck had stood there and watched the man sop every last morsel of the poison into his body.

Then, after they were pushing basically a dead herd north and just waiting for the last of them to drop and become buzzard scat, two mountain men saw their troubles and had shot off their Hawken rifles, sending the frightened herd into a stampede in which all the authentic cowpunchers were killed, and so was Davidson Lord of Tate's crew. He had broken his leg, a bad compound fracture from which he had seen many men not recover, but one of the mountain men knew some Injun medicine and he'd fixed him up, straightened out the leg with a bunch of whiskey in Tate, and then a bunch of poultices which pulled any poison from the open wound of the break.

Tate was feeling better, he was able now to get up on a horse, and if he had enough men—with the blind O.B. Thomas, Buck, himself, and the two mountain men, they only had six men to push over a thousand head of longhorns and in perfect circumstances over perfectly known ground that might have been okay, but they were going where Jack Tate had never been. And sure, the mountain men had been there, but too little, too late. Brownley was going to be pissed if he showed up at Wolf Point and there were no cattle there, and worse than that, he, Jack Tate, would not get paid, and he had been counting on this influx of cash to help himself get his own spread down San Angelo way. Heck, his wife had basically told him, if he didn't settle down fairly soon, she would be done with him.

And if that weren't enough, one of the mountain

men, the old skinny one, had said he knew some plainsmen who could help them move the herd, and he had been gone for two weeks, and no sign of any plainsmen. When Tate questioned the younger mountain man about it, all that was said was to keep the faith, whatever that meant. Jack Tate was about to take things into his own hands and leave with the skeleton crew of five and see how far he could get with the thousand-plus herd.

All this was going through his head when he looked up to the north, hoping against hope that Immanuel would be coming with the plainsmen. There was a bunch of dust. Like maybe fifty men or more were on their way south. They could be Injuns, they could be, and that would be the last straw for Jack Tate.

"Say, don't ya have a pair of binoculars with ya?" he rode over and asked Uzziah, who was eating more of what was left of breakfast.

"Yeah," Uzziah said, reaching into his saddlebags and pulling the binocs from them, "Help yerself!" he held up his arm with them at the end of it.

Tate rode over and, taking the binoculars, looked north. Surely, he couldn't be seeing what he was seeing. He brought the binoculars down and rubbed his eyes. He held them to his face again.

"Injuns! Injuns!" Jack Tate shouted, and Buck burst from his dreams and sat up fast, he'd forgotten he was under the chuckwagon. His head hit the bottom of the chuckwagon so hard, it sounded like a dull bell. He knocked himself out and flopped back on his bedroll.

"There's Injuns coming, and they ain't exactly in a hurry, there must be a hundred of 'em," he said.

O.B. Thomas was walking in circles looking for a

gun to shoot, and Uzziah, for one, was glad he hadn't found one. Uzziah stood up and went to Thomas.

"Don't worry, I think I know these Injuns," he said to Thomas.

Over this, Tate was still screaming. Grabbing his Winchester, he set himself up using the chuckwagon as a shield.

"Buck, get yer lazy ass up and act like a man in the last few minutes of yer life! Damn it to hell!!" Tate screamed under the chuckwagon.

Buck rolled out from under the wagon, holding his head. "What ya hit me fer?" Buck asked Tate, rubbing his head.

"Injuns, Buck, Injuns!" Tate screamed.

"Where?" Buck asked.

"There!" Tate pointed out the many riders who were basically dog-trotting their ponies toward their camp.

Tate looked again with the binocs and saw the skinny mountain man, and he was dressed like the Injuns in nothing but a breechcloth and a fancy beaded chest ornament.

"They've captured yer partner and have him stripped naked," Tate said, trying to hand the binoculars to Uzziah.

"No thanks, there are certain things ya seen 'em once, yer good," Uzziah said as he mounted up on Shadow and rode out toward the advancing party of Injuns.

"He's got the right idea," Buck said. "Might as well run right into the teeth of 'em and be done with it!" he shouted, punching the air to make the point!

Uzziah met up with the advancing party, and greetings were exchanged between him and Buffalo Warrior and some of the others he knew from the buffalo run, then he and Immanuel, who was indeed dressed as a Crow, rode fast toward the chuckwagon.

"What the hell?" Buck asked Tate, who was standing there with his mouth open.

"Prepare to die, Mr. Krieter," Jack Tate said as he raised the Winchester to his shoulder and pointed it at Immanuel and Uzziah. "They're 'bout to steal a stolen herd!"

10

St. Louis was a bustling city by now, well over 200,000 people, and with the Missouri right there and the Mississippi not far away, the city was filled with business opportunities. As Ned Brownley and the extremely tall Franklin Rivers walked down the gangplank and waited for their horses to be unloaded, Brownley remembered he had business right outside of St. Louis that in no way concerned Mr. Rivers.

"There's a nice hotel downtown, it's called The Southern Hotel, it's on the corner of Walnut and 4th Street. I'll meet you down there. There should already be rooms in my name there. I've taken care of the hotel bill. Go into the saloon on the first floor, it has a magnificent mahogany bar, and order a drink or two. I'll join you there later," Brownley said, thinking of the six-story hotel which ran two city blocks and was a block wide. It had 350 guest rooms and apartments and employed about the same number of people to keep it running.

Brownley rode away from the dock area, knowing

that a man like Franklin Rivers would find the hotel. Brownley had business to do that would ensure the success of his cattle operations in the northern Montana territory.

Ned Brownley had been in communication with John W. Basye, who had settled in what would become known as Bowling Green, just north of St. Louis and twelve miles from the Mississippi River. Basye had started a family store there selling sundries, mercantile stuff, lumber—you name it, Basye had it. It soon became evident to John Basye that the sale of whiskey was where the real money resided.

He started his own distillery, and by the time Brownley made it to St. Louis, Basye distillery had been busy filling fifty barrels of his distilled whiskey for Ned Brownley. The story of how the Native Americans could not resist the smell, taste, and imbibing of alcohol had met Brownley's ear with a certain ring to it. He knew that if he got enough liquor to the northeastern parts of the Montana territory that he could rule there in spite of all the resistance that was supposed to be there by the different tribes. He figured, correctly, that if he brought in enough of the magic potion to those tribes that resistance to his cattle ranching up there would soon be lost in the doldrums of alcoholic dementia, and the undermining of the very peoples and cultures which he thought might keep him from being a cattle baron.

Hours later, when he rode into Basye's store, he was greeted by the man himself, John W. They had a drink, and then the enormous amount of money was exchanged for the fifty barrels of whiskey. They were loaded onto two different wagons, and John W. himself guaranteed the delivery the next day. They would be loaded onto the paddle wheeler that Brownley and Rivers would be taking to Wolf Point. And Brownley was no fool, they labeled everything from flour to molasses and other things that settlers would have need of. He wasn't going to be caught taking whiskey to the Injuns, but whiskey was definitely on its way to the Montana territories.

Just before Brownley mounted his horse and went back to St. Louis, he turned to John W. Basye.

"Sir," Brownley said, now with his born-to-English accent, "I wonder if you and your wife would see fit to join me and one of my business partners at The Southern Hotel for dinner tomorrow night. I have reserved a table for us, and also a room for you and your wife to stay the night. No sense in driving back in the horrors of the night, if you can stay within the confines of a luxurious hotel, right? I'm hoping this arrangement can turn into as many barrels as the territory can support."

"We'd love to join you," Basye said, his eyes growing big, thinking of all the whiskey which a territory like Montana could use, "It will get me off the hook for a while. My wife, she's a bit younger than me, and is always wanting to go into the city," Basye said, smiling.

"Wonderful, then it's a date," Brownley said as he turned his mount and rode toward St. Louis with the sun about an hour from going down.

The rooms at The Southern Hotel were spacious with lots of modern accoutrements. There was a bathroom in each of the more expensive suites, and Brownley didn't mind spending money when he foresaw the future, which was bright and full of money.

The next day, Brownley slept in as he had no other business to attend to here in St. Louis. He had several interesting dreams, but a few minutes after getting up, he couldn't remember any of them. He decided he would fast until the evening meal.

About suppertime, Brownley met Franklin Rivers at the staircase leading downstairs. One entered the dining room through a grand archway from the lobby, which had Corinthian columns with the tops overlaid with gold leaf descending into alabaster poles going into black granite supporting feet. The bar was off to the left as they walked toward the arch that led into the dining room.

"We will be joined by friends of mine at dinner tonight," Brownley said casually to Rivers as they made the archway.

"Is it someone I know?" Rivers asked.

"Hardly, unless of course you've been up this way before?"

"No, this is my first time," Rivers admitted.

"I thought so, by the way," Brownley said, then switched to his native tongue with the British accent, "I will be speaking in this manner tonight with my guests, the Basyes."

Franklin Rivers stopped dead in his tracks and looked at Brownley, and Brownley returned the look and raised an eyebrow.

"Yes?" Brownley said in his perfect high-English way.

"Why would *Texas* Ned pretend to be English? I

mean, it's a good accent, I have to admit, but I don't understand," Rivers said.

Brownley surveyed the dining room and whispered something to the maître d'hôtel, then turned back to Rivers, "Let's have a drink, we'll be informed when our guests arrive," he said and, taking Franklin Rivers by the arm, led him into The Southern Hotel's lounge. Franklin was guided over to the end of the bar, where they were the only two customers. Not that the bar was empty—this time of evening, all of the rich St. Louis was out and about.

The barkeep came over and Brownley thought for a moment concerning the mixologist's recipes for Tanqueray.

"We'll have two Tanqueray Mules, and go light with the ginger beer, please," Brownley said to the man behind the bar.

Franklin looked at Brownley like he was staring at someone from another planet.

"Come, come, in Texas it's beer, whiskey, or rye," Brownley said in his practiced Texas accent, then he switched to his English upper-class, "but in the civilized world, mixed drinks are all the rage, my good man!" Brownley said and pulled out a pack of tailor-made Player's Navy Cut. He offered one to Rivers, who stared at it as if it, too, were from another world, put it in his mouth as Brownley produced a cigarette lighter and ignited the smoke for his business partner and then his own.

Franklin drew the smoke into his lungs, then exhaled with a smile.

"Please tell me what's goin' on?" Rivers asked as he

sipped the Tanqueray Mule that had been set in front of him.

Brownley took a long drink from the mule and motioned to the barkeep and held up two fingers, meaning two more Mules.

"Okay, my name is Neddy Brownley. I was born in East Peckham in Kent, England, on the River Medway. I made my way to this country because I was not royalty, nor did I have any royal blood in me. I read about this country and all men being equal and all that, and decided this was for me. As soon as I landed in New York, I hired a voice coach who gave lessons to actors on Broadway to teach me the Texas accent." Then Brownley switched to it. "And I hafta tell ya, I know it well, like it was me own dang tongue."

"And the Great Northern Cattle Company?"

"Yes, you would ask about that, wouldn't you?" Brownley said, going back to his homeland accent and taking a long drag on the Player's Navy Cut.

"Thank you," Rivers said as the barkeep set the second Tanqueray Mule in front of him and Brownley.

"It's a legitimate company, registered in Texas, and you and I, my good man, are going to make—as the Texans say—a shite load of money from it."

"And the other members of the board?" Rivers asked with some trepidation.

"You know about the unfortunate, not so much, accident arranged by Sheriff Kingsley, and the loss of my own dear wife along the way."

"Was she English, too?"

"Oh, heaven's no, I married her in Dallas, she was a down and out madam from a house of prostitution which was folding, and she agreed to be my ruse as my wife of many years."

"And the boy, Kelly Jones?"

"The sheriff's money turned him. It won't be the first time money had done its worst. You see, as the Good Book says, it's not money that has its roots in evil, it is the love of it, which twists and turns the soul toward Satan himself," Brownley said, extinguishing his first tailor-made and extracting another. Graciously, he offered another one to Rivers, who was still working on the first.

Rivers watched as, either the smartest man in the room or the only one he knew who belonged to Satan's legions, lit another tailor-made Player's Navy Cut.

"Oh, there they are, let's go enjoy some dinner, shall we?" Brownley got up, and holding the smoldering cigarette between his lips, walked toward the maître d'hôtel desk with his unfinished second mule in the other hand.

Through the archway and past the maître d'hôtel desk, the dining room was a spacious and palatial room with Saltillo tile set in white with black squares separated by two white tiles throughout. The chairs were straight-backed with two spade designs in the backs and cushions on the seats. They sat at a table for four next to one of the five floor-to-ceiling windows, which had curtains of sheer gossamer covering the windows but allowed the outside city gas lights to shine through. The maître d'hôtel came over and Brownley whispered something to him, and the man smiled and left.

The next man to appear was the wine steward. Brownley whispered more things to this older man, who was elegantly dressed, and he, too, disappeared.

When the wine steward returned, he had a Madeira from Portugal, vintage 1825. It was one of the dry Madeiras that could be consumed on their own as an aperitif.

Brownley tasted it, then asked the wine steward to let Basye taste it, and when Basye did so, he nodded approvingly to Brownley.

The meal went on without a hitch. Brownley, in his amazing English accent—which it turned out wasn't fake—left Franklin wondering what else about Mr. Brownley was not quite right. His Texas accent was affected, perhaps even the long marriage which he and Eloise had purported to have had, perhaps that too was fake. Of course it was, he had said as much in the bar.

And the deaths of Sheriff Starr Kingsley and the missing Steve Hudley? Why would the sheriff do such a thing and for what gain, only to be caught and hung, and didn't the boy keep ranting on how it was Brownley who had hired him to run down the banker, but nobody was interested in that particular story because of the salacious tales told so willingly by the voluptuous Nelly Jones on the stand, and he remembered seeing each of the male juror's licking their lips or swallowing during her testimony. He, Franklin Rivers, was beginning to think that he was in the company of a man who killed without much consideration, and twisted the truth, if he even had a notion what that might be, into whatever scenario he wanted it to be and would best show him as the innocent.

Franklin Rivers's blood began to run cold. He had had way too much to drink, and the convivial company aside and the laughter and the joking which he imagined was real, but at this point, who could tell?

"I do hope you'll excuse me," Franklin said as he stood up, and literally looked down upon the table. All eyes were on him, and it seemed to Franklin that Brownley's eyes especially betrayed a warning. "I find," Franklin continued as he scooted his chair back in, "that I have imbibed too much and I must retire. It's been a long journey up the Mississippi, and I need some rest. Mr. and Mrs. Basye, I am delighted to have made your acquaintance, and I do hope we see each other again," Franklin said, and he turned without looking at Brownley and walked from the dining room.

Franklin took the steps two and three at a time, with his long legs, it was easy. He felt as if he were a child and was having a bad dream about some monster chasing him. When he got to the room, he fumbled with the key, looking furtively down the hallway, expecting, he wasn't quite sure what. Once the door was opened, he slammed it shut and locked it. He was safe, or so he thought.

Back downstairs in the dining room, the Basyes had no idea what was going on. As far as they were concerned, they were being treated to a lovely evening at The Southern Hotel, and Mr. Basye made a point that he would have to give Brownley a discount on the barrels the next time he was in town. And yet a discount on so many, well, maybe he would and maybe he wouldn't, it seemed Ned Brownley had the money and was willing to spend it.

Brownley sat there making polite conversation, thinking of the key to the Basyes' room, which was still in his coat pocket. He would pretend that he hadn't gotten it when they left for their rooms and get another key, a better key—the key to his last partner's room!

As the Basyes and Brownley left the dining room, he spoke up.

"Oh, goodness, wait right here," Brownley said. They were at the foot of the stairs. "I forgot to get your room key, I'll be right back."

Brownley left the couple at the foot of the stairs and walked with purpose to the hotel desk.

"Do you have another key to room 508? I seemed to have misplaced mine," Brownley asked the man at the desk while slipping a twenty-dollar gold piece across the counter to him. There wasn't a question, after all, Brownley was well known at The Southern, and he had rented three rooms that night. He walked briskly back to the Basyes and handed them their room key from his coat pocket, keeping the one to 508 in his pants pocket.

"I'm going to have a nightcap in the bar, you two lovebirds go on up," Brownley said as they giggled and began ascending the stairs. Brownley went in, had another Tanqueray Mule, and, finishing it, left the bar.

Brownley walked the five flights of stairs and was amazed that he wasn't short of breath. He would be getting on the northbound paddle wheeler tomorrow morning early, and would more than likely be gone before what he was about to do would be discovered.

He tapped gently on the door to 508, Franklin Rivers's room. He waited, he tapped a bit harder, then used the key he'd obtained to enter. He locked the door behind him.

He could hear water running. The door to the bath was cracked open, and as he approached, he could hear singing. Franklin had had enough to drink to engender such behavior, and he was thrilled it was going to be this easy, or so he hoped.

Strains of *Jeanie with the Light Brown Hair*, a Stephen Foster song, were drifting from the bathroom. *Why do people sing in the tub?* wondered Brownley. Well, really, it didn't matter. All the bathrooms were the same, the tub faced away from the bathroom door, and as Brownley snuck up behind Franklin Rivers, he'd taken off his jacket in the bedroom and was rolling up his sleeves.

"As *Jeanie's hair was floating like a vapor, on the soft summer air*."

Brownley struck. He wasn't a big man, but the strength in his arms and hands was amazing. Franklin didn't have time, beyond a momentary gasp, to get air, and as his long legs kicked and his hands reached for Brownley's neck, which he'd tucked close to his body, it was apparent that everything Franklin had imagined about Brownley was true, and then some. Brownley could see Franklin's eyes widening with fear and horror as they struggled, causing the air to escape from his lungs.

Water was being splashed everywhere, and twice Brownley was scratched on the face as the man attempted to free himself from the grave of his bath, but eventually, Franklin took in a big breath of water, and his eyes froze open as the long, hairy legs stopped kicking, slipping back into the elongated tub and Franklin's hands fell away from Brownley's face.

Brownley was pleased. Franklin had admitted to the Basyes that he'd had too much to drink, and now as Brownley cleaned up the water with the remaining towels in the bathroom, and hung them up to dry over the radiator, Brownley realized he was the sole owner and President of the Great Northern Cattle Company, well, except for Nelly Jones and her father-in-law, but that could be taken care of later. The important thing was that all the money from this enterprise would be mostly filling his coffers and his coffers alone.

He relocked the room with the key he'd been given by the front desk and went to his room to sleep. He dreamed of money, of all things, and also of the Injuns who would be supplanted from their lands by fermented spirits. Well, God had created whiskey so the Irish wouldn't rule the world, and for that, Brownley, as an Englishman, was eternally grateful, but perhaps he had also created it so that the Injuns would fall prey to the Whites. Who knew and who cared, as long as his plan worked.

The Basyes told their story to the St. Louis Police, how Franklin had gone up to his room early after having admitted that he was drunk. People slipping unconscious into warm bathwater was common enough, the police said, and Brownley just sat there and looked aghast at the whole thing. The police asked about the band aids on his face, and Brownley admitted he'd cut himself several times that morning while shaving.

When they brought Franklin's body down the long flight of stairs, it slipped off the gurney and tumbled down the last flight, landing naked in the lobby. There were screams and hollers, and Brownley had to suppress a smile as he thought the entire matter had ended up more like a farce than a drama.

When he had managed in spite of everything to make the early paddle wheeler, he was delighted. He checked to make sure that all fifty barrels of whiskey were on the boat, and he gave instructions to the men who ran out to get the wood at each wood station. Once they got into the Upper Missouri, each time a wood station was engaged, a barrel of whiskey was to be left on the wood station dock.

"Let me get this straight, a barrel, fifty-three gallons, of this bonded whiskey is to be left at each wood station on the Upper Missouri?" an incredulous man asked.

"Yes, it's my way of paying the woodcutters, after all, where would we be without them?" Brownley asked and walked away.

The men decided that some of the barrels would be tapped early and stored away for the crew. Well, it was illegal to damage or use any of the passengers' belongings, but since it was just going to be left, what difference would it make?

11

The Crow had always been good with cattle, after all, they grew up chasing the cattle of the plains, the buffalo. They had gathered the reluctant herd of longhorns up and gotten them to move toward the next watering hole, which Immanuel and Uzziah were both glad the Crow knew its location.

Jack Tate, Buck Krieter, and the blindman, O.B. Thomas, had grown used to the Crow within the first day, and O.B. was treated with reverence since the Crow believed that those who could not see in the physical world saw better in the spiritual one. Instead of being ignored like O.B. had basically been by the Whites who surrounded him, the Crow warriors gave him amulets and helped him dress as a Crow warrior.

"What the hell's goin' on?" Jack Tate asked Uzziah at the end of the first week on the new trail picked out by the Crow.

"What d'ya mean?"

"The way they're treatin' O.B. What's with that?"

"He should consider himself blessed," Immanuel said, and Uzziah looked at Immanuel and wondered, *Who is this man?*

"Would the Crow women be the same way with O.B.?" Tate wondered out loud.

"Probably," Uzziah said. "We saw some mighty healin' when we was with these Crow women who took care of a White woman who'd been raped."

"Raped by Injuns?" Tate asked, bending down and pouring himself some coffee.

"No, by murderin' thievin' Whites!" Immanuel spat out.

"What happened to 'em, the bad hombres?" Tate wondered.

"They was dealt with," Immanuel said, and the way he said it had Tate wondering no more.

"Anyways, Thomas is useless to us, but he's treated like damned royalty by the Injuns, I don't get it," Tate admitted.

"I'm sure it's not the first thing ya haven't understood," Immanuel said.

"What's that supposed to mean!?" Tate asked, bowing up a bit.

"Yer feelin' better, ain't ya?" Uzziah asked.

"Yeah, so, I ain't gonna put up with no shite from neither of ya, understand?"

Uzziah and Immanuel looked at each other. It was a common enough experience out here in the wild. Men are injured, need your help, help is rendered, then they go back to their belligerent ways, not remembering who had been there when they needed them.

"Understand?" Tate was not going to let go of it.

"Understood, partner, understood," Immanuel said.

"And I ain't yer partner, got it, I'm the trail boss!" Tate said, and all he was really thinking about was the fact that nearly 500 head had been lost, and Immanuel had told him that he had promised enough beef to the Crow to get them through the winter. He knew Brownley, and he knew he wasn't going to be all soft and fuzzy about giving the savages meat to eat without them paying for it. And yet, Tate's stance in the cattle drive was negligible now, because he didn't know where they were going. He had heard Rudley Quatrain speak of Wolf Point, but hell, he had no idea where that was, and he wasn't even sure the Injuns did either. Maybe they were taking the entire herd someplace where Brownley would never see them and that whole dream of the Great Northern Cattle Company was just that—a dream.

Tate scowled at the mountain man partners one last time and headed away from the fire. He was going to get O.B. so he could get up on his horse and sing to the cattle. That was another thing that the Crow thought about when they thought of O.B.—here was one man who could not see, but without any help at all, he rode around the entire herd at night and sang them cow songs. Well, they'd never heard of the music, but it was soothing, and maybe that was the whole point.

"What burr has gotten under his saddle blanket?" Uzziah asked Immanuel.

"Brother, I'd hate to have to tell ya, the way he's actin' right now is one of the reasons I can't stand being 'round White folk too long, 'ception bein' ya, a course."

"He ain't grateful, that's all there is to it," Uzziah said, putting a name to it.

"Yeah, well, we did stampede his cattle—"

"Who was dying a thirst and goin' away from water!"

"But other things happened—"

"But we done our best to take care around those things," Uzziah said.

"Hey, I know I'm a soundin' like ya, when I says, doin' stuff and expectin' anythin' is probably like shittin' in one hand and hopin' in the other—I mean, guess which one fills up first?!?"

Uzziah just looked at Immanuel. The two men smiled at each other.

"Ya done learnt it good, old son," Uzziah said.

"Ten years ago, that old son stuff was okay, but lately..." Immanuel just trailed off.

By the time the paddle wheeler had reached the Upper Missouri, one of the barrels was almost empty. The crew had been helping themselves with no sense of proportion or abstinence.

Brownley walked by one of the saloons where the crew was being talked to by the captain.

"I don't know which of ya blaggards brought whiskey onboard, but I've noticed a decline in the rigor and form of how things are being done on this ship," he said as Brownley went on down to the main deck and began tipping barrels to see how many had been tapped. It was just one, and it was way in the back. They had hidden it well.

When Brownley got back up top, the meeting was

being dismissed and the captain was headed up to the pilot house.

"Captain, may I have a word with you?" he asked in his British accent.

"Certainly, please follow me up," the captain said.

Within the pilot house, the man piloting was relieved of his duty, but not before the captain spoke harshly with him.

"Ask the others what was said, and pay close attention," he said sternly to the man.

The captain took over the wheel and seemed most at home in piloting the vessel. The two men were easy with not talking, and Brownley let him enjoy his being captain before he spoke.

"I'm afraid what you were just lecturing your crew on is my fault."

The captain turned on Brownley as if he'd just told the man he was sleeping with his underage daughter.

"What ya mean, yer fault!?!"

"There's fifty barrels of whiskey on yer main deck," Brownley said.

"What!?"

"Don't you examine your cargo?" Brownley asked, a bit put off.

"Well, no, not most times, I mean as long as it ain't dynamite or black powder, what do I care?"

"Well, one of the barrels is almost empty," Brownley commented.

"Fifty-three gallons of whiskey and we've just got to the Upper Missouri?"

"Yes, that's about right."

"What ya mean to do with it?" the captain asked, then added, "Trade it to the Injuns?"

"No, no, I'm giving it to them," Brownley said as he took a sheaf of banknotes from his inside pocket and handed them to the captain.

"What's that fer?" the captain asked.

"Just my way of saying thanks for not caring," Brownley said.

"Hell, ya don't have to pay me not to care. Why, I had a wife and three girls raped and murdered by the savages, and anything that can help destroy them, I'm all fer it!"

Brownley extended the sheafs of notes once again. "Well, let's just call this an insurance payment for your unfortunate loss," Brownley said.

The captain looked at the notes, it was a lot of money. Then, looking straight down the Missouri, he swiped the notes from Brownley's hand without looking and put them in his coat.

"Let's just say this conversation never happened. Good day," the captain added.

From then on, certain crew members were put on guard duty with the barrels of whiskey and the tapping stopped.

At each wood station, the captain would watch from his roost in the pilot house as a barrel was unloaded and left sitting forlornly on the dock.

Word of the whiskey being left at wood stations reached the ears of many in the Blackfeet Confederacy. The Blackfeet Nation consisted of three peoples: the Kainai, Piikani, and Siksika peoples. They ranged over the plains and prairies of the Montana territory and the land further to the north in Canada. Their wandering nearly always had to do with the search for sustenance, and that sustenance was buffalo for hundreds of years. The bison not only afforded them meat to eat and to jerk for later consumption, but it also gave them tallow, buffalo robes, and horns—no part of the great bison was seen as unusable.

These wandering hunters had often seen the smoking canoes, as they were sometimes called, and they also knew where the wood stations were, using them from time to time, if they were in proximity and needed the wood.

On one such occasion, a big barrel was discovered. Being childlike in their assumptions that what was left behind and not guarded must indeed be a gift, the first of these barrels was loaded upon a travois and taken to the nearest village. When they got there, the barrel had cracked and most, if not all, the whiskey had drained out of it. The little that was left was enjoyed by the chief and a few of the worthier braves. They enjoyed the strong water very much and sent other scouting expeditions out to look for more barrels.

The travois used this time was cushioned by buffalo robes, and when they got back to the village, the entire barrel was intact. The celebration that ensued lasted nearly two weeks, and when all was said and done, it looked like the village had been bombed. Trash was blowing everywhere, unattended children wandered around, dogs ate what foodstuffs that had been left out, and all in all, it was decided that the next time they discovered a barrel, preparations should be made for the aftermath.

Tribal jealousy for the barrels became a problem

as several different scouting parties from different Blackfeet Confederacy tribes argued over whose barrels they were. Arguments turned to weapons, and when the barrel made it back, one scouting party had been wiped out, and the other had several losses of life.

While all this was happening, Brownley knew nothing of it. What he knew well enough was the avarice of man, and no matter what country you lived in, there were always those who would wield it over others in a chance to get what they wanted and keep it from their neighbors.

Brownley didn't know one single Injun, but what he did know was the darker side of the human heart, and that, it seemed, would further his dream of having the Great Northern Cattle Company take root and survive in the Montana territory.

Just about the fastest news that travels is bad news. Buffalo Warrior and his band of cattle-driving Crow guessed they were about half a week from arriving at Wolf Point, the place where Jack Tate said the cattle must be delivered. That afternoon, with the sun high and the dust roiling up from behind the herd of some thousand longhorns, Buffalo Warrior spoke to Uzziah and Immanuel.

"This man, Tate," he said in Crow, "does he know that nothing exists where we are taking the cattle?"

"Guess he does, what d'ya think, young son?" Immanuel asked.

"The White man knows a lot of things, but he may

not know eventually what he's doing," Uzziah spoke in Crow.

All three men laughed at that. In the distance, a rider was coming fast from the south. Buffalo Warrior saw the dust trail behind the horse and pointed it out to the mountain men.

"Someone comes," he said.

They watched as the rider got closer, and they all noticed the deportment of the man on the horse. He almost fell off several times, then, when he came to a halt, he did slide off the pony and started laughing uproariously.

"This is Grows Lonely, he is from my tribe," Buffalo Warrior made the introduction while the man was still laughing.

"He's touched, or drunk as a skunk," Immanuel said.

"There was nothing wrong with his mind when I left the village," Buffalo Warrior said, then talked to the warrior on the ground.

"What is the meaning of this? Where have you come from?"

Grows Lonely sat up and looked at the three men, and the huge herd which kept moving on.

"From our village, I..." He looked around and realized who he was talking to. "Buffalo Warrior, I am no longer lonely," he said, and taking a canteen, he raised it to his lips and took an enormous gulp, the brown liquid spilling down his chest. He put the stopper in the canteen, then fell over dead drunk.

That evening, as they made camp, they took Grows Lonely off his horse, which he had been tied across. They laid him down as the chuckwagon pulled up, and Buck jumped down from the seat and tied the reins to the brake of the wagon.

"What happened to him?" he asked, and then, when he was walking toward where they'd laid him down, he exclaimed, "Damn, he's drunk, and I'll bet there ain't a saloon in a hundred miles of chere!"

O.B. got busy riding around the herd as soon as it got dark and the rest of them—except for a smattering of Crow, maybe five, who rode the herd at night—sat around the campfire after supper. Grows Lonely had told them all, well, the Whites who didn't speak Crow had to be translated to, but he told the story of the big whiskey barrels and their discoveries all over the Upper Missouri.

No one knew what to think, but Jack Tate seemed like he must know something, so Immanuel just asked him outright.

"Do this have somethin' to do with this Great Northern Cattle Company, ya think?"

Tate looked at him with a dark brow and shook his head.

"It's got something to do with it, don't it?!?" Uzziah asked fervently, wanting to know.

"Maybe, I don't know. I'm not a drinker myself, I mean, I'll take a drink, but don't everyone know what drink does to the Redman?"

Everyone knew, and Immanuel and Uzziah were beginning to suspect that some devil, literally, was dropping off barrels of whiskey along the river at the wood stations, and as much as Immanuel appreciated the gesture, he didn't know what to think of it.

Tate started talking, and the tale he told was an old one, perhaps as old as the devil himself. He had been hired by a man named Ned *Texas* Brownley, and his mission was to draft some not-so-good hombres, and O.B. and Buck were the only ones left from the hiring, and go along with a herd of beef, Texas longhorns, to be exact. Somewhere along the way, take the herd over from the original trail boss, Rudley Quatrain, and steer it past Cheyenne, bringing it eventually on to Wolf Point. Tate didn't know exactly what was going to happen there, but all he knew was, Brownley was going to meet them there, and he would be paid then, along with all the men he hired.

"So, what yer sayin' is ya rustled these cows from the trail boss, but then didn't know where the waterin' holes was?" Uzziah was trying to wrap his honest mind around all this. It sounded to him like the most cockamamie scheme he'd ever heard of.

"I sometimes wish you guys would have just let us die out there. I only came on because of the money Brownley was promising, and now, I'm beginning to think that it was all in vain," Tate said with a troubled spirit.

Later that night, Immanuel and Uzziah were lying on their bedrolls and sipping coffee. Both had their pipes out and were smoking. The tale that had been told them sounded like something out of a Shakespearean play. A man was grasping for greatness and fortune, but his sense of hubris—pride grown from overconfidence—was so overgrown that he was willing, and it seemed able, with his resources, to obliterate the native cultures along the Missouri simply because he wanted to corner the beef market. His overreach was both troubling and out of character with what the West was all about.

"What ya think's really goin' on chere, partner?" Immanuel asked.

"The End Times?" Uzziah said with a sense of irony in his voice.

"Ya done told me only Father knows that."

"Ya was listenin'?" Uzziah said, smiling.

"A man, by hisself, has decided to run the table on our red brothers, why?"

"I don't know, old son, I really don't," Uzziah said, blowing smoke into the air above his bedroll.

"But it don't make sense, do it?"

"Chaos is the hallmark of Satan," Uzziah whispered.

"What ya whisperin' fer?"

"It's his world and he's always listenin', brother?"

"But I thought God so loved the world and all that?"

"Yeah, but we're just traveling through, like I been tryin' to tell ya," Uzziah said.

"So, all this," Immanuel said, his arm sweeping across the Milky Way, and the billions of stars and galaxies that it consisted of, "all this is just a test?"

"Well, it's more acourse, it's Father's way of seeing where our hearts lie. Father's way of seeing if we love 'im."

"Well, it seems an awful waste of whiskey," Immanuel finally said.

Uzziah just looked at the only man, besides his brothers and father, that he had ever loved, and he realized, in a sense, in Immanuel's sense, yes, whiskey was being wasted, but men would always try to conquer God, wouldn't they? Wasn't that what the tower of Babel had been about, pride—overweening pride—reaching up and trying to pull God from the throne and have a seat there yourself?!? There was only one God, the Lord God Almighty, maker of heaven and earth, and the rest was a mystery shrouded in a conundrum hidden within our terrible and troubled pride.

12

When the paddle wheeler got to Wolf Point, there was little there but a dock and a wood station. Brownley didn't expect much more. The crew, mostly those who held inferior positions on the crew, and mainly those who had broken into the barrels without permission, they were the ones who had to unload it, and since only about six barrels had been dropped at wood stations and one barrel drunk by the peons on the crew, Brownley took an especial enjoyment in seeing them sweat and grunt.

He sat on the lower deck where the barrels were being unloaded from and the captain joined him there.

"So, this is yer destination?" the captain asked, his eyes scanning the bleak and foreboding horizons.

"Yes, yes, it is," Brownley said, taking his pack of Player's Navy Cut from his coat and offering one to the captain, who took it and looked at it strangely.

"These are tailor-made," the captain said as he rolled the cigarette between his fingers, holding it close to his ear and listening to the tobacco crunch inside.

"Yes, they are, Captain, so convenient, you want a smoke, have a smoke, doesn't tie up your hands or anything," Brownley said and lit the captain's and then his own smoke.

"There's Injuns out there, ya know that, don't ya?"

"I should hope so, I've been sending out my invitations up and down the Upper Missouri for the past week. If they don't know I'm here, I'm going to be very disappointed."

The captain drew the smoke in and stared at the side of Brownley's head. He had met all kinds coming up this way, and for a certainty, this man was the strangest.

"Yes?" Brownley had turned and seen the captain staring at him.

"Oh, just ponderin' things, Mr. Brownley, just ponderin'," the captain said, looking away. He didn't like the look in Brownley's eyes, and would be glad when the whiskey—all of it—had been successfully unloaded and they were steaming upstream. Maybe Brownley was right about the natives, and maybe he wasn't, all in all, it wasn't a bet that he, the captain, would have taken, and that was for sure.

"That's the lot of it," one of the stevedores said, perspiration pouring from him as he mopped his brow.

"The supplies, also, you didn't forget my supplies, did you?" Brownley asked. He wasn't worried about the Injuns, but he was worried about not having enough to eat.

"No, they's on the other side of the barrels," the man said.

"Good," Brownley said.

The captain stood, and so did Brownley. Brownley

stuck out his hand for the captain to shake, and the captain simply looked at it, then he looked up for the last time into the living eyes of Ned *Texas* Brownley. He was glad he was an anchored man, there was a million miles of falling darkness in those eyes.

"Thanks for the smoke," the captain said. He didn't want to be rude, but he also didn't want to touch the man. "Ya take care, understand?" the captain said as he turned his back on Brownley, who still had his hand out, and walked up the stairs to the hurricane deck.

The longhorns were getting fatter, and Wolf Point wasn't that far away, possibly a day or two.

Buck Krieter cooked supper that night, and Uzziah knew it wasn't as good as his own food, but ate it anyway.

"Don't see why ya ain't cookin' fer us," Immanuel said.

"I will eventually, but what ya don't understand is when a man had been doin' the majority of the cooking fer nearly ten years, anybody's cookin' tastes good, as long as he ain't the one cookin'," Uzziah said, digging into the beans and dragging a biscuit through the juices.

"Ya make it sound like I never cook," Immanuel complained.

Uzziah just looked at him and went back to eating.

"Okay, okay, I rarely cook, but I do cook."

"You're alive and you were up in those mountains a time afore I came, and then a time afore I got back, so I knows ya cook."

"Ifn yer tryin' to guilt me—"

"How long we been partners?" Uzziah asked.

"Long 'nuff."

"And in that time, have I ever tried to guilt ya 'bout anythin'?"

"Hell yes!"

"Well, guess what, this ain't one of 'em."

"What I wouldn't give to have yer johnnycakes or biscuits. I swear, Uzziah, yer torturin' me."

"Without intendin' to."

"I don't know, I wish I did, but I just don't know," Immanuel said, tearing off a corner of a biscuit which could have been thrown and used as a lethal weapon.

"We should be there tomarrie," Tate said as he walked up.

"Ya think?" Immanuel said, trying to chew the biscuit.

"Yeah, I do, say, Uzziah?"

"Yeah?"

"Why don't ya cook fer us more often?" Jack Tate whispered, keeping an eye on the chuckwagon, making sure Buck was out of earshot.

Immanuel just sat up and looked at Uzziah as if to say, *See!*

"Maybe when we get to Wolf Point and meet yer boss, I will," Uzziah said, taking a sideways glance at his partner, who looked like he wanted to jump up and scream.

"Buck's a good, ole boy, but half the time he's cookin' he's so slouched I don't think he knows what he's doin'."

"I'll keep it in mind, okay," Uzziah said, smiling as Tate turned and walked away.

Immanuel just kept looking at his partner until Uzziah finally spoke. "What?"

"Ya'll cook fer a total stranger, and not me?"

"Sometimes, you are just an old woman, ya know that, don't ya?" Uzziah said and went back to sopping the gravy, such as it was.

The next morning, Brownley had made a fire to cook his bacon and beans over. He sure hoped Tate had hired a good cook for the trail, he wasn't looking forward to having this sort of repast much longer.

He'd set his tent up, and it looked all right. A corner was slouching, and the wind liked to whip it over in the night. He had no idea it was this windy up here in the middle of summer. The bacon was frying nicely when he looked up and saw some dust in the distance, coming from the northeast. Probably just the wind, he told himself, surely, the longhorns wouldn't be coming from that direction!?

He looked back down at the bacon and it was burning. Damn! He tried to flip it over with the fork, but got splattered by hot grease and burned his hand. He dropped the fork and swore.

"Mother of God!" he yelled as he ran to the dock and dipped his burned hand into the Missouri. The bacon was still burning when he noticed the dust was being made by a whole lot of Injuns. Good, they had received his invitation, and the sooner they got this over, the better. Of course, he was referring to the introductions, their gratitude, and then on with the business of giving them as much whiskey as they could carry so they would go away and leave him alone to become the cattle baron he'd always dreamed of being.

They had had breakfast, and Uzziah had told Buck he wanted to cook that morning to give the man a break. Buck appreciated it. He knew his cooking sucked, but he had been hired to do the job, and by God, if nobody got in his way, he would do it. The offer came at a point in the drive when Buck needed a drink, and there just didn't seem to be a drop of it in the camp. Truth be told, the more sober Buck got, the worse his cooking.

Buck, Tate, Immanuel, O.B., and Buffalo Warrior sat around the fire as Uzziah dished up their plates. Buffalo Warrior's braves were happy with the jackrabbits they killed the night before, and frankly, Immanuel was on the cusp of going over and eating with the Crow if Buck was going to continue cooking.

They sat around eating and enjoying the johnnycakes, the biscuits, the bacon, the beans, and even some quail eggs, which Uzziah had scared up that morning before anyone had gotten up. The mother quails had squawked about it, but there'd be other matings and other eggs. As everyone was eating and thinking how good it was to have Uzziah back cooking, one of Buffalo Warrior's braves ran over speaking Crow so fast that neither Immanuel nor Uzziah could understand him. Buffalo Warrior stood and looked to the west.

Then, they all stood. Black smoke was roiling into the morning sky, and the sunlight at one point was passing through it, but none too successfully.

"What the hell is that?" Buck asked, everyone else

fairly sure what was happening, or at least they had a notion.

They drove the longhorns toward the smoke, a sure beacon of where they were going. It took them the better part of the day. Well, they stopped at a pond for the cattle to drink, and to make some coffee at noon, and the smoke was still shooting skyward.

By the time the sun was about an hour from being set, the herd forded the Missouri and got on the northern bank, then drove them toward the dwindling fire. Well, by that time, it was simply a big smoldering pile of barrels, and the dock was gone, and so was the wood station.

Brownley had been hung naked by his feet, from a big Silver Maple tree, the lower branches had been cleared away so that his upside-down body could swing nicely in the breeze. No one counted, but there were probably over a hundred arrows in his body, and from the bleeding in his extremities, it looked like they had started there and then worked their way into the torso. After the arms and legs had been filled with arrows, the scrotum and penis had been removed, and his torso and head looked like they had been painted black, the blood turning that color after it had sat in the sun for a while. The beating heart had almost bled the man out, it was a death of a thousand cuts, so to speak.

Brownley's eyelashes had been cut off, so that he witnessed everything, and in his mouth was stuffed an entire pack of Player's Navy Cut, tailor-made, which no one had ever seen before. Well, that wasn't entirely true.

"Those were the smokes he liked. Even offered me one at Fort Belknap," Tate said.

When the smokes were removed, Uzziah noticed the man had no tongue, and looking below where he hung, they found it, cut out and discarded.

"He must have died a coward's death," Buffalo Warrior said, knowing that torture was to see if a man was honorable and able to suffer without speaking.

"Evidently, he must have had plenty to say," Immanuel said in Crow.

"Until he didn't," Uzziah replied in Crow.

The money that Tate, Buck, and O.B. were supposed to be paid was scattered around the site of his execution, well, that's what it was. All three men spent most of that evening searching for the coins and paper money. Tate said it wasn't nearly what they had been promised.

When the body was discovered, Buffalo Warrior had a Brave climb the tree and bring down some arrows.

"They are from both Blackfeet and Crow quivers," Buffalo Warrior said in Crow to Immanuel and Uzziah. He didn't have to tell them that those tribes were enemies, and only united to fight a common enemy. In this case, it was surmised that the enemy of my enemy is my friend, and Brownley had definitely been seen as the enemy.

"Sons a bitches!" Jack swore openly as he rolled out his bedroll and the Crow made their camp further from the White men.

"Will they come back and finish us off?" Buck asked a question that all the White men wondered, well, the ones that didn't know the Crow way.

"We'll see 'em tomarrie, fer sure," Immanuel said, and that didn't help anybody sleep any better.

As the sun set, Uzziah joined Immanuel down at

the burned-up dock and wood station, the remains, the rims and stays of the barrels were still red hot.

"What a waste of whiskey," Immanuel said.

"I think that was the point," Uzziah whispered, hoping Jack Tate was far enough away.

"What ya mean?"

"There's a Bible verse that mentions this," Uzziah said.

"No, there ain't, that's just foolishness to think so!" Immanuel exclaimed, but not too loudly.

Uzziah just looked at Immanuel and shook his head.

"Ya need yer Bible to tell me?" Immanuel asked.

"No, it was one which my pa sort of drilled into me."

"Say it to me," Immanuel said.

"Ya sure?" Uzziah asked, and Immanuel nodded.

"*But these people blaspheme in matters they do not understand. They are like unreasoning animals, creatures of instinct, born only to be caught and destroyed, and like animals, they too will perish.* That's from Second Peter," Uzziah finished up.

"I wonder what they done with his First Peter?" Immanuel said, joking badly.

Uzziah just looked at his partner and smiled. He had to love the man, always seeing something funny.

"Then, the Blackfeet and Crow done us a favor, young son."

"Yes, yes, they did."

"But what 'bout Tate, and the others?" Immanuel asked.

"When they come, the Injuns, and they will, we'll

fix it, I know we will," Uzziah said, and Immanuel was worried if that were possible.

They had left the body hanging.

"We gotta cut the poor sonofabitch down!" Tate demanded.

"This death is a ritualistic one," Buffalo Warrior said in Crow. "We must honor their wishes until we see them."

"I can't let it swing all night," Tate said.

"Don't do it!" Immanuel said to Tate.

"Sure can't stop me," Tate said, and he started climbing the tree with a knife between his teeth.

Uzziah threw the lasso and pulled Tate down. He hit hard and grabbed his leg, the one that had been broken.

"Bastard! I think ya broke my leg again!" Tate yelled.

It wasn't broken, and Immanuel put a poultice on it to bring down the swelling, but that ended the idea that they were going to cut Brownley down.

They camped upwind from the swinging body, and in the night, when the wind started up, Uzziah looked, and the moon was reflecting off the river, and shining on the swinging body like it was a silver fish. He watched for a while, the when he turned to roll over in his bedroll, Immanuel was also watching.

"Ifn he falls, he'll burst open like a ripe watermelon," Immanuel said.

"I think he'll hold," Uzziah whispered back.

They ate breakfast, sort of, mostly it was jerked meat, pemmican, which Uzziah and Immanuel always carried. They didn't think the Crow had even had breakfast.

Shortly after sunup, they could hear the thundering of unshod ponies coming their way, well, from two separate directions. The Crow came from the south and the Blackfeet from the north. They rode in, and tensions were obviously high. Uzziah and Immanuel had already decided what was to be done to escape a massacre.

The Crow Chief was there, and so was Buffalo Warrior's father, the Crow medicine man. The Blackfoot chief was the same as at the buffalo run a few years before. He was the one whose son had been buried under tons of dead buffalo. Both fathers had weathered well.

They talked, the Blackfeet and Crow, in sign back and forth, then Immanuel spoke up. "We wish each tribe to have 250 longhorns from the herd," Immanuel said in Crow and Buffalo Warrior who spoke Blackfoot translated.

The Blackfoot chief spoke back quickly and harshly.

"He says what's to keep them from taking all the herd for themselves?"

"We are!" the chief of the Crow said in English. It was well known that both the Crow and Blackfoot spoke some English, they just didn't like to.

"So," the Blackfoot chief said, "again, you wish to fight for what we could have all of?"

"What's that mean?" Immanuel asked Uzziah.

"I think he's saying ifn they kilt all the Whites, they could divvy up the herd half and half!"

Immanuel gulped hard and marveled at the soundness of such logic.

"What the hell's goin' on!?!" Jack Tate asked, then added, "Sounds like they gonna take the cattle!"

"Some of them, yes," Immanuel said.

Tate's hand went to his revolver, and Immanuel turned his Hawken toward Tate's chest.

"You'll never know how it's gonna turn out ifn I shoot a hole in yer chest," Immanuel whispered.

Tate's hand came off his gun.

Much signing was going on between the two tribes, and neither Immanuel nor Uzziah could keep up. Finally, they made the sign of a sweeping hand, palm down in front of them, and the deal was done.

Without further ado, both tribes, and Buffalo Warrior's braves joined with the other Crow, and the herd was halved, then halved again as each tribe drove them in opposite directions, one north, the other south.

"So, that's it!?!" Tate asked, fairly pissed off and limping a little. "They take half our herd, which we drove up here at great loss, just like that, they take half!?!"

"Yeah, but I know how to breed cattle and ifn we stays with ya this winter, by spring, we'll have half or at least a quarter back agin," Uzziah said, and Immanuel just looked at him.

"We're goin' back to the mountains, young son," Immanuel said.

"No, no, we ain't. We're gonna help these poor bastards breed these cattle, build fences, harvest some of the summer grasses, and hunker on down here in the east Montana territory, and turn this thing around," Uzziah said.

Immanuel didn't like it, but that's what they did. They dug a hole beneath where Brownley was hanging, cut him down, then buried the bastard right where he fell.

Then they dug out cabins in the hills surrounding the Missouri, and as the paddle wheelers made their ways north and south, they placed orders and paid for them with the cash they found in Brownley's tent.

By fall, fences had been erected, cows had been impregnated, and calves were on their way. They scoured the hills for wood and supplies, and hunted and jerked meat, and all in all, Jack Tate had himself four partners: a bad cook, a blind wrangler, and two mountain niggers. It looked like the Great Northern Cattle Company was not dead yet.

And in the evenings, when the lamps burned brightly in the cabins built back into the hills, and it felt to Immanuel that they'd never get back to their own cabins, Uzziah would read the old newspapers that had arrived on the paddle wheelers about the wake of destruction that one, Ned *Texas* Brownley had carved all the way from San Angelo, leaving his wife and banker run over by a boy who had supposedly conspired with the local sheriff and both were hung for that. Then, the murderous trail continued up the Mississippi, where the body of his former partner, railroad man, Steve Hudley, and the body of a soiled dove had washed up on the banks of the Big Muddy.

The drowning death of another partner in the bathtub in room 508 at The Southern Hotel in Louisville had been changed to murder, and Brownley was the prime suspect. Then, getting off at Wolf Point,

Brownley seemed to have disappeared into the Montana territories, the papers said. Behind all this reading, O.B. Thomas could be heard warbling the cows to rest as he blindly rode around the ever-increasing herd and soothed them to sleep. Winter was approaching, it was as sure as the river flowed south, and the two mountain men and the other unlikely partners wondered what the heck a winter in this desolate place would look like.

"Well, partner, I never thought we'd be cattlemen," Uzziah said to Immanuel, who was sitting in the doorway, sipping coffee and looking out on the vast prairie and the herd.

"Hey, truth be told, as long as yer cookin' I'm okay with just 'bout anythin'," Immanuel said, looking back over his shoulder where Uzziah was bringing a cake from the Dutch oven.

As Uzziah took it out, the aroma filled their cabin. He set it aside on the table, making sure the tablecloth was out of the way, and it was just sitting on the wood. As he sat down and looked at Immanuel smoking in the doorway, and waited for it to cool, he thought, *Sometimes, life came at you full tilt, and sometimes, you were on the sidelines, watching the creation and destruction of it all, and really the only thing you were called to do then was witness and say, Amen!*

"What'd ya say?" Immanuel turned back to his partner, his face a happy smile.

"Nothin'," Uzziah said, and just like two people growing older together, they had begun to think each other's thoughts.

A LOOK AT BOOK EIGHT: WOLF POINT

A UZZIAH MOUNTAIN MAN WESTERN DOUBLE

Some battles are fought on the trail. Others, in the heart.

Uzziah O'Bannon and Immanuel Jones settle in at Wolf Point to help Jack Tate, a rustler-turned-rancher, build a cattle operation along the Missouri. But when Father De Smet rides in with a plea for justice, the mountain men agree to investigate a string of thefts plaguing a mission in the Bitterroot Valley. What they find in Wisdom is darker than expected—and getting out may require more than just bullets and backbone.

As the West threatens to pull them deeper in, the East calls them home. War has broken out, and the O'Bannon men are rallying to defend Virginia. Uzziah and Immanuel ride for the Shenandoah Valley and join General Johnston's army just in time for the First Battle of Manassas—where not everyone makes it out alive.

As grief settles and the war deepens, loyalties are tested. Immanuel questions the cause, while Uzziah fights to hold his family—and their friendship—together. Meanwhile, Uzziah's sister Hanna joins the fight disguised as a boy in Jeb Stuart's cavalry, only to discover love and danger tangled in the same uniform.

This two-book bundle includes the fifteenth and sixteenth novels in the Uzziah Mountain Man Series.

AVAILABLE MARCH 2026

THANK YOU

Thank you for taking the time to read *The Promised Land: A Western Double*. If you enjoyed it, please consider telling your friends or posting a short review. Word of mouth is an author's best friend and much appreciated.

Thank you.
J.J. Bonham

ABOUT THE AUTHORS

He was good looking and could sell ice to eskimos. But ... writing asked something else from him. He would have to corral his interest in being free. Writing would take him to a place where he was tamed, but also able to actually tell a story.

After the first two weeks at the Yale School of Drama, he called the head of the playwriting department, Milan Stitt and told him he was quitting. Milan invited him to lunch at a nearby Mexican restaurant in New Haven. He told the man who had had plays on Broadway that he wanted to be a free writer. Milan smiled, then explained the way to freedom was always through discipline.

Something in him clicked and it all began to make sense.

Three years later, when he received his MFA in playwriting, he received the much coveted Cole Porter Prize for Excellence in Writing.

Enter a woman, years later, when the first 'J' in J.J. Bonham, Jack Bonham, had written thirty screenplays in 7 years and had one optioned which looked like it actually might be done.

Unlike Milan Stitt, this woman had no plays on Broadway, but was a divorced mother of four grown children. She loved soaps, and was an ardent watcher of the same. In the years of her devotion to watching she developed an uncanny ability to discern plot and analyze character. Uncanny, really better than any of his teachers at Yale.

They, Jack & Judy, the other 'J' in J.J. Bonham, married in Buffalo Springs, Colorado. While teaching elementary school in Denver they read the same novella and looking up and into each other's eyes, realizing something. They could do that.

Thirteen years later they had written nearly 200 novels. Westerns mostly because that was who they were – a misplaced couple from the 19th Century who saw life in a western justice sort of way. They danced in Virgina City, Montana. Dances from a different time and place, but still their time and place.

Now, they live in the Bitterroot Valley on five acres and looking out the office window as he puts this together for them, he can see the thunderstorm marching across the Sapphire Mountains. Earlier, sitting on the porch, she had said something about the crack of lightning years before as they said vows of love in Buffalo Springs. He remembered.

www.ingramcontent.com/pod-product-compliance
Lightning Source LLC
LaVergne TN
LVHW040216110826
845146LV00005B/1309

* 9 7 9 8 8 9 5 6 7 3 5 7 7 *